A bright SUMMER

A Seasons Novel

Kate Smoak

DEDICATION

For those chasing their dreams,
and for those supporting mine – you
know who you are.

– Kate Smoak

CONTENT WARNING

This book contains scenes of graphic sexual content, depictions of alcohol and drug use, and deals with mental health issues like anxiety and eating disorders. We advise readers accordingly.

Please note: this is the first book in a series of four where the HEA develops over the series.

CHAPTER
ONE

ELISSA

The shrill ringing of my alarm blares into the quiet of my bedroom, drowning out the sound of the soft drum of rain on the window.

I'm naked.

Something hard and warm squishes against my bosom as I lay on my stomach. I've buried half my face in my pillow, which is now damp from sleeping with my mouth open, and a sheet is haphazardly draped over my waist. I reach blindly for my phone and tap around the screen until the ringing stops. Sucking in a deep breath, I blow my hair out of my face and roll my eyes open. The room materializes in front of me, and it takes me a minute to realize where I am as my eyes adjust to the lighting.

"Uuughhh," I moan. My head throbs and my mouth feels like it's filled with sand.

I squint over at the hard body next to me and the night comes flooding back. The loud, pounding music, the lights and colours blurring around our sweaty bodies pressed together — and that was only at the club. His name has temporarily escaped me, but I'm sure it will come back to me eventually. I push off his chest, slink out of my bed, and stumble to the washroom.

I lean on the vanity to steady myself as I rub my face, trying to make the dizziness go away. Swinging the mirrored cabinet door open, I rustle through the assortment of bottles and boxes, trying to find the aspirin.

"Come on, come on…Riley!" My head tips back between my shoulders and my knuckles are white from gripping the mirror. I slam the cabinet shut, questioning why I drank my weight in liquor.

"Riley! Where the hell is the aspirin?"

Riley darts into the bathroom wearing an oversized navy t-shirt, her once sleek lob now standing up like a peacock, looking as rough as I feel.

"Can you be any louder?" Riley hisses at me. "It's not like you're the only one with a massive hangover. This is the last time I drink tequila excessively." She grunts as she lowers herself to the toilet to take a piss. I scoff at her empty promise, knowing full well that tonight will be the same for us.

"I think the aspirin is in the kitchen. Doug took some last night before sleeping." Nodding my appreciation, I march to the kitchen for a glass of water and the pills to cure my headache. The flush of the toilet echoes down the hallway and Riley emerges a moment later with her hair smooth and perfect. I'll never understand how she can tame her hair with such ease — and that's without a shower or any product. Lucky bitch.

"God, I am craving carbs and maple syrup," I call out over my shoulder as I fill a glass of water at the sink. "Do you want to go for breakfast?"

I turn to Riley and toss the aspirin back, chasing them with a slug of water just as my bedroom door creaks open. The hard body from my bed walks up to me, stark naked, wraps his arms around my waist and places a gentle kiss on the side of my head. Riley wiggles her brows with astonishment and approval when she notices his thick, glorious eight inches and Viking body, and I have a brief flashback to him filling me to the brim as my legs draped over his shoulders. When he notices Riley standing there shamelessly checking him out, a smug grin pulls at his lips, and he grabs her hand to shake it.

"Liam. And you must be…" he pauses for just a moment, not long enough for Riley to introduce herself, and saving me the nervous stuttering and awkward tension of not remembering his name.

"…Riley. Right? Elissa's roommate and bestie?" My mouth forms a small "o" in surprise.

"Yeah, that's me. And good morning to you," she says. With a wink, she spins on her heel, marches toward her bedroom, and slips through the door, closing it behind her with a soft click. I turn to Liam and give him a small smile.

"I'd love to join you guys for those pancakes if you don't mind. Last night's activities have left me rather... ravenous." He grins as his eyes darken, clearly recalling the memories of last night's frolicking. Suddenly, he yanks me into his chest, fists my hair in one hand, and pushes his tongue through my lips, kissing me hard. After a few moments, he pulls away and smacks my ass before turning and walking to the washroom. I hear the telltale sputter of the shower turning on.

"You coming, babe?" he shouts from the bathroom. A shiver shoots down my spine in distaste at the pet name, but I decide to join him. Knowing I won't see him again makes everything simpler. I don't do back-to-back, and I won't let him join us for breakfast. Then again, this *technically* wouldn't be a back-to-back since it hasn't ended yet... it's just more of last night. Right?

My glass clinks as I set it in the sink, and I follow the sound of the shower stream bouncing off this guy's chiseled chest.

• • •

Riley stares at me, eyebrows raised, from across the booth as I pour an unhealthy amount of sugar into my coffee. Griddle Cakes, our pancake house of choice, is alive and humming with chatter as the rain pelts down on the asphalt outside. Riley is practically bouncing out of the booth to hear everything about this guy...Liam, right? She's been seeing Doug more frequently, so she claims she's living vicariously through my flings, although I know for a fact she and Doug aren't serious.

"How was it? He has an enormous dick, so he must have been good," she says brightly, anticipation written across her face. The clinking of cutlery against the plates grates on my nerves as my hangover rears its ugly head.

"Just because he has an enormous dick doesn't mean he's automatically good with it. He could've been terrible," I reply distractedly, scratching my spoon against the bottom of the mug as I stir in the mountain of sugar I poured into my coffee. Riley grimaces and sneers in my direction.

"So, in other words, you blacked out and don't remember?"

I shoot her an affirmative finger gun and click my tongue. "Yep. You got it."

I pick up my coffee and take a gulp. "Oh, ever-loving God, bless you for this delicious coffee," I say as a quiet moan escapes my lips. Riley shakes her head and laughs. A few moments later, a pile of steaming, fluffy pancakes is sitting in front of me. I grab the bottle of syrup — real maple syrup — and douse the cakes in the golden, sticky nectar. After a moment of us wolfing down some much-needed carbs and sugar, Riley breaks the silence.

"So, about tomorrow…"

I shoot her a pointed look as if to say, "Don't go there." She sighs.

"Look, I know you don't want to talk about it, but we need to plan for how to deal with your parents at graduation."

I laugh scornfully at her and shake my head, pretending I didn't hear her as I continue to shovel pancakes into my mouth. Unlike most people, the thought of my parents attending my graduation doesn't appeal to me. They don't deserve to sit there and be "proud" of me. I haven't even spoken to them since before Christmas, and it's now April. My body tingles with anxiety as Riley drones on about my parents. A cold bead of sweat threatens to trickle down my spine, and a wave of dread washes over me. My feet twitch with the need to get away, to run. It's a feeling I know well. I've been running from my parents my entire life, or trying to. My therapist once said that my body doesn't know the difference between fight or flight, which sometimes triggers panic attacks. So, I've used actual running as my coping mechanism.

It's easy to explain. Running is like breathing for me. Most people struggle with breathing when running, but for me it's the opposite — running is the puffer for my metaphorical asthma. When I'm under stress or feeling anxious, it feels like I'm suffocating when I'm not running. Once my feet hit the pavement, all the tension drains out of my body, swirling around as it pours out from my feet, and I feel light again; weightless, like when you've reached the precipice of a rollercoaster and then it drops you over the edge. Running is one of the few things that allows me to clear my mind. I've tried meditation and yoga; they didn't work for me. They're too quiet of an activity, and that quiet just opens my mind for chaos to grow. I need exertion, I need to push myself to the limit.

Any fast-paced activity or sport will do when I need to release steam. Volleyball, ball hockey, lacrosse, I'm in. But running is where I feel I can soar; just fly away from here. The ultimate freedom. So, I lock my mind in brain jail and run. I know this isn't healthy, and I need to distance myself from them, but I can't say no to my parents because deep down, I just want them to love me. There's an incessant hollowness inside that gnaws at me. Although I crave love, I keep myself far away from any attachments, because in my mind, I can't give what I've never had.

The only thing getting me excited about the ceremony tomorrow was my parents' request for an extra ticket to my graduation. My heart flutters knowing they thought of bringing Lana with them. I miss her so much. She didn't let me know she was coming, but I think she's just trying to surprise me. She's the only one I care about coming to the ceremony and seeing my speech.

"I don't think I need to worry about it. They're sitting with your parents, and we'll take a few group shots together for the press. Then, we'll go out for an early dinner with your parents and Lana and end our night at the bar, picking up some hot asshole for me to fuck," I say around a mouthful of pancake.

Riley cringes at the harsh words and my emotionless tone, but she says nothing. She knows better than anyone how my relationship (or lack thereof) with my parents is. She's been my best friend since we were in diapers, and even though I sometimes get jealous of her relationship with her parents, she loves me anyway. Her parents love me too, and have been kind enough to welcome me into their family. If I'm not spending my holidays and breaks with Lana, I'm tagging along with Riley and her family.

Riley takes over the conversation and starts describing what she is wearing under the gown and how she will style her hair, and I nod as if I am paying attention. She moves on to how she wants to style my hair, because mine is much longer and it's fun to play with it, when my phone beeps in my purse. I pull it out and groan when I see the name lit up on my screen.

Mother Dearest: *Congrats on graduating. We'll see you tomorrow. Please make sure Riley does your hair and makeup if you refuse to hire someone to do it for you.*

I wrestle with a pang of loneliness in my heart at seeing the message from my mother. A reminder that she hasn't reached out since Christmas. I suppress the moisture springing to my eyes — just a moment of weakness. Another beep comes from my phone, and I look down at the screen.

Mother Dearest: *Oh, your father wanted me to remind you that you need to pack up your suite. You have a week before the movers arrive and bring everything to your condo in Toronto.*

The tears rimming my eyes evaporate faster than water in the desert. My fists clench as I squeeze the phone and my vision clouds with red. Only twenty-four hours left until I lose the last bit of temporary freedom I have. I need to make these twenty-four hours count before I am a prisoner within my family once again.

CHAPTER TWO

ELISSA

It's 9 PM, and I am getting ready in the bathroom, swiping some eyeliner onto my lash line, creating that smoky look I love. I step back and pull my curly hair away from my face. In the mirror I see Riley at the end of the hall, in the living room. She holds up two dresses, with a towel wrapped tightly around her slender frame. Her phone sits in the middle of a ring light on a tripod, and she's talking to her voiceless viewers live.

"Now, this backless, black cocktail dress is from Chanel," she says, as she swings the dress in front of her body, tilting her head back and forth. Her lips are pursed in thought as she debates how it looks against her complexion.

"I feel this might be a tad too dark for me. Since it's only April, I haven't worked on my tan, so I feel as though it might wash me out." Her lips pull into a pout before she swings the second option in front of the camera.

"This one," she explains, "is an emerald green silk strapless dress with a sweetheart neckline. It totes gives me Bella Goth vibes from *The Sims* franchise. I only wish Versace sent me this in a red! My black lob with this dress in red…hello?? I would drip sex appeal and cosplay at the same time!"

She chatters to her silent audience, and I smirk to myself. Riley is popular with her social media channels because she's gorgeous, realistic, and has hints of nerdiness thrown in. She's a down-to-earth girl, although some people think she's pretentious. She is an ambassador for the Canadian Mental Health Association because of her ongoing battle with anorexia, and she's been very candid with her journey and recovery on social media. The past four years have been successful for her.

Riley blows kisses to the camera, asks them to vote in her story about which outfit she should choose, and signs off. I turn back to fixing my hair until she appears behind me.

"So, what colour do you think? Black or green?" She asks me this knowing full well I am colour-blind in my left eye, but only partially in my right eye. Only shades of blue and some hues of green are missing in my right eye's vision. The green hues I can see are always dull and lacklustre. I don't answer her, knowing full well that her viewers will choose anyway. Instead, I flip her off and blow her a kiss.

Moments later, I am wriggling into my jeans, which are like a second skin that hugs every curve of my ass and hips, when Riley lets me know the car she ordered will be here soon. I slip on some black pumps and throw open my closet door, sliding hangers across the rail trying to find my favourite shirt. When I find it, I hug it to my chest and then pull it over my head. The amethyst halter top complements my dark blue eyes, or so Riley always tells me. With a scoop neck and low cut back, it fits my torso and breasts perfectly. The low back inhibits me from wearing a bra. Thankfully, I'm perky enough and don't need one. The silky texture of the top glides across my nipples, forcing them to pucker. With a quick glance in my full-length mirror, I ruffle my long, chestnut hair that smells of warm vanilla shampoo, shake loose the curls so they're more of a beach wave, and head out the door.

Our favourite haunt, Xion, is right in downtown Kingston on Princess Street. It is a fancy little place that has cheap booze, quality service, and hot patrons. It even has a rooftop bar and lounge for the VIPs. We arrive just before 11:30 PM, and the place is overflowing. We walk straight up to the door, ignoring the line, to talk to Teddy, the bouncer. We smile and flirt with him, and he lets us through, as always. When we found this place as freshmen in university, Teddy was working here, too. He is a couple years older than us, and Riley went home with him that night. We know everyone who works here and we always get exceptional service.

The first stop is the bar. We each grab a stool and wave at Liza, the bartender. She comes over with our drinks in her hands, shimmying to *Belly Dancer* by Imanbek and BYOR as the song pumps into the room from the DJ stand. We needn't order, as she already knows what we're having.

"Cosmo for Riley and a Johnnie Walker on the rocks for 'Lissa."

"Thanks Liza," I say. "Open a tab for us and keep them coming!"

"As per usual," she chortles. "Oh, there are quite a few good-looking men here tonight. You'll have them buying you drinks all night. You girls look smokin' hot."

Sure enough, not even five minutes later, two guys walk up to us, one on either side of me and Riley. I feel the burn of their eyes undressing us as they flag down Liza.

"Another round for the ladies," the one beside Riley says. He oozes masculinity, with a sharp, defined jaw and a clean, short beard with a few days of growth. He's also got what I assume to be stunning crystal blue eyes, because of the way they reflect any bit of light that hits them. His hands are big and strong as he grasps his beer, with his broad shoulders emphasizing his tapered torso as he leans against the bar. He flashes us a bright smile.

"I'm Kessler, and he," he motions to his buddy beside me, "is West."

I turn to the guy beside me to say hi and my stomach falls.

"Uh, yeah. We've...already met. Last night," I say, giving Liam a small smile. I excuse myself from the conversation and head for the bathroom. Kessler and Liam chat with Riley as I disappear into the crowd. When I walk into the ladies' room, I kick open a stall, slam it shut with my foot, and flick the lock. I hover over the toilet as I relieve myself, thinking, *Is this it? Have I slept through so many guys at this bar that I'm circling the same ones the very next night? What the fuck?*

It seems Toronto can't arrive soon enough. After flushing the toilet with my foot, I walk out of the stall to wash my hands. I stare at myself in the mirror and let out a sigh, then drag my feet back to the shit-show at the bar.

Riley looks to be about three drinks deep already when I return. Her cheeks are tinged a slight pink, and she is flirting up a storm with Kessler, touching his hand and running her fingers along his biceps. I clear my throat behind her. She whips around and when her eyes land on me, they light up.

"'Lissa! You're back!" she squeals. "C'mon, let's get another drink and dance with these studs."

She pulls Kessler by the collar of his light grey button-down, leading him to the dance floor. I shift my eyes to Liam, who looks way too pleasant to be seeing me again after I tossed him out of my apartment so unceremoniously this morning. I shrug and head to the dance floor with Liam in tow. When we find Kessler and Riley on the floor, she is grinding her ass, hard, in a figure eight against his crotch. He's looking over her shoulder, and by the look on his face, I can tell he can see right down her dress into her cleavage. His left hand slides up her thigh while the other one holds his beer. I saunter up in front of Riley and start grinding on her, crotch to crotch, when I feel Liam press his body against mine. We dance like this for a few songs until I motion for a drink and walk away, leaving Riley with the two men. My plan tonight is to make myself numb for tomorrow's festivities.

I catch Liza's attention and order another whisky and a tequila shot. I slam the tequila back with no chaser and take my drink back to the dance floor. When I spot Riley, she is still rubbing her ass all over Kessler and he is marking his territory over her neck. I look at Liam, who is swaying to the music all alone, awkwardly drinking his beer. I assume he is waiting for me when I feel a tap on my shoulder. I look behind me and grin. My night has gotten better. This guy is about a foot-and-a-half taller than me, with mousy brown hair that is shaved on the sides, with just a bit on top to spike. He's sporting a chin strap and his face is broad, with sharp cheekbones. His full lips would feel heavenly sucking on my clit. He's wearing a black t-shirt and some dark-wash jeans. He holds out his hand and I take it, following him back to the dance floor.

We're a few feet away from Riley, Liam, and Kessler, but I pay them no attention. Instead, my legs are straddling one of this guy's muscular thighs, grinding against him, and I can feel the tension building in his jeans. I smirk when I look him in the eyes, swinging my hips to *Thunder* by Gabry Ponte, LUM!X, and Prezioso. *I picked the right leg to rub against.* I sling one arm around his neck as his enormous hands grip my waist, pulling us closer together. After a few more songs, I feel his hot breath and tongue lightly running up the shell of my ear.

"Wanna get out of here?"

Oh, boy, do I ever. I nod my head and tell him I just need to let my friend know. He follows me over to Riley. The music is so loud, but I shout to her that I'm leaving, and nod toward where the guy is standing. She gives me a thumbs-up, but darts her eyes over to where Liam is standing. I glance at him out of the corner of my eye. Liam's eyes dim and his body slouches when he realizes I came over to say goodbye. I shoot a hand in the air to signal my goodbye to the boys with Riley.

The hot guy I am leaving with comes over to me, snaking his arm around my waist, pulling me out of the club. I'm not as inebriated as I planned to be to end up with a hangover, but I'm definitely tipsy enough to lose some of my inhibitions and fuck this guy all night long without worrying about seeing my parents tomorrow.

CHAPTER

THREE

BRANDT

I hate nothing more than being issued ultimatums. Yet, here I am.

The board wants to look at other ventures in order to expand our portfolio. They've decided it should have something to do with media and publishing, as it is the only sector we haven't invested in yet. I agreed to it with the caveat that I had explicit control over what company we invested in. I mean, it's my fucking company. No vote should stand in the way of what I want.

Currently, I am looking at the profit-and-loss statements of Black & Wells Publishing and Press, the company I've chosen to expand with, just for a chance to be within close proximity of Elissa. It's probably a bit strange that I've chosen to invest in a company because of a woman, but I've waited for this opportunity for a long time. Maybe luck will be on my side, and I'll have a chance to run into her; a chance to talk to her. I feel the heat of Harold Black's stare boring into my head. I glance over at him from under furrowed brows, and he shifts his stare elsewhere. The server of the restaurant in the hotel I'm staying at places an egg white omelette and black coffee in front of me.

"Well, it seems everything is in order," I say, picking up my fork and cutting into my omelette. "I have some things in mind that will help you really expand into the digital market with my tech company's expertise," I assert. "Specifically, I want control of the new division you're thinking about creating, and that I would invest in. I'd take seventy percent control."

Harold grunts and strokes his moustache, a fucking disgusting habit of his.

"I'll need to do a lot of work to make sure things integrate properly and seamlessly. You're trying to converge all of your print media into digital, while also creating new content, and —"

Harold interrupts me.

"I think a sixty, twenty-five, fifteen split is fair."

Huh? What the fuck? He reads my mind and continues explaining.

"I'm creating this division for my daughter specifically. I'd like her to have fifteen percent of it to learn how to control shares before…" he trails off and shudders, "…before she gets the rest of my company."

"I don't give a flying monkey how the shares break down. But I'm holding seventy percent. What you do with the remaining thirty is up to you. Take it or leave it."

Harold made a *humph* noise, and suddenly his eyes spark. *This cannot be good.*

"Fine," he sneers, seemingly coming to a decision. "But I have a final stipulation." His lips press firmly together for a moment, then he continues.

"Word on the street is that the board and your family want you to settle down. I have a daughter who needs a husband." My pulse quickens. I chose this company because it presented the perfect opportunity to see her again, but what was that about a husband? My face remains completely neutral, as I don't want to give him any leverage or the benefit of a reaction.

"I'm sorry. You want me to marry your daughter?" I ask flatly, my expression not betraying a hint of my racing thoughts. Harold smirks at me.

"Yes. She is a pretty and smart girl, but she lacks direction and is a bit...wild. I've been hesitant on handing over my company to her ever since she was little." His eyes harden as he tries to hide his frustration. I grab my coffee and take a drink, not breaking eye contact.

"If I had a son-in-law, someone like you, I'd happily let her keep control of the company, with the other shares going to her betrothed." He says this as if I am a greedy prick, only looking for money and still operating business deals like some slimy gangster from the 1920s.

"I don't understand. So, you want to arrange a marriage for her?"

"Yes and no." Harold pauses. "I want you to seduce her into accepting a proposal. My daughter graduates from Queen's University this afternoon. I have an extra ticket and would like you to join me and my wife at the ceremony and meet Elissa. What do you say? Then you can take the week to think it over?"

Ah, that's why he wanted to meet me in Kingston and not Toronto.

I nod my head, letting him know I am interested in meeting her.

"My assistant will email the details. See you at 2 PM, Nixon Field." Harold flashes a victorious smile as he gets up and shakes my hand. I watch him walk away and take stock of what just happened. I notice a definite uneasy feeling in the pit of my stomach at the thought of this marriage ultimatum, but to deny I'm considering it would be foolish. She's all I've really thought about for the last eight years.

When I return to my suite, I flop down on the bed and stare up at the ceiling. I couldn't believe what Harold was offering; I only sought to bring Black & Wells into my portfolio because the board wanted a publishing and media company. But to see Elissa Black in person? *Yes, please.*

Just thinking about her has my pulse racing and my groin tightening. No other woman has ever interested me in the slightest. I remember everything about her from the first time I saw her eight years ago. It was my senior year of high school, and she was just a freshman. I remember her being assigned to the group Rhys and I handled. The way she giggled at her friend's whispered comment, the way she tucked her bronze hair behind her ears while biting the inside of her cheek, the way her ass shook when she walked down the hallways, her kilt swishing against her thighs. I remember finally understanding why guys were always into the "schoolgirl" bit with the Catholic uniforms.

Elissa was one of the most popular girls in the ninth grade, but it didn't make her one of the mean girls, even though she hung out with them. There was one moment in particular that made me fall in love with who she was. It was just before Christmas break and her friends were picking on some girl who had a second-hand uniform and shabby book bag. The mean girls took her backpack, threw it in a slushy puddle, cackled, and walked away. The girl was fighting back tears as Elissa let her friends walk ahead. Suddenly, she bent down and picked the girl's belongings out of the slush. Elissa took everything out of her designer messenger bag, put the girl's stuff in it, and handed her the messenger bag. It was the sweetest thing I ever saw, and my heart fluttered.

Elissa won every academic achievement, she was always the top performer in the competitive dance team, and she carried the track and field team too. She was even captain of the volleyball team as a freshman. Elissa really was that good, though most of the gossip floating through the hallways insinuated that "daddy paid her way into the captaincy." My eyes sought her out, the same way I need air to breathe. It was like my entire being was aware of where she was at all times. I could spot her in a crowd in a second, without fail, just like I did the first time I saw her back in my senior year.

It was the first day of classes after the summer holidays, and September always brought a certain hum of energy throughout the halls. Teachers and students alike didn't grumble or groan when they entered the school, but instead were having animated and happy conversations.

My buddy Rhys and I volunteered to show the incoming freshmen around for the week, like most seniors do, to get a few of the volunteer hours that we needed to graduate. A sea of navy, white, and ocean blue uniforms covered the school's front quad, each uniform worn by a nervous and excited teenager, eagerly showing their class schedules to their friends, seeing who was in which class together. The freshmen class size was the largest it had been in the last five years, with over 231 students. Which left Rhys and me with thirty-three students to help.

When the warning bell rang at 8:10 AM on that warm September morning, a few stragglers without their designated groups started rushing around in a panic. One geeky-looking kid was smashed into, and his books, class schedule, and contents of his backpack spilled everywhere. The kids around him pointed and laughed, but one girl walked over, swept everything up off the ground, and helped him organize his stuff. The girl's face glowed pink, as though it embarrassed her to be the only nice person in the crowd of laughing teenagers.

When she stood up, our gazes locked for a minute. Her sapphire eyes sparkled in the sunlight, and I couldn't look away. From a distance, her eyes were as clear and blue as the sea. Her skin flushed a deeper pink, bordering on red. She bit down on the corner of her lip and shifted her attention back toward her friends as she rejoined their circle. From then on, every molecule in my body could find her in any room. I only fell more in love with her — from a distance — from that day on. Her name was called at every award ceremony throughout the year, and I could finally put a name to her beautiful face. Elissa Black: Best in Class, Highest GPA in Grade Nine, MVP Girls' Volleyball, Vice-Captain of the Competitive Dance Team…the list went on and on.

My dick was straining against my slacks at the thought of her prancing around on stage in her ballet tights, the muscles of her perfect, round ass pulled taut when she was in her pointe shoes… Like I've done a thousand times before, I pull up her friend's social media page and find a recent picture with Elissa in it. She posted a photo twelve hours ago of both women standing in a bar. It was one of those promotional photos for the bar, where the photographer makes the women stand out with lights streaking around. Elissa was in tight dark jeans and a purple top. Her nipples pressed against the tight shirt, almost demanding to cut through the material. *Fuck.*

I unzip my slacks and pull them and my boxers down, letting my cock spring free. I toss my phone across the bed, wrap my hand around my thick, pulsating cock, and focus on the fantasy of having her.

When she slips away from the dance floor, I trail behind her, watching her ass sway as she leads us to the restroom. She steps inside for a few moments, then pokes her head out and flashes me a playful grin to let me know the coast is clear. I shut the door behind me and rush to her. I pull her against me and smash my mouth down on hers, devouring her. I grip her ass and hoist her up as she wraps her legs around my waist. I walk us into one stall, slam the door shut, and press her against it, anchoring her there with my knee. One of my hands grips the nape of her neck, deepening the kiss, and when I part her lips with my tongue, a whisper of a moan escapes her.

The same hand then trails down the length of her neck like a feather, a small shiver erupting down her spine. When my hand palms her tit, they fit perfectly as I massage and paw at her breast. I then flick her puckered nipple with my index finger. My lips trace the trail my hand left along her neck earlier, finding their way down to her cleavage. I pull her shirt down, further and further, until a tit pops out, revealing her perfect, creamy skin and a pale rose nipple. An eager sigh escapes my lips before I take the nipple into my mouth and suck on it hard. She writhes against the stall door, lacing her fingers in my hair and pulling tightly.

I bite her nipple, not too hard, but enough to elicit a feral moan. My cock twitches in my pants and I can feel the heat of her pussy against my leg getting warmer. My hand seeks the heat like a missile and rubs her clit through her jeans. I can feel the dampness soaking through…

A heat swirls in my stomach and my balls tighten. *Fuck.* I snap back to reality and as my hand slams down the length of my cock, I reach over and grab some tissues from the nightstand. I keep pumping until my cock is throbbing my release into the tissue.

CHAPTER

FOUR

BRANDT

I arrive at the Nixon Field soccer pitch at 1:45 PM, waiting at the end of the rows of chairs for Harold Black. By the grace of God, it was only the end of April, so it wasn't swelteringly hot in Ontario yet, but the warm sun beaming down sent a pleasant shiver over my body. The smell of freshly mown grass fills the air. I'd chosen a navy button-down shirt and cuffed it at the crook of my elbow, paired with charcoal slacks and a matching sport jacket. Back at the hotel, I had to rub one out another two times before I could collect myself and get ready. I'd stood in the shower, bracing myself against the wall with my left hand while my right stroked my length. The muscles in my thighs were taut and my ass was clenched as my mouth was agape, panting, sucking in the shower's steam as I pumped myself to euphoria.

It was like my libido was that of a teenager again, who was figuring out his cock for the first time. The idea of seeing her with my eyes, in person, and not through a memory or a screen made my cock ache and my heart race. No other woman has ever roused my dick the way she does. I don't know why, but there's something about Elissa; something natural, chemical, that pulls me to her.

For the last eight years, I have been yanking my dick to fantasies of her. I've never been a very overtly sexual guy, and I've never understood why Elissa has only ever been the one to capture my attention that way. Focusing on my education, then later growing my business, has always been my direction, my focus. Of course there's been a few girls I've seen a few times, but it never leads to anything. With my limited experience, I've always been a giver. It's never interested me enough to have a woman touch or suck my dick — let alone shove it in someone's hole. Even though no one understands what happens behind closed doors, I'm often seen with a rotation of new women at functions and whatnot, which led the board and my family to think I was some playboy. Hence, their desire for me to find someone and settle down. And it plays right into Harold's agenda, which sort of irks me in its own way.

Closer to 2 PM, Harold and his wife arrive. He is the loudest person here, and his entourage of media people follow him. When he meets my eyes, his gaze brightens, and he places his hand on his wife's lower back and ushers her over to where I stand.

"Glad you could make it, son." Harold greets me with a handshake, placing extra emphasis on "son." I suppress a flinch at the *son* comment, as if he's insinuating the marriage proposal is a done deal.

"This is my wife, Collette."

"A pleasure to meet you, Collette," I say warmly, enclosing her into a small embrace and giving a polite kiss on the cheek. She murmurs a hello and saunters off to find three seats near the front row. Harold chuckles and slaps a hand on my shoulder.

"This shall be interesting. You'll have to join us after the ceremony for dinner and drinks," he says. I only nod and follow the path to where his wife found seats for us. I wait at the end of the row for Harold to come and sit next to his wife, with me on the end of the row beside him. The dean of the university greets everyone and starts the proceedings. It is about an hour before the valedictorian is called up to speak for the graduating class of 2023.

"Please give a warm welcome to this year's valedictorian. She is a headstrong and hardworking woman whose tenacity knows no bounds. Captain of the track and volleyball teams, she has helped Queen's University hit some outstanding records in tournament wins. She has double-majored in English Literature and Business, and graduates with honours…" The crowd murmurs with approval and awe. *She is a magnificent woman, that's for damn sure.*

"…Please welcome Elissa Black to the stage."

The entire audience breaks out in a round of applause as Elissa walks up to the podium to deliver her speech. She is every bit as graceful, poised, calm, and collected as I thought she would be. However, her beauty is nothing like I remembered — it's better; she's perfect. Her auburn hair gleams underneath the graduation cap, soaking up the sunlight as it radiates behind her. The quickening of my heart is almost audible. Thankfully I grabbed a program to fold over my lap, as I feel my slacks tighten at just the sight of her. Even eight years later, she does something to me that is supernatural; something I'm unable to articulate. It's like my body lights on fire when she's in my vicinity. My soul tingles when she's nearby. If our eyes connect, my heart squeezes in my chest.

I wish I could say that I enjoyed her speech, but that would be a lie. I couldn't focus on anything other than the way her lips moved and the lilt of her voice. Imagining how those perfect, heart-shaped lips would feel pressing against mine, or the sound of her moaning my name while I'm ramming into her.

"Here's to the graduating class of 2023! Thank you!" When she ended her speech, she did a little curtsy and shook the dean's hand before sitting back down in her chair on the stage. The dean then calls a list of names for their degrees. When he calls Elissa's name, she glides over, takes his hand, and shakes it for the cameras. A polite applause ripples through the crowd, and I glance over at her parents to see their proud faces as their daughter collects her diploma. To my surprise, neither of them are paying attention.

Collette seems to be flicking through posts on Facebook, while Harold keeps glancing at his watch every few moments, brows furrowed, clearly growing more irritated with each time check. *Seriously? The audacity of these people…but then again, they're from old money and came from generations of wealth. So, achievements like graduating — as valedictorian, at that — from Queen's University likely mean nothing to them.*

As the dean comes to the last of the graduating names, the audience's energy shifts. People are murmuring and squirming in their chairs by the end of the three-hour ceremony. I am one of those people. But not for the same reasons as the others. My pulse quickens as I grow more nervous to come face-to-face with Elissa, the woman of my dreams.

CHAPTER

FIVE

ELISSA

Another long night, a satisfying romp with a strange, desirable body, and a hangover is what I should have avoided before seeing my parents today. More specifically, the hangover. After we got home from the bar, I broke out the whisky in my liquor cabinet, and the stud and I drank half the bottle. I squeeze my eyes shut to block out the harsh sunlight, but the glow still filters through my lids. I groan in pain as my head pounds, screaming at me for (A) all the alcohol, and (B) allowing dehydration to set in.

A debilitating wave of nausea crashes over me, and I can't decide if it's from mixing the tequila with the whisky I drank last night, or the nightmare of the past that haunted me in my dreams. Last night, memories from when I was about eight or nine replaced any sweet dreams.

As I slept, I remembered tiptoeing downstairs to get a glass of water, and my parents were busy hosting a gathering. I've always had great hearing, so it's easy to pick up on conversations a few feet from me in a crowded, loud place. When I try to focus on one or two voices, the other noises just fade away. As I padded toward the kitchen, I heard my name and froze.

For a second, I thought I was hearing things, or that I was about to get in trouble for being out of bed. But when I glanced over my shoulder, I realized the voice was coming from my father's study. I heard my father say my name again, and I changed my direction to head toward him. I could hear my parents arguing, but they didn't argue by raising their voices. They talk low and quiet when they're mad or fighting. It's kind of unsettling; sometimes, you just want them to yell at you. I could hear my father stomping around his office.

"Shit, Collette. Stop with this crap about having another one," my father said. I peeked through the tiny sliver of the open door. He was pacing back and forth, one hand on his hip and the other rubbing his dark goatee in frustration.

"Well, I'm sorry I gave birth to Elissa," my mother cried as she threw her hands up in the air, exasperated. My tiny brain and heart stopped working. One felt like it cracked and the other shot a spring.

"But, if you want a successor, and one that is blood-related, let's just have another."

My father was now facing away from my mother, toward his bookshelf, his fist pressing against his forehead.

"No. I'm not taking that risk to end up with another needy girl. I don't have time for another one hanging off my leg for attention. I'll just need to make sure her future husband will be acceptable, or I'll need to live long enough to have a grandson to pass it to."

I jumped as a soft hand rested on my shoulder. I looked up, still trying to process what was just said. It was our housekeeper, Lana. She put her finger to her lips to make sure I knew to stay silent and jerked her head to the side, letting me know it's time to go back to bed. She escorted me upstairs and tucked me in, stroking my rusty hair.

"You know you shouldn't be eavesdropping, right Liss?" She gave me a half-hearted stern look. My vision blurred a little as I fought back tears and just nodded my head. She sighed.

"How much did you hear?"

"Enough," my little voice whispered. "But I don't understand. Why am I not a boy like they want?" Lana stared at me with soft eyes, grazing two fingers down the side of my face and across my jawline.

"Hon, I want to say that things get taken out of context when people eavesdrop." She paused briefly. "But sometimes people have expectations when they want to start a family, and things don't always go as planned. Some people only want boys, and some only want girls. Some people just don't care. It's neither right nor wrong. People can't help what they want." She saw me scrunch up my brows in confusion, so she paused again, biting her lips together to collect her thoughts.

"Your father's job has created tension, and your mom and dad have become frustrated. Your mom and dad don't always say the nicest things, and being frustrated doesn't excuse it. I don't think they meant what they said. You are the sweetest little girl. Anyone would love to have you."

She gave me a soft smile and kissed me on the forehead. When she was about to close the door, I stopped her.

"Lana?" She popped her head through the open crack of the door.

"Would you love to have me?" She smiled softly.

"I already have you, baby girl. I'm not going anywhere. G'night, love."

Her head disappeared and the hallway light flicked off. I rolled over onto my side, and before my eyes adjusted, I forced them shut and stayed like that until I drifted off.

Over the next few years, I tried hard to be the kid they wanted, vagina or not. I kept my head down and rarely asked for anything. I worked my ass off at school and had the top grades to prove it. I collected every academic achievement there was in high school. But even the highest grades and the most prestigious of awards didn't seem to matter to my parents. It was like I was a ghost in the house, one who would occasionally cross the veil between the living and dead when they would notice I was there, possessing a chair or something.

Lana was more like a mother to me than a housekeeper. Her official title was housekeeper, but she did little housekeeping. She did basic chores, grocery shopping, or prepping meals during the day when I was off at school, while another actual maid did most of the housekeeping and cleaning. Lana would shuttle me back and forth, from home to school, to sport tournaments, to friends' houses, and to whatever appointments I needed to attend.

Lana started getting worried about how much I had retreated within myself over the years. Whenever she inquired about my day, I gave her short, generic answers, typically accompanied by an eye roll or a shrug. Over time, I stopped asking to hang out with my friends, other than Riley, my best friend since birth. The summer before I started high school, Lana took it upon herself to set me up with a therapist. I hadn't known, but she paid for it out of her own pocket.

Thinking back, I was such a bitch to her about it. I thought it was my parents' idea, and I resisted it. I skipped sessions, did whatever I could not to attend. *I didn't need a therapist. I needed my parents to pay attention to me.* Thankfully, I had Lana. Wait, she's not gone! Don't misunderstand; I just mean that I am so thankful for her presence in my life, especially during the formative years. I'm not sure when it started, but at some point I started calling her "mom." Usually when it was just us, but sometimes when Riley was around, too.

I always kept my grades high and familial expectations low. Sometimes, I felt there was a glimmer of hope; when I felt that there was a turning point coming. Times when my parents would show up at my dance recitals or track meets, but then, when the main events were over, I would notice the press there, and they would stage loving photos of a proud family. Being the unwanted daughter of the CEO of one of the world's top publishing and press houses came with a lot of expectations and obligations I could not avoid. I even tried to become emancipated at seventeen, but my father had his lawyers kibosh that quick.

"Elissa," my father addressed me in a mediation conference room back then. "Why? Are you purposely trying to hurt your mother and I?"

My eyes flickered with anger as I stared at them, willing myself not to cry even as the tears burned in my eyes. I stayed silent, but he continued.

"Just what are you thinking? The ungrateful brat, seeking attention again! Do you have any idea what would happen to me if word got out about this?" he scoffed.

"I can see the headlines now: *'Heiress of Publishing Press House Closes Chapter on Family,' 'Rewriting History for an Heiress,' 'Real-Life Princess and the Pauper.'*" He shook his head as he rattled off the supposed headlines.

"Of course, Father. It is once again about you," I spat, venom thick in my voice. His bewilderment was the tiniest spark of happiness I had felt in a very long time. Seeing an emotion on his face other than disdain was a victory.

"Yes, it is about me. It's all about me. I'm the one who pays for you. I'm the one who built this company from *nothing*, and all you have to do is *nothing* just to inherit the damn thing! My life's work, in the hands of an ungrateful girl!"

"Well, I never asked for the company. I don't want it. I don't need it, or your money!" My father rolled his eyes at me.

"I'm serious! Why else would I attempt to emancipate myself? I want no ties to either of you. I've only ever tried to be what you wanted, and it was never enough. I'm finally done giving a shit, and I want out."

I glanced over at my mother and could smell the boredom rotting out of her as she swept a file across her long, artificial nails. My father smirked at me and declared that he would not let me be rid of my name or familial obligations, and he would oppose me at every turn in my attempts to gain freedom.

Fan-fucking-tastic. A prisoner within my family. And it has been that way ever since. Little freedom, little responsibilities, little self-respect. Dealing with them daily was never an issue. They weren't always around. I spent most of my time with Lana, especially during the summer and holiday breaks during high school. While most kids my age would've loved having next to no supervision, that wasn't me. I craved the attention and love of my parents. Some of my classmates saw it as absolute freedom, but the only real dose of freedom I felt I had was when I entered university. I could remove myself from the toxicity of my loneliness and move into a dorm. My parents and I fought on this, but they relented when I made a compromise: If I could go to a school of my choice, live in the dorms and room with Riley, and have more autonomy over my life during school, I would follow along with their choice of major and be part of the family business after graduation. I lost a hell of a lot more in that deal, but I also gained freedom, however temporary it may have been.

I tear myself away from the memories and shake the guy beside me awake, telling him it's time to leave. Getting out of bed, I stagger to Riley's room and bang on the door in an attempt to wake her up. We have a graduation ceremony to get ready for.

• • •

Once the ceremony was over, I rushed to find Riley so we could meet up with our parents. I was actually rushing for one reason: to see Lana. My parents thought of bringing her, which is surprising, because who knew they could be thoughtful? I was too busy focusing on the ceremony and proceedings, so I didn't think to look at my phone until after the ceremony. Grabbing my phone from my clutch, I tap the screen to see two notifications. One from Lana, and one from my father. I read my father's first, saving the best for last.

Disappointed Father: *We are over on the left-hand side and ten rows from the front. Riley's parents are near us as well. Please check your face to make sure it is decent before coming over here.*

What a dickhead. What kind of father says that to his daughter on the day of her graduation? And why the hell does it matter what I look like? I know there are going to be photos, but it's just my parents, Riley, her parents, and Lana. Then, I look at the message from Lana and my heart sinks. Tears sting my nose and eyes.

Mom: *Happy Graduation Day, darling. Hope you have a fantastic day. We'll celebrate the next time we get together. Sorry I couldn't be there. Love you. Xo.*

But...if Lana wasn't here, who was the third ticket for? Who could be so important to bring to a *family* event? Fuming, I grab Riley's arm and drag her along to find our parents.

CHAPTER
SIX

ELISSA

We finally spot our parents in the crowd. As we walk over, I notice that Riley's parents have their backs to us, and they are standing next to a tall man with broad shoulders. Riley elbows me in the ribs.

"Psst…look at the buns on him!" she squeals quietly. I snicker and wiggle my eyebrows at her. Once we get close enough, my father notices me over Riley's mom's shoulder and a too-wide grin appears on his face, emulating the image of a proud father. He sidesteps the group, spreads his arms wide, and struts over to us.

"There she is! My amazing daughter!" my father boasts. I groan inwardly, suppressing the urge to vomit up my breakfast. Riley perks up and shrieks when her parents turn around. They both run over to squeeze her and jealousy twists uncomfortably in my gut. My father pulls me into an awkward embrace, and I lightly pat him on the back twice before stepping back. Mother then saunters over, places one hand on each shoulder, and air-kisses me like the French.

"Good to see you, baby," my mother murmurs as lovingly as she can muster. I grit my teeth.

"Hello, Mother," I say as I reciprocate the air kisses and step away. Once I'm out of my mother's grasp, I see the man my father has invited to my graduation in place of Lana. Sadness, frustration, and curiosity bubble inside of me, fighting for release. My father is chatting with Riley's parents and this mystery man until Riley's parents excuse themselves. My father leads the man over to my mother and I; the warm April air thickens as they walk closer.

"Elissa, please meet Brandt Collins. Of Collins Global Collective. Brandt, it's our pleasure to introduce you to Elissa," my father says, oozing feigned enthusiasm. Brandt peers down at me, with a slight smile that tugs his full lips slightly higher on the left. When his eyes lock on to mine, I'm suddenly temporarily paralyzed. Only when he steps closer do I realize his height. As I take him in, I notice the muscles of his shoulders and arms flexing beneath the fabric of his suit jacket. A sudden urge to climb him like a tree comes over me.

When Brandt extends a hand, I hesitate to take it. Instead, my gaze pulls away from the extended hand to his face. The sunlight highlights and bounces off his natural bronzed skin, giving him a divine glow, like a god cast down from the heavens. His eyes are a shade of green that seems lacklustre, though I'm sure my vision impairment is hindering their actual vibrancy. Brandt's golden-brown hair is precisely styled, though the breeze gently ruffles the gentle "swoop" of the style. His hair looks as soft as a cloud, and my fingers tingle with the need to run them through his shiny locks.

When I take his hand, it's like an electric current courses through my body. All my senses seem to heighten, time seems to slow, and everything around us fades away. I notice he is still staring at me and hasn't blinked yet. With urgency in his eyes, he gently shakes my hand, and I feel his grip is ever so slightly clammy. *Strange. A big, strong, confident man like this has clammy hands? Why would he be nervous?*

"It's nice to meet you, Elissa," Brandt says, his voice deep, clear, and powerful; a sound that vibrates down to my core. I feel a slight heat rising on my cheeks, among other places.

"Yes. It's nice to meet you too. However," I say tightly, shooting a glare at my father, "I was not expecting a business associate of my father to be joining my parents at a family occasion." No matter how good-looking this man is, I can't allow the swirling arousal in my lady bits to distract me from my anger toward my parents for neglecting to bring Lana.

"Oh," Brandt says, his brow lowered in confusion. "So, this was a…surprise?" Leave it to my parents to trap this guy in the thick of their schemes.

"Yes. I was under the impression they wanted the third ticket for Lana."

Brandt raises his eyebrow and turns his gaze to my parents. My mother rolls her eyes, clearly annoyed I brought up Lana's name, and my father shrugs off the comment just as his assistant leans over and whispers something in his ear.

"Ah, yes. The press is ready to take a few shots of us as a family." My father waves the photographer over and tugs me between him and my mother, as both of them look at the photographer like professionals. They even sort of look like they are actually proud of me. As the photographer snaps away, my father glances over at Brandt.

"Ah, Brandt. Why don't you hop in a few of these photos?"

Brandt looks slightly uncomfortable but doesn't refuse the request. He stalks over and my father walks around to the other side of my mother so that Brandt can stand beside me. Brandt sidles up against my side and his arm lightly rests against my lower back.

His touch is so light, anyone would barely notice his arm is there...except there is a coursing, hot electricity humming around me from him being so close. My mouth pulls into a forced and awkward smile. After a few more shots, my father steps away with my mother and insists on the photographer getting a few of just me and Brandt. I shoot my father a death glare and he returns the look. I sigh in defeat and just do as my father wishes.

The photographer gestures for us to stand a little closer together. Perhaps assuming we're a couple, she positions our heads, tilting them toward each other, and places my hand on his chest. Brandt and I simultaneously freeze. I feel the thunderous pounding of his heart underneath my hand, and when I look to his beautiful face, his sun-kissed skin now blushes a reddish hue.

"Now," my father says jovially, "Brandt, why don't you meet us at our hotel's restaurant for dinner? We can't have our guest dining alone." I frown at the suggestion.

"Sorry, Father. But I already have plans to have dinner with Riley and her parents…I was unaware that you'd be inviting a…guest." My father's jaw clenches as I side-eye Brandt.

"Well, just invite Riley, Brianne, and Connor. They're always welcome," Father says tightly, his teeth gritted. Brandt clears his throat to get our attention.

"Just as well. I'm not here alone. I have two friends with me as well."

My father tenses at Brandt's words, but my insides melt at the soothing baritone of his voice.

"Bring them along! The more the merrier." Father clasps his hands together. "We'll see you there, Brandt. Elissa, message Riley and let her know. I believe her parents are staying at the same hotel."

● ● ●

The Frontenac Club in Kingston was my parents' stay of choice on the rare occasion they came to visit me at school. They like it because it's swanky, and even though it is a small place, it makes my father feel important and exclusive, boosting his already inflated ego. Riley and I arrived at the hotel lounge approximately forty-five minutes later to see our families sitting at a bank of tables pushed together to accommodate nine people.

We glide across the white marble tile toward the group. My father glances up at us and plasters on a forced smile as he stands to welcome us. The three other men that were my father's guests stand up, their backs facing us. I immediately recognized Brandt, as he was wearing the same suit from the ceremony. The other two men beside him look vaguely familiar, and when they turn around, Riley and I gasp and exchange shocked glances.

In front of us stand Kessler and Liam. Their eyes light up as they recognize us, and Liam saunters over to me, pulls me in, and places a kiss on my cheek. My father's brow furrows and I shoot Liam a hard stare. Kessler follows suit with Riley, and both accompany us to the table. I slide into the booth next to my mother, the cool blue leather feeling smooth against my thighs. Riley plops down on my right. Sitting across from me is Brandt, who is staring at me with cold, hard eyes; beside him is Liam. Kessler pulls up a chair and sits at the end of the table, right next to Riley. He leans over to her to whisper something and she giggles.

My father flags down the waitress and asks for a bottle of the nicest wine they have for the table. I can feel a burning stare boring into me, and when I glance up, I notice Liam and Brandt are focusing on me. My mother also takes note, her gaze flicking between the three of us.

"It appears there's no need for introductions between you, Riley, and these two?" my mother inquires. I cringe and Riley's face lights up.

"No, Collette. We met Liam two nights ago at a club, and last night he was at the club with Kessler," Riley explains, keeping her eyes locked on Kessler's. But Kessler speaks up and extends a hand toward Riley anyway.

"Rhys is my first name. It's Rhys Kessler," he says, flashing a hundred-watt smile at Riley. My father glares over at me, jaw ticking, from where he sits between Brandt and Riley's dad Connor. I shift my gaze and see Brandt's icy stare still frozen in my direction. *What is wrong with my father and Brandt?*

We engage in small talk around the table while we wait for our entrées to arrive. Everyone, that is, but Brandt. He sits across from me with a vacant stare and is impossibly still, like a gargoyle. Suddenly, he speaks up, interrupting the flow of the conversation.

"Elissa…"

Everyone turns toward him, surprised that he's finally spoken, and with such a commanding voice.

"What do you plan on doing with an English Lit and Business degree, anyway? Seems strange to double major in both."

I feel a challenge behind his words, as though he's suggesting that I am missing a few brain cells to combine those two degrees together. I meet his challenge, knowing full well how hard it is to combine those two majors — plus, a bit of googling before coming here told me Mr. Big Shot dropped out of the University of Toronto after two years.

"Yes, it seems a bit…*strange*. But I'm sure you already know how *difficult* a business major can be…imagine a double major. And I'm sure my father has told you all about his *plans* for me."

I sit up straight, cross one leg over the other under the table, and fold my arms together, putting up an invisible barrier. Brandt doesn't seem phased by my response; instead, he seems rather entertained. The corners of his mouth twitch and a sparkle glints in his eyes.

"He might've mentioned some of his ideas for your future to me in passing. We talked about the division you're supposedly heading when you move to Toronto in a week."

He levels his gaze at me, waiting for a smart-ass remark, I'm sure. Goosebumps pepper my skin under his stare. I plaster on a polite smile, turn to Riley, and whisper in her ear. She just looks at me in confusion.

"Well, dinner was great," I say, as my eyes lock on Brandt for a few beats before I turn my head to my father.

"However, Riley and I have a previous engagement scheduled for tonight, so we need to head out, unfortunately." My father grits his teeth and I see his hand tighten around his wine glass.

"Interesting how you assume dinner was great," Brandt interjects flatly, "Considering we have yet to receive the entrées." He raises one of his eyebrows, egging me on. I purse my lips to hide my smile.

"You're right. But it seems I am rather full after the appetizers. In fact, I couldn't possibly eat another bite." I take the napkin off my lap and daintily wipe the corners of my mouth to drill the excuse home. A rising red flush burns my father's neck and creeps up to his ears, like a thermometer. His upper lip and nose start to twitch.

"I'm sure the bar and alcohol can wait until after we finish eating," my father grunts through his teeth. I shift my eyes to him and shrug.

"It's not the bar, Father. Rather, I have only a week to pack my apartment and it will not do itself. So, while we'd love to stay and chat...we must be off." I nudge Riley to move out of the booth so we both can exit. Brandt stands up to acknowledge our departure when my father speaks up.

"I'm sure I can have my assistant arrange something — to have someone come over and pack you up. It would be rude to leave the dinner to pack," my father counters. Brandt buttons his sport coat and my dad looks at him, concern swimming in his eyes at Brandt's readiness to leave.

"You know, I wouldn't mind helping Riley and Elissa pack their place. I, too, am quite full from the appetizers." Brandt looks over at Rhys.

"Let's go help these girls pack their things. We can stop and grab a bottle of something and make it fun." Brandt turns to my father and shakes his hand.

"Maybe we'll stop by the bar, and I can see what's so interesting about it."

With a tight smile plastered on my face, Riley and I stand up and make our way over to hug and say our farewells to Mr. and Mrs. Jaimeson before heading out.

CHAPTER

SEVEN

ELISSA

When the five of us arrive at the apartment building, I head in first, twisting my keys in the lock of the lobby door. Liam comes up behind me and places his hand gently on the small of my back. Goosebumps rise on my skin as I feel a wave of chills roll over my body. I risk a quick glance over my shoulder and see the ice in Brandt's eyes. When the key finally clicks in the lock, we pile into the lobby and I smash the button to the elevator, praying it comes fast. When the lift arrives, we all squeeze in and I swipe my key card, taking us up to the first penthouse.

Riley is all over Rhys, and Liam is hovering over me, his brawny arm clamped around my waist as though he's worried I'm about to flee. To be fair, I do really want to flee. Brandt is at the very back of the elevator and I can feel his frosty glare, causing a shiver to run down my spine. I look into the shiny reflection of the doors and see Brandt exactly as I thought I would. He's leaning against the gold rail of the lift, ankles and arms crossed. I raise my gaze to see his stormy eyes are narrowed as he stares back at me in the reflection. Heat suddenly rises to my cheeks and I look away. Wishing the elevator would move faster, I close my eyes and centre myself with a few deep breaths. The elevator dings when it reaches our floor and I leap out and book it for my door.

It's an hour into packing and we all seem to have made some progress. Most of the shelves in the living room are all packed up, half of Riley's closet and dresser, and all the kitchen stuff. Boxes are neatly stacked wherever we can fit them. I'm heading toward my bedroom to get started on my dresser when Liam falls into step behind me. He clears his throat to alert me and I turn to face him.

"Want any help in there?" He gives me a mischievous look. I feel my stomach knot at the suggestion.

"Um…no thanks, I can handle my room by myself. How about you start on the linens?" I counter, praying he'll take the hint. A flash of disappointment dims his eyes, but he quickly recovers, nods, and turns to head back to the living room. With a sigh of relief, I grab a couple of empty boxes and open my bedroom door to start packing, only to find a gigantic body sitting on my bed, flipping through some of my high school yearbooks. I almost jump out of my skin.

"Shit!" My hands fly to my chest. "I didn't think anyone was in here."

Brandt closes the yearbook, lays it across his lap, folds his hands over top and looks at me, his expression unreadable.

"Uh…so, I'm going to pack some of my room up now."

He nods, stands, and gently takes the flat boxes from me. He unfolds them and starts taping them, the sticky-sounding ripping of the tape gun filling the silence. I stand there for a moment, taking in how his hands move and the flexing forearm muscles that are on full display, straining against the cuffs of his rolled-up sleeves; how he's slightly bent at the waist because he's still too tall to assemble the boxes, even with them on the bed. I feel the hair on the back of my neck rise and notice he's taking me in as well from his periphery. I shake my head, walk over to my closet, and slide the door open to one side.

I decide to start with the top shelf of the closet. I stretch upward, on my tiptoes, to grab a box that I think contains unworn heels. Struggling to reach the very top box, I hop to knock it forward a bit. Suddenly, a shadow darkens the space around me, and I can feel a hard, warm body lightly pressing against my back. A long, muscular arm and big hand reach past my head to grab the column of three shoe boxes from the shelf, and a breeze of sandalwood fills my senses. Brandt moves closer in order to get a better grip on the boxes, and when his body is more firmly pressed against me, I feel a prominent hardness at my lower back. I tense up, and my heart starts pounding. I don't even notice I'm holding my breath until he moves away from me with the boxes. The air rushes out of my lungs, leaving my head feeling light and fuzzy.

"Let me help with the top shelf," he mumbles. Still facing the closet, I nod. I don't trust myself to turn around and look at him at this moment. After a few more steadying breaths, I excuse myself and head to the washroom without making eye contact. I close the door, lean my back against it, and twist the lock. I take a few more breaths and look up at myself in the mirror. My face is beet red. I can feel my pulse racing as the blood pounds in my head.

I see my running gear hung up on the wall hook from the last time I wore it. There's just too much tension in the apartment. Sexual and frustration, and sexual frustration. I feel my throat closing and I'm struggling to breathe. Making a quick decision, I quickly change into my running clothes, which smell funky from the sweat of my last run, but in this moment I don't care. I walk past my room without glancing in, continue straight down the hall to the foyer, grab my AirPods, slip my phone in my legging pocket, slide my feet into my shoes, and head out the door while tying my hair up.

"Uh oh," I hear Riley say as I close the door behind me. "Someone's freaking out…"

I slam the door shut behind me. The elevator will take too long, so I opt for the stairs instead. Twenty-two floors later, I am on the pavement outside of my complex and I immediately take off, pounding my feet into the pavement. My heel strike has always been hard, so it is no surprise that I can hear my footsteps through the drums of *Hail to the King* by Avenged Sevenfold. I focus on the lyrics to try to clear out my mind of everything that has happened today. However, I just can't keep Brandt off my mind. And then there's Liam, who's hanging around like we've become something over the last few days, even though I made it perfectly clear nothing is going to happen when I kicked him out of my apartment two days ago.

Then my mind is back on Brandt. His demeanour seems to change from hard and cold to warm, then back to cold again. He's the one who offered to help, and at the time I assumed it was just a way to push my buttons. But then there was that moment in the bedroom, where he was pressing up against me. Warmth swirls in my lower abdomen. There was no doubt in my mind that I'd felt the hardness of his cock pressing against my back...and however hard it was, it wasn't hard to tell just how big he was. I keep running, faster and faster, trying to push these thoughts out of my head before I have to return to the tension of the apartment.

CHAPTER EIGHT

BRANDT

I hear something coming from the washroom. Suddenly, the door whooshes open and a blur streaks by Elissa's bedroom doorway. A few seconds later, I hear the apartment door slam and Riley muttering something about Elissa freaking out. *Did she just...leave?* I get up and walk to the living room to see what's going on.

Riley is standing next to the sofa with Liam and Rhys, seemingly discussing something. Liam watches Riley with wide eyes, full of concern. I clench my jaw at the affection he seems to have toward, or with, Elissa.

"She does this often when she's stressed out," Riley says quietly. I shift closer to the conversation to listen in.

"I think with the end of school, and having to move so quickly, and being under her father's thumb again…it has her on edge." Rhys nods his head, like he understands what Riley is talking about.

"It can be a hard transition," he agrees. I'm not sure what to think. Over the last few hours, I have seen a totally a new Elissa; nothing like the girl she seemed to be in high school. Riley shrugs and looks over at Liam.

"I wouldn't take it as anything personal. She just doesn't get clingy, or make many emotional connections. I'm really the only relationship she's ever had," Riley says with a faltering laugh, trying to console Liam. He nods and shoves his hands deep into his pockets.

"I just thought that when fate threw us together again at the bar the second night, then at dinner again, that it meant something. I sort of just took the lead because I had a feeling she was distancing herself."

Jealousy courses through my veins, scorching hot and burning like acid. Liam had been with Elissa.

"It's nothing personal, just know that's how she is. And it's hardly the first time she's had the issue with guys sticking around when she…isn't looking for attachments," Riley explains gently. Liam exhales in disappointment. The three of them get back to packing up the last bits of the hallway closet and living room. Hearing that Elissa hasn't had attachments previously fills me with curiosity. *Is this why her father wants to arrange a marriage? To keep her out of trouble?*

Two hours pass before Elissa walks back into the apartment. She's slick with sweat. Her already tight clothes are now sticking to her, defining her body even more. My cock pulses at the sight of the sweat rolling down the valley of her cleavage. Her face is flushed, and her tongue darts out to lick a bead of sweat that has formed above her lip. The action draws me in, and I can't look away. I think about how her Cupid's bow would taste on my tongue instead. Running my tongue along her perfect heart-shaped lips before completely devouring the swollen pink petals. I notice my trousers tightening, so I move into the empty kitchen and adjust myself to hide my lust.

Half an hour later, the bathroom door opens and a cloud of deliciously scented steam billows out behind Elissa. A white towel is all that stands between her and my eyes, and I am instantly hard again. She tiptoes toward her bedroom, and I can see droplets of water trail down her toned, fair legs. I am torn from my thoughts as Riley calls out, "'Lissa! I was just talking to the guys and we're planning on going out to the club. Get your ass ready and let's go."

I swivel toward the three of them and raise my eyebrow at Rhys, silently asking him, *What the hell?* Rhys smirks at me in response, shrugs, and then grinds his hips, humping the air. I roll my eyes.

"So, since we're going out, Liam, Brandt, and I will head back to our hotel and meet you there."

"We really only ever go to Xion, if you're okay with that?" Riley asks Liam and Rhys. They look at each other and nod.

"That's good with us. It was a pretty decent place," Rhys says agreeably. Riley smiles sweetly at him.

"Excellent! We'll see you guys there!" She kisses Rhys on the cheek and skips off to her bedroom to get ready for the evening out. Rhys walks over, claps my shoulder, and leads me out of the apartment, with Liam trailing behind.

Back at the hotel, Liam is in his room getting ready. As I step out of the shower, I hear Rhys walk into my room using the door joining our rooms, then the squeak of the bedsprings as he lays back on my bed.

"Man, let's go. Why are you taking forever? You and Liam primp and preen like no one else I've met."

I exit the washroom with a towel hanging low on my hips, my locks freshly tamed.

"Chill out, all I have to do now is get dressed."

I know he's antsy to see Riley again, but I had things to take care of. This afternoon, being so close to Elissa made things *hard*. So, taking advantage of the shower, I sought relief, making sure I wouldn't cream my pants tonight if I were to be up against her again. The thought of pressing my body against her tonight sent my mind racing back to earlier in the evening, when it was just the two of us in her bedroom. When I grabbed those boxes from the shelf, I knew she could feel my erection. It wasn't intentional, but I can't say it didn't excite me even more. I felt her tense the moment she knew, and the way she exhaled afterward teased me with the idea that she might have been as excited as I was.

I tug on a fresh pair of boxers and some dark Levi's, run a black leather belt through the belt loops, and stuff my wallet and phone in the pockets. I finish buttoning up the baby blue dress shirt and shove my feet into a pair of black low-top Converse sneakers. I bend down to tighten the laces and then straighten back up, ready to go.

Rhys jumps up off the bed and shouts, "Fuck! Finally! Let's grab Liam and dip." He wiggles his eyebrows at me.

"Two hotties are waiting for us."

I roll my eyes at him, knowing he's only thinking about getting his dick wet. A bolt of jealousy hits me, as I wonder if Elissa will gravitate toward Liam tonight. My hands clench into fists and my knuckles whiten just thinking about them together.

CHAPTER
NINE

RILEY

Climbing out of the cab, Elissa and I take a minute to adjust our dresses. I'm wearing a short, black Michael Kors dress. It reaches about a third of the way down my thighs, and hugs all my curves perfectly. My slender waist gives the illusion that my breasts are bigger than they actually are in this dress. The halter straps cross in the front and tie neatly at the nape of my neck, and the entire dress has golden studs decorating it. My red pumps are tethered to my ankle and the strappy laces wrap tantalizingly around and up my calves.

I look over at Elissa as she adjusts her Lucy in the Sky body-con dress. The ruching of the dress accentuates her hips and ass, with the hem reaching just under the curve of her cheeks. Thin strings hold up the front of the dress and run along to the back, where they meet under an enormous, decorative bow. The dress perfectly displays the swell of her breasts, and it is quite obvious that there is no room in there for a bra, but her breasts are perky and firm. The powder blue of the dress highlights the sparkle of her sapphire eyes.

"Damn girl, you fiiiiine," I drawl. She pops a hip, winks, and blows a kiss at me.

"You're on fire, too!" She links her arm through mine and we strut over to the door. The long line twists around the side of the building. I notice the guys standing in line a few feet back.

"Yo, what are you guys doing waiting in line?" I shout over at Rhys and the other two. All three turn around and all their eyes light up when they see us strolling toward them.

"We're holding our spots in line. Come join us," Rhys responds. I giggle and shake my head.

"No, no, silly. Get out of line and follow us."

Elissa and I head over to the door while the guys exit the line and follow suit. Teddy nods his head when he sees us, giving us a big smile.

"Ladies," he embraces us both at the same time, his huge arms giving us a gentle squeeze. "Last hurrah before you guys leave for T.O.?" I give Teddy a small, sad smile.

"Yep, unfortunately. But we'll definitely come back and visit. We can't stay away from our favourite club and bouncer too long," I say sweetly, batting my lashes. Teddy blushes, but then his face hardens as he sees the three men approach behind us.

"Do you mind letting them in with us, Ted? They're here on business with 'Lissa's father." Teddy's pinched face relaxes and he nods.

"Have fun, ladies. Don't forget to say goodbye before you leave." He unclips the velvet rope and steps out of our way. Teddy nods to the guys.

"Gentlemen…"

The men nod in return and thank him as they walk by. All of us make our way to the bar and I flag down Liza. When Liza finally arrives, she already has our drinks ready. She slides our regular order across the bar to us. I notice Brandt eyeing Elissa with interest when he sees her glass of amber liquid. A smug grin pulls at my lips.

"Hi Liza! We also need two rounds of tequila — for each of us — to start off the night, please," I say. "It's our last night here for a while."

"Ah, it's finally time to leave for Toronto! Well, ladies, the first drink is on the house," Liza replies.

"Isn't our first round always free?" Elissa teases the bartender, running her tongue along her teeth. Liza smirks at her and raises her hands in defeat.

"My best customers always get the good perks. What will the guys be having?" Liza says, slowly rolling her eyes over the men, eye-fucking them in the process. The boys place orders for their beers and Elissa asks her to put everything on a tab. Liza winks at her and starts setting up ten shot glasses of tequila. My mind drifts off briefly, wondering if 'Lissa and Liza ever hooked up. The way they flirt suggests that they may have had a fling before.

I'm brought back to the present moment when Liza places the saltshaker and a plate of lime wedges on the bar beside the shots. The guys prep themselves for the shots while Elissa and I wait until they're ready. The three of them look at us questioningly. Liza laughs.

"You guys are gonna be in for a long night trying to keep up with these two."

We all grab our shots, Elissa and I double fisting our two, do a quick cheers, and slam them back. The guys chase theirs with the lime, while Elissa and I chase ours with a second shot of tequila. We all grab our assorted drinks from the bar and start sipping them. Just as I'm about to move the party to the dance floor, I feel someone wrap their arms around my waist and whisper, "Hey baby," in my ear. I turn around in surprise and realize it's Doug, my fling for the past two weeks. I groan and steal a quick glance over at Rhys. His eyes narrow and he pushes up from the bar, straightening to his full height, fists curling at his sides.

"Hey, Doug, nice to see you," I reply, kissing his cheek. "Doug, you know Elissa. But this is Rhys and Brandt. I think you might remember Liam," I gesture toward the guys. "He was over the other morning when you were."

Doug tenses and nods over at the guys. I wave off the group and let them know I'll be right back. I lead Doug away from the group.

"Doug, you know that this is just a fling, right? Because 'Lissa and I are leaving in a few days, and we won't be back." Doug's shoulders sag as he realizes what I'm saying.

"It was really nice fucking and stuff, but I'm afraid this is as far as it goes. No hard feelings, I hope?" Doug runs his hands through his hair, straightens, and puffs his chest out. He gives me a rueful smile and a small hug.

"It was nice meeting and fucking you too, Riley." He kisses my cheek goodbye and walks over to a group of girls. I sigh in relief, happy that things ended well. I turn around and walk back over to the group. As they chat, I down my drink and turn to the bar to order another one. When it arrives, I grab it and Elissa's hand and drag her to the dance floor. We sway and bounce to *Miss You* by Oliver Tree and Robin Schulz, making our way deeper into the crowd of sweaty dancers.

The guys stand behind me and Elissa, swaying to the beat. Near the last third of the song, Rhys presses his body up against me and starts moving his body with mine, one hand gripping my hip, the other arm snaking around my ribs, with his cold beer pressing into me. The heat on my back from his body contrasts the cold glass bottle under my breasts, igniting a fire below, and goosebumps blanket my skin. *Tonight is going to be a good night.* I meet Elissa's eyes, lick my lips, and give her a wink.

Elissa gives me a nervous, uncertain look and jerks her head in the direction behind her. Liam and Brandt are both towering over her. A giggle escapes me. I turn my head to meet Rhys' handsome face, letting him plant a kiss on my brow.

CHAPTER
TEN

BRANDT

The moment Riley calls out to us, we all turn around and my heart stops. Elissa looks gorgeous. I don't know how I will survive the night at this point. Rhys notices me staring at Elissa and nudges me in the ribs. I shoot him a thankful glance for distracting me before I start drooling. The three of us leave the line when Riley invites us to follow her directly to the door.

Walking behind the girls was a mistake. Riley has a nice ass, but Elissa's is magnificent. The dress is so short that if she were to bend over, she would be completely on display. I try to distract myself again and look around the club before my cock can get any ideas.

When the bartender asks us what we want, I order whatever is on tap, but I am full of surprise when I see the bartender slip Elissa a tumbler of whisky. I would never have pegged her for a whisky drinker. I find myself more intrigued with her every moment that passes.

After the round of tequila shots, Riley pulls Elissa to the dance floor. Rhys, Liam, and I follow the ladies. The girls sway their hips to the flow of the music, and I am mesmerized; I can't take my eyes off Elissa. She dances like a goddess. What I would give to wrap my arms around her and feel her hips against my crotch, moving like that. Rhys is suddenly behind Riley and doing exactly what I'd like to do with Elissa. I glance over at Liam, who is distracted by two ladies talking to him, though I can see him stealing glances at Elissa, like he's making sure she's still alone. I notice Elissa's glass is almost empty, so I down my beer and head over to get another drink for her at the bar. I don't know what her whisky of choice is, but luckily the bartender does.

After fighting my way back through the crowd, I notice Elissa is still dancing by herself, completely lost in the music. She's wiggling her ass and shoulders opposite of each other and whipping her head back and forth, her hair swishing like curtains over her face as the beat of *Deep Down* by Alok, Ella Eyre, Kenny Dope, and Never Dull reverberates through the club. I quickly Shazam the song to keep for later if I end up leaving alone. I approach her, tap her shoulder, and offer her the drink. She eyes me for a second, takes the drink, and thanks me. My heart is pounding rapidly, even from that minor exchange.

I lean in and ask her if she wants to dance. She stiffens slightly, then shrugs and nods. Placing myself behind her, not entirely sure what to do, I start to sway slowly, trying to match her moves. She grabs my free hand and places it on her hip, and a zing of electricity sparks between us. My breath catches, and I try to remain calm. I look over at Rhys and he gives me a giant grin and a thumbs-up.

I let Elissa set the pace, mirroring her movements. When the song changes to a slightly slower pace, she rolls her ass into my crotch. I feel my pants strain and I am sure she feels it too. She pauses for the briefest of moments, but then continues. I down my drink, trying to get rid of my nerves. Elissa turns to me and motions toward the bar, quirking one eyebrow in question. I nod and follow her.

"Want a shot?" she asks me, as she flags down Liza. I'm not sure if she even acknowledged my answer, but she orders four shots of Patrón anyway.

"Four shots? There's five of us," I holler over all the noise. She grins at me, and my heart stops beating. I wish I could capture that smile and save it forever.

"Oh, Brandt. These four shots are just for us." My cheeks heat as my mouth falls opens slightly.

"Okay, I see. I just…rarely drink a lot of hard liquor," I confess. She laughs and throws back both shots.

"What? A businessman that doesn't drink hard liquor? Has hell frozen over?" She slides the other two shots toward me and raises her eyebrows at me, waiting. I shake out some nerves and pick up both shots and down them, like Elissa, with no salt or lime chaser. It takes a second, but I have to hold back the urge to vomit. My cheeks puff, but after about a minute, I'm good. Elissa is laughing her ass off at me and her eyes are sparkling through the club's darkness. She flags down Liza again and asks for one more round.

"Oh no, I can't do another shot. I'll end up puking," I shout to her. I feel a buzz taking hold of my body and mind.

"C'mon, Brandt. Loosen up a bit."

Liza slides us each another shot. Elissa raises her shot glass and says, "To working together in the near future."

My smirk tugs at my lips. I lift my glass and clink hers. Then, we both down the shots at the same time. I hold back the urge to vomit again, and she laughs again. I shoot her a playfully dangerous look, and something dark flashes in her eyes. She grabs my hand, waves to Liza, and drags me back to the dance floor.

I feel the warmth bloom through my body from the shots. Elissa dances and wiggles in front of me as she pulls me to a spot in the centre of the floor. She's facing me, popping her chest and ass as she bounces her weight between her feet to *Friday* by Riton. My nerves melt away, and my mind can only focus on her body moving in front of me. She dances toward me, turns around, and places her ass on me again.

With my hands now free of drinks, they slide up her thighs of their own volition. My fingers briefly toy with the hem of her dress before continuing up her body to gently grip her hips. She leans closer to me, feeling the music and using my body as a human stripper pole, grinding all over me. She twirls around me, dancing behind me for a moment to slide her hands down my thighs, and continues to twirl until she is facing me again.

The song shifts into *Your Love (9PM)* by A7S, ATB, and Topic, and Elissa's arms snake around my neck, pulling me closer to her. The tequila is working its magic as I feel my limbs loosen up and I bend down slightly, resting my forehead against Elissa's, still dancing and following her lead. The rest of the club melts away until it's only the two of us in this moment.

CHAPTER

ELEVEN

ELISSA

This night has taken the strangest turn.

I am currently grinding up against my father's future business partner (which also, technically, makes him my future business partner). The vibrations of the music flow through me and my body translates the vibrations to dance movements. I press my ass into Brandt's pelvis and roll my body along his long, hard torso. When my ass is at the top of the roll, I slowly bend over, one foot slightly forward, giving him a fantastic view of my ass with his hands on the sides of my hips. I instantly feel his hard-as-steel cock pressing into me. I smirk to myself and slowly stand back up, transitioning back to a body roll against him.

I toss my hair back and see Liam dancing with some other chick a few feet away, and I can't help but notice the sadness in his eyes when our gazes meet. I disconnect from the tension and start twirling around Brandt like he's a pole and I'm putting on a show. I run my hands up his back to his shoulders and down again to his thighs. I twirl away until I meet him face to face. I entwine my arms around his neck as the song changes. Our eyes lock for a moment and it's like our bodies click into place, swaying together perfectly. Brandt leans down slightly and rests his head on my forehead. It's a rather intimate gesture, but somehow I don't feel the urge to run like I normally would. So, I continue to dance as one song melds into the next in a blur of noise.

Another four rounds of tequila later, and the guys are smashed; Riley and I are just slightly less trashed than them. The bar is closing, and we're being ushered out by Teddy and Liza. Riley and I hug them goodbye and gush about how much we love them. As we reach the door, Riley leans against me and stumbles slightly. Rhys comes up from behind and slides his arm around her waist to steady her. Liam and the girl he was dancing with are on the sidewalk ahead of us, flagging down a cab.

"I'm out, guys. See you back at the hotel," Liam says to Rhys and Brandt. They wave to Liam, and just as he opens the cab door, I call out to him.

"Liam, wait!"

I walk over to him and give him a quick hug.

"Sorry for how I am. It's just…who I am. Take care of yourself, okay?" Liam gives me a smile, nods, and wishes me the same back. He climbs into the cab with his date and the car takes off. I feel an intense energy pulsing around me, and I feel my muscles contract. Sure enough, when I turn around, Brandt is staring me down with a dark look in his eyes.

Riley's high-pitched cackle breaks the tension and I walk over to her and Rhys, who is busy sucking and licking up her neck. Watching Rhys do his thing to Riley, an unexpected stab of loneliness comes over me. I shake it off.

"Well, I'm out. See you back at the apartment, Riles." Rhys disengages from Riley for a moment and shares a look with her.

"We're coming too," Rhys answers for Riley. He looks to Brandt. "You coming, man?"

Rhys glances at me and Brandt, who is also looking at me. I shrug to let Brandt know I don't mind if he tags along. Brandt turns to Rhys and nods. I walk to the curb and flag down a cab.

Brandt takes the front seat of the cab while I slide into the back with Rhys and Riley. I'm being squished up against the window as Rhys' large body takes the middle seat and Riley perches on his lap. The only way this is bearable is that her back is to me and her feet are facing the opposite direction. Unfortunately, I can still see Rhys' hand sliding up and down Riley's backside, squeezing her ass every few seconds. I groan to myself and look ahead, catching Brandt's stare in the oversized rearview mirror. Thirty seconds pass and I feel a blush creep up my neck to my cheeks, so I turn my head to look out the window.

The four of us stumble out of the elevator toward my apartment. I struggle with the keys, finally find the right one, and grind it into the slot. Once we're in, I lean against the wall and kick off my pumps, letting out an overtly loud moan by accident.

"Mmm, fuuuuuck."

Riley snickers and tugs Rhys with her as she walks past me to the living room. She flicks on the stereo system and grabs a bottle of who-the-hell-knows-what from underneath the TV stand, one of the few items we haven't packed yet. She takes a drink straight from the bottle, starts dancing to *Do It to It* by ACRAZE and Cherish, and passes the bottle to Rhys. He takes a big gulp and makes a face.

I shrug, walk over, and take the bottle from Rhys to take a long swig. I turn to Brandt and hold out the bottle, raising a brow in question. A cocky smirk stretches across his face, and I notice his full lips always seem to tug a bit higher on the left side.

Riley twirls around, hands in the air as Rhys watches her. I join her, twisting my hips to the beat of the music, and notice Brandt takes a seat on the couch, enjoying the private show. Riley dances to her bedroom and comes back a moment later, a joint perched between her lips and flicking a lighter. She lights the joint, takes a big drag, holds it in, and passes the joint to me. Rhys' eyes widen with excitement, as if he's never seen two beautiful girls party before.

I wet my lips and press the joint to my mouth. I roll my eyes back into my head when I take a drag, like it's the most euphoric thing in the world. I hold it for a moment and exhale, still holding the joint when I start to dance again, swinging my hips, shoulders, and head. Rhys takes the joint from me and indulges as well. He moves to hand it to Brandt, but he just shakes his head, refusing.

After we each have a few more puffs, Riley giggles and moves closer to Rhys. She takes the joint, stamps it out, and starts dancing with him. They slowly sway together, kissing and caressing each other, as they move closer to her bedroom. My eyes drift shut as I continue to dance, and I don't even realize they've disappeared until I hear the soft click of her bedroom door closing. My eyes shoot open, and I notice Brandt is missing too. Just as I turn my head to look for him, I feel him press against me from behind. His hands run up my thighs and gather the hem of my dress, then he fists the silky material and yanks me close.

We start dancing together again, and I reach back to gather my hair and move it all to one side. I guess Brandt takes it as a signal, and I feel a feather-light kiss where my neck meets my shoulder. His beard gently scratches against my skin. A delicious shiver runs down my spine and I know he feels it, because I feel his lips smile against my skin and his crotch pulse. He trails his tongue lightly along my shoulder, up my neck, and traces the shell of my ear. His hot, ragged breath blows against my ear as his hand slides up my body and stops just below my breasts, while his other hand slips down to my pelvis. He blows gently along my neck where his tongue left a trail. Electricity shoots through my body and a small gasp escapes my lips.

Brandt spins me around and his hands cup my face as he lowers his forehead to mine. He tilts his face slightly closer, his lips barely brushing against mine. My heart races with anticipation as I struggle to breathe. He holds me like this for a few moments, neither of us moving. His chest is rising and falling as fast as mine, and I know we both feel a charged intensity radiating between us. Finally, I can't take it anymore, so I decide to make the first move. I place my hands on his face, pull him into me, and kiss him hard.

CHAPTER

TWELVE

Brandt

Elissa's lips crush against mine, and she tastes better than I could ever imagine. It's a closed mouth kiss, but it is the best I've ever had. Thanks to the liquid courage from all those shots, I fist her hair with one hand while I slide the other down to the small of her back, pulling her close — close enough for her to feel just how much I want her. My tongue sweeps across her lips, pleading for them to part. When her mouth opens, my tongue darts inside and tangles with hers. The rush of endorphins tightens my balls and I almost blow in my pants, but I clear my mind and hold myself back.

Her hands run up and down my chest and she sighs as she feels the taut muscles of my abdomen. Her hands trail down around my waist to my back, making a home in the back pockets of my jeans and sending my mind reeling. My hand moves from the small of her back to palm her breast. She moans into my mouth as I rub my thumb across her nipple a few times until it stiffens. I gently roll her nipple between my forefinger and thumb as I trail kisses along her jaw and neck. Her head tilts back and she gasps for air. She moves her hands back to my face and pulls me back to her lips. Our mouths meet in a heated clash and she sucks on my bottom lip.

My hands shoot down to her ass and squeeze before I lift her up. She wraps her legs around my waist and I growl into her ear, "Bedroom?"

It's clear Elissa can barely breathe, let alone speak, so she just nods her head. I walk us to her bedroom, still holding her while she sucks on my neck. I slam the door shut behind me with my foot and toss her onto the bed. Towering over her, I slowly unbutton my shirt, not taking my eyes off her. She's lying on her back, knees slightly bent toward each other. I focus on her face, taking in how beautiful her skin is as it glows in the moonlight streaming through her window, and the shine of her hair on the pillow. Her lips are red and swollen, and her eyes are full of desire as she watches me take off my shirt.

Elissa licks her lips and clambers to her knees to help me remove my shirt. Her hands slide up my abs, around my shoulders, and push my shirt off. I let it fall to the ground. She moves her hands to my belt and undoes it while kissing the line of hair that trails down to my waistband. After fiddling with the button and zipper of my jeans, she hooks her thumbs in the front pockets and tugs them down. I help the rest of the way and step out of them. Her hand trails up my knee to my thigh, then she runs her hand along my erection, palm flat on the outside of my boxers.

I crawl onto the bed, forcing her to move back with me until her head is on the pillow again. I lower my head toward her, pressing my lips against hers again. I slip my tongue into her mouth, and her lips part eagerly. The muscles of my shoulders strain slightly as I hold myself above her, and I trail a finger lightly up her thigh until I reach the apex. My hand glides over her and grazes the outside of her underwear. *Fuck. She is so wet already.*

As my hand is hovering there, her breathing becomes harder, almost panting. I press down a little harder and start rubbing small circles. My balls tense up, begging for relief. It hurts. I growl as I push aside her panties and dip my middle finger into her wetness. A moan leaves her lips as I hook my finger, trying to find her sweet spot.

She grabs my cock with her free hand and squeezes it through the boxers. I have to rip my hand out of her and pin her hand down on the mattress. I'm breathing hard and trying to gain composure, because just that brief touch almost sent me over the edge. She tilts her hips toward me with a moan, begging for my fingers to make another appearance. I oblige her, dipping two fingers into her this time and using the heel of my palm to rub against her clit as I stroke inside. I kiss down her neck as her hands fist the bedspread. Suddenly, her chest tenses and her back arches, and I can hear a moan clawing up her throat until it comes out. She shouts out "Brandt!" and

I feel her muscles clench around my fingers as her come rushes down my fingers onto my hand.

Both of us are breathing heavily as I slowly pull my fingers out of her and lick her come off my hand, sucking my fingers clean. I move my head down to clean the come that is glistening on her thighs and lips. She tastes sweet, like a velvety, musky honey, a taste that instantly creates an addict out of me.

I almost lose it again. I moan as I taste her come right from the source. It takes all my strength not to shove my tongue in her. She tastes incredible. As I finish cleaning her up, she pulls me up to her and kisses me on the mouth. She reaches over to her nightstand and tears open the drawer. Her hand paws around blindly in the drawer, looking for a condom. Struggling to find one, she breaks the kiss and rolls toward the nightstand. She lets out a massive sigh and rolls onto her back again.

"Do you have a condom? I forgot I already packed up my nightstand."

I freeze, looking directly into her eyes. My heart stalls. *Fuck*. I groan and shake my head.

"No, I don't have any on me." Because why would I? I never thought that this would happen. I rarely need to carry any because I never let it get that far. I'm never quite interested enough to go further. No one has ever caught my attention like Elissa has. She bites her lips, clearly contemplating. I hesitate, then take a chance.

"I'm clean. Are you on the pill?"

She nods her head and I instantly go back to kissing her feverishly. Just as I am halfway done pulling down my boxers, her eyes flash open and she pushes against my chest. I rise up and kneel on the bed. She sits up and looks me in the eye.

"Oh, my god…we can't do this." Elissa runs her hands through her hair, then jumps off her bed and backs away.

"Shit! Fuck! What the hell. Fucking alcohol. We're supposed to be business partners soon." She paces back and forth. I slowly get up and start dressing.

"Christ…this could have been a big mistake," I heard her mutter to herself. I wince at the repulsion I feel emanating from her, and my cock is straining hard against the zipper of my jeans. She turns to me.

"I'm sorry. You should go."

CHAPTER THIRTEEN

Elissa

What in the ever-loving fuck did I just do? I almost had sex with a business associate. Someone I will presumably be working closely with, once the department is up and running.

Fuck. Fuck. Shit. Fuck.

Hopefully, Brandt takes this in stride and we can work professionally together in the future, I think to myself, trying not to panic. I look over at him and watch him get dressed, his face expressionless and emotionless. Meanwhile, I pace back and forth, muttering to myself and chewing on my thumbnail. Brandt clears his throat and I snap my head to attention. He gestures toward the door.

"So, I'm just going to head out.... It was nice meeting you, I guess. I look forward to working with you." He strides out of my room, and a moment later I hear the click of the apartment door closing.

The next morning, my head is throbbing, and I automatically go through my hangover routine. I stalk to the bathroom, lean against the vanity, and rip open the mirrored cupboard to locate the aspirin. I uncap the bottle and swallow three of the little white pills dry.

I sink down onto the toilet, elbows on my knees and my face in my hands as I retrace my drunken steps. After I flush and wash my hands, I stagger to the kitchen to find some water and some bread to soak up and dilute whatever is left in my system. As I pass the living room, pieces of what feels like a really screwed up dream flash in my mind.

Stumbling into the apartment, Riley blaring the stereo and passing a bottle around, and then passing around a joint. Me dancing with Brandt, and Riley and Rhys disappearing from the room. Kissing Brandt. Brandt carrying me to my room. Making out with Brandt. Brandt's large, strong fingers inside me. Clenching around Brandt's fingers and calling out his name. The visions burst in my head like a strobe light, making me dizzier and dizzier, until I'm running to the kitchen and heaving into the sink.

It was just a dream. A really vivid dream. I know I can be reckless, but hooking up with a business associate would be too much, even for me. Right? As I'm trying to make sense of what happened last night, Riley's door creaks open, and she backs out of her room in a t-shirt and panties, holding hands with Rhys. My stomach immediately drops. *It wasn't a dream…it all really happened…*

Riley walks Rhys to the door. They linger there for a few minutes, kissing and whispering to each other. Something about texting later and meeting up again when she's in Toronto.

That's all well and fine, but I need to talk to Riley, right now. I clear my throat and yell from the kitchen, "Have a good day, Rhys!" They both giggle and I hear the door click shut. Riley floats into the kitchen, a hazy, dreamy look on her face. Her head is way up in the clouds, and it'll be a while before she comes back down to solid ground.

"Elissa, I'm in trouble," she whispers to me. I make a "hm" noise, asking her to elaborate.

"I think I love him. I know we just met…what, two days ago? But I think I've already fallen."

I slowly nod my head, not giving her any words of affirmation or negativity. When she comes down in a day or two, or when he doesn't call or text, she'll shake off this post-orgasmic high and realize it was just her hormones talking.

"So, you wanna get dressed and go grab some pancakes?" I ask her, changing the subject.

"Sure. I'm starving. And I want to hear about your night! How was Brandt? It looked like you guys were getting close!" She wiggles her eyebrows at me. I roll my eyes at her, toss my hair over my shoulder, and head to my bedroom.

"Just go and get ready. We'll debrief after I've had some pancakes."

Friday mornings at Griddle Cakes were always super busy. It was their "Friday Flaps" day, when you can get all-you-can-eat flapjacks for $12.99. There was always a line-up. We had to wait outside for about twenty minutes before we could get inside and grab a table. Becca, the owner of Griddle Cakes, jogs over to our table as we're getting settled. She greets us with a bright smile.

"Hey ladies! It's so good to see you. I'm gonna miss seeing your faces all the time."

On Fridays Becca always seems more frazzled. It's one of the busiest days of the week, and Riley and I both knew she would have been here in the kitchen at the crack of dawn, prepping things for the day by herself. The dark circles under her eyes usually resembled the black paint footballers paint under their eyes before a game. For a while, she was trying to use concealer to cover the dark circles, but eventually gave up, because it was just adding another task to complete.

"We're gonna miss you too, Becca!" Riley gushes. "I would be your first customer if you ever consider opening another location in Toronto!" Becca laughs.

"Oh man, that would be a big undertaking. I'm already so busy here, I doubt I could find the time to open one in Toronto," she replies. "But, tell ya what. If I ever consider opening another location, I'll call you, and you can help me pick out the perfect place. And maybe I'll even let you have free breakfast once a week." Riley's eyes light up with adoration.

"It would be an honour to help you. And I would post daily to my Insta and tag the shit out of the new location.

You'd have to clone yourself." Both the girls laugh at that, and I join in.

"I would also be so into you opening a branch in T.O. I don't know how I will get through my hangovers without your delicious pancakes."

A sadness washes over me at the thought of not having her pancakes, or seeing Becca, for a while. The three of us are quiet and thoughtful for a moment, until my stomach growls loudly and ruins the moment. We all burst out laughing, and all kinds of people are looking over at us, wondering what the hell is so funny. Becca recovers first and wipes a tear from her eye.

"Lemme go get you a plate of cakes and a bowl of fruit," she offers. "And today, it's on the house, ladies. So, eat your fill, and I'll also pack you some for the road. Put 'em in the freezer and pop them into the toaster when you need a fix. They're still amazing after they've been frozen."

Riley and I stand up and squeeze her for what seems like an eternity. When we pull away, it's as clear as the tears streaming down our faces that we're all crying. We break into a silly, awkward giggle as we wipe our tears away.

Riley and I slide back into our booth and request some coffee. Becca walks away for a moment and comes back with two mugs and a carafe, and leaves it on our table. Grateful, Riley and I fill our mugs to the brim with black, bitter goodness. I inhale the intoxicating scent of the go-go juice, closing my eyes and listening to the bustle happening around us while *Walls* by Kings of Leon plays softly over the speakers.

"Spill," Riley demands, as she shovels fluffy, golden pieces of pancake into her mouth. I grab the maple syrup bottle and drown my pancakes in it. I lick the stickiness off my thumb and forefinger.

"There's nothing to say, really."

Riley gives me an annoyed look that clearly tells me she doesn't believe a word of that. I let out a long sigh.

"We…made out. And then he took me to my room. Things got heated, but we didn't go all the way." Riley looks confused.

"What do you mean, you didn't go all the way?"

"I realized that I'd already packed up all of my night-stand stuff, and he didn't have a condom on him. We were gonna do it bareback, but the thought sobered me up and I realized he's a partner for my father's business. I ended up kicking him out." Riley stares at me, wide-eyed, in disbelief.

"You…kicked him…out?" she asks slowly, drawing out the question. She shakes her head. "Ouch. I feel bad for him."

My face goes red and a cold bead of guilty sweat forms on the back of my neck.

"Yeah, I kind of do too. But honestly, it was a blessing in disguise. I'm gonna have to work with this guy. I mean, yeah, the chemistry was off the charts, but…how would I face him every day? Most of my one-nighters I never see again. And that's by design."

Riley bobs her head in understanding. I grab my mug of scalding coffee and gulp down about half of it. Thinking about how this might affect my work life once I move to Toronto, I can only hope that Brandt was blackout drunk and doesn't remember a thing.

Riley and I spent all our time over the next few days packing up the rest of the apartment. The only great thing about having to move to Toronto is that my father bought my apartment, and it has two bedrooms, so I can have Riley move with me and be my roommate still. Being able to keep Riley close is one of the few luxuries that my father doesn't control. That's probably because our parents are friends.

Riley's parents still live back in our hometown of Chatham, Ontario. They're both surgeons at the hospital there, and because there is a shortage of doctors and nurses across Ontario, they stayed local, and are now the chiefs of their respective specialties. Her father and mine met at the University of Toronto during their undergrads, and they met the women who would become their wives at around the same time too. Our mothers became inseparable, so, when Connor Jaimeson finished medical school, Brianne convinced my mother to move to Chatham to start their families. My father had already started his small media empire in Toronto, but he followed my mother anyway and ended up commuting from Chatham to Toronto twice a week. He would spend four days in Toronto and three days at home. I rarely saw my father growing up. And, when I was finally old enough to be on my own, even though Lana was always around, my mother always ended up going to Toronto with my father.

Lana also lives in Chatham. She quit being the housekeeper when I graduated from high school. Instead, she started working as a property manager for the handful of real estate holdings my father owns back in Chatham. She eventually settled down and has a family of her own now. Her little boy is almost three years old. Riley and I are supposed to be heading back home soon for a visit, to see her family, and to see Lana for her son's third birthday. It will be nice to visit home again.

My eyes sting with the emotion building in them. *Home.* I always get emotional when I think of this. Most people envy the childhood I had, but it doesn't mean it was great. Money means nothing if you're constantly lonely. Except for Riley and Lana, I was very lonely. One of my major flaws is borne from that constant loneliness. I don't form any meaningful attachments. Ninety percent of my relationships are superficial.

I plop down on my bed and stare off into space. I glance at my dresser and notice the yearbook haphazardly tossed on top; the one Brandt was flipping through. I reach over to grab it. I take the pages between my fingers and let them cascade. I flip a few pages from the front and realize this is the yearbook for my first year of high school.

I turn to the page where my face, eight years younger, stares back at me. I run my fingers across the glossy paper and a sad smile curls my lips. Sitting so still, with a genuine smile on my face, metal braces sparkling on my teeth, and one side of my copper hair French-braided around the top of my ear, giving it the fancy tucked-behind-the-ear look. I was wearing my navy polo uniform shirt with our school emblem on the left side of the chest, and I remember Riley was behind the camera person, pretending to air hump her to get me to really smile.

I read the caption underneath the photo.

Quote: *One day I'll fly away. – Randy Crawford*

Most likely to be: *A pretty bird in a pretty, golden cage — with my wings clipped.*

God, I was I depressing when I was fourteen.

But, let's be honest…I wasn't wrong.

I toss the yearbook into one of the open boxes at the side of my bed, roughly rub my hands against my face, and reluctantly get up to finish packing.

CHAPTER

FOURTEEN

BRANDT

After the crap-fest that was last weekend, Harold calls me a few days after I returned to Toronto to set up a lunch. He wants to meet to go over our last conversation and, as per his email, we're to meet at a small bistro downtown at noon tomorrow. I'm not sure I want to continue down this path after the humiliating end to the night Elissa and I had last week. If I invest, I will have to see her every day for the foreseeable future, or at least until the department is up and running.

It's been a long day, and it's not over yet, as I still have to go over the documents for the investment again. Struggling to focus on what's in front of me, I toss the files onto the coffee table and head to my bedroom to change into some pajama pants and make myself more comfortable. I rummage through one of my dresser drawers to find a pair, then pull them on and cross my arms in front of me to lift my shirt over my head.

As I stand in front of my mirror, I take a hard look at myself. I know a lot of women find me attractive. My eyes slowly take in my appearance. My grassy green eyes are vibrant when the light hits them just right, I have a defined nose, and at the moment, a maintained beard carpets my sharp jaw. It's not a long beard, rather more like I haven't shaved in a few days — which I haven't. Still, I've made sure it's respectable, neat, and distinguished. Hell, I'd even say that, depending on what I wear, it makes me look ruggedly handsome.

I trail my eyes over the rest of my body — my thick neck, broad shoulders, and wide chest, complete with toned pecs and an abdomen that looks like an ancient Greek artist chiselled it out of marble. A thin line of dark golden blond hair runs down the length of my abs toward my pelvis. My arms are thick, muscular, and the veins bulge, especially when I'm working out. My back and shoulders are defined; my ass is firm and looks great in any pair of pants. Before I go back out to the living room, I lower myself to the ground and do a few push-ups to re-energize myself and help boost my levels of concentration.

Going through the paperwork is tedious, but necessary. I haven't always been as successful as I am today. I had a humble upbringing, middle-class, in Hamilton, Ontario. However, as things changed in the development of Hamilton, my family relocated to Chatham during my first year of high school. My dad runs a construction and roofing company. The benefit for my parents was they could build a new home and use it as their "model" home to show prospective clients, complete with all the bells and whistles.

We moved halfway through my first year of high school. It was the second semester, and my first period was gym class. I was always tall for my age, but still somewhat scrawny at the time. In the change room, all the guys were laughing and goofing off before class started. Two of the guys rough-housing bumped into me and I fell backward over a bench, landing sprawled in the middle of the floor. The room went eerily quiet, and a hand reached out toward me. The guy in front of me was about the same height and stature as me, but he had muscles. His messy, inky black hair wasn't quite a shag, but it wasn't short. He flicked the front of his hair to the side and looked at me with crystal blue eyes.

"Sorry, bro," he said, his voice cracking slightly. I took his hand and he helped pull me up. I've never been a huge conversationalist; I'm usually quieter and more reserved until I really get to know someone. I nodded my head at his apology. He extended a fist.

"I'm Rhys, and you're new." I bumped my fist against his.

"Yeah. And, Brandt," I mumbled. Rhys clasped his arm around my shoulders and howled. My face turned slightly red.

"Yo, everyone, listen up! This here is Brandt, my boy. You fuck with him, I'll kick your ass," he triumphantly announced to the entire locker room. A sharp, shrill whistle from the doorway broke up the commotion.

A man stood at the door with a whistle around his neck, wearing a Ursuline Catholic College Lancers athletic department cotton t-shirt. A small potbelly was tucked underneath the band of his navy basketball shorts.

"Get your asses in the gym," he barked. "Now!"

The guys slammed their lockers shut and jogged toward the gym, each grunting, "Yes, Coach." Rhys winked at me with a mischievous grin.

"Welcome to UCC. See ya out there."

Suddenly, my phone beeps, pulling me from the memory of when Rhys and I first met. Little did I know he'd grow to become my best friend. I reach over to pick up my phone and see Rhys' message pop up.

Rhys: *Yo. You got plans tomorrow? Was thinking of shooting some hoops.*

Me: *Maybe in the late afternoon. I have a meeting with Harold at noon. Going over some merger info.*

Three dots appear on the screen, indicating Rhys is typing a response. They bounce for a few minutes, then disappear. I drop my phone onto the arm of the couch. With a sigh, I pick up the merger documents again, reading the same paragraph for the tenth time. My phone beeps again.

Rhys: *Omg, his daughter's friend... Riley.*

He finishes his message with a gif of a chef kissing his fingers.

Rhys: *Shoot me a text when you're done. We'll play for a bit and go for drinks later.*

I reply to his message with a thumbs-up emoji and

set my phone back down on the arm of the couch. I sigh again and rub my face roughly. Rhys' mention of that night floods my mind with flashbacks...

How wet and eager Elissa was for my fingers. Her riding my hand urgently. The sound of her moans and panting echo through my mind. I feel heat stirring inside me and when I look down, my pajama pants have a tall tent pitched. I pop the fly button open and let my cock spring forward. Tilting my head back and resting it on the couch, I fist myself, pumping hard and gradually picking up the pace. My hips thrust in tandem with my hand as I bring myself to the precipice and find release.

• • •

The next day, I arrive at the bistro ten minutes early. I loathe people wasting time and being late. Unfortunately, Harold has a reputation for his tardiness. *Prick*. I sit and place the documents I was reviewing last night on the small circular table. I pick up the menu, a little folded piece of cardstock in the centre of the table, just to give myself something to do before Harold arrives. The waitress comes over and purrs, "What can I get you to drink?"

One of her perfectly manicured hands runs along my shoulder. I look up at her, and her artificially blonde hair looks too well-maintained for her to be a waitress. Her makeup is heavy enough that I can tell she's wearing it, but it doesn't look trashy. She's got that smoky eye thing going on, and it makes her cool grey eyes stand out. Her lips are full and seductively pouty, and again, they look like maybe she's had some work done. Regardless, she's got a beautiful face that would attract any horndog man, and her frame is slender, with curves in all the right places. Unfortunately for her, this man isn't a horndog. While I can appreciate her beauty, she just doesn't get me going. I gently dip my shoulder to slide her hand off me.

"Just a water for now, please. I'm waiting for a business associate," I respond curtly. She nods silently and walks away. I hear a bell ring across the bistro, above the door I walked into not so long ago. I glance over and it's Harold. *Only five minutes late. That's got to be a new record.* I stand up gracefully and wait for Harold to approach. When he is in front of me, we both reach out to take each other's hand with a firm grasp. I motion for Harold to join me as I sit down.

He unbuttons his blazer and sits down opposite me. We stare at each other for a moment, each waiting for the other to relent, to relinquish their power. Luckily for me, the waitress reappears with my water and Harold breaks eye contact to greet her. Thankfully, her focus is on me, so she doesn't notice his creepy gaze undressing her with his eyes. I clear my throat, and he orders a rum and Coke. She leaves to head to the bar to fulfill his order, and Harold ogles her ass openly as she sways away. With a dirty smirk, he turns back to me.

"So," he starts. "How was your weekend out with my daughter?"

I shrug, not wanting to give anything away. I'm not sure how this conversation is going to go, and I certainly don't want to show my hand too early. Harold's eyes narrow.

"Any more thoughts on the business proposal I sent over?"

"Yes, and I am interested. I think the new division

would be a perfect fit for our expanding profile at Collins Collective…" I lean back and hook my ankle over one of my knees, folding my hands in my lap. Harold's face lights up.

"Excellent. This is good news. But, about the other condition?"

I didn't actually think he was serious about that.

"Which was what, again?"

"You need to marry my daughter. Only then will you get full control of the entire company, and if you're not married to her within a year, you lose all claim to the new division. Regardless of how much work you have put into it."

"I don't think you can offer an ultimatum to marry your daughter, especially if she doesn't want it. She doesn't strike me as someone who would be okay with this." Harold smirks and lets out a small chuckle.

"Well, you're right." His hand pushes through his dark hair. Some grey is peeking through at his temples.

"She definitely will not like the idea of being forced into a marriage. Unfortunately, she knows what is at stake. And, even if she could live with being cut off, she has this innate and annoying habit of wanting to please me. Pathetic, really." I feel my blood boil at the casual cruelty of his comments.

"Then why not just let her leave?" Harold's eyes narrow at me, a reaction to the bite in my tone.

"She's a Black. That carries weight in our society. If the 'heiress' were to walk away or get cut off, it would create too much chaos." He rubs his temples and pinches the bridge of his nose with one hand. "And she has been in enough tabloids and social media posts thanks to her reckless, party-girl behaviour. If she has a stable man, things could settle down." His face slowly grows hard.

"And dammit if I can't even control our own press. *Journalistic integrity*," he spits. "They're tabloids and papz. There's no integrity in that." He rolls his eyes and folds his arms across his chest.

"So, my role is an image stabilizer for your company?" I say flatly.

"Yes, and no. Besides, I saw the way you looked at Elissa. You're certainly not getting the shit end of the stick. I just need her reined in. And that division will give her something to do within the company, without actually having any real control. Then, eventually, her husband, which would be you, would take over all operations." Harold was oozing with pride, like his little scheme was completely genius.

"I don't see how this will work with Elissa. She doesn't seem like she'd be interested in an arranged marriage." He smirks at my rebuttal.

"That's because it won't seem like an arranged marriage. You're going to woo and court her, like you would in any other relationship." I stare at him, my face blank. *How the hell would that work?* As if he could read my mind, he continues, "You'll be in proximity. You'll be taking the reins on setting the new division up. There'll be lots of chances for late nights, work dinners, and whatever."

The waitress returns and we place our orders. Harold and I say nothing for a few minutes. My phone vibrates and I slide my hand into the inside pocket of my jacket and silence it. I sit and stare off into space, one arm across my chest, the other resting on top, with my fist pressing against my lips and my thumb anchoring my jaw. Harold starts talking again, but he's moved on to discussing the business aspect in further detail, going into what he envisions for the department.

When our food arrives, I eat in silence as he continues the shop talk. I finish my food before him and sit patiently, listening to what he has to say. When he finishes, his cutlery clangs to the plate and he stares at me intensely. A devilish grin stretches across his face as he reaches a hand across the table, waiting, like the devil offering a deal, just begging for me to get burned.

"So…do we have a deal, *son*?"

CHAPTER
FIFTEEN

BRANDT

"So, what happened the other night with Riley's friend?" Rhys asks as he shoots the ball from the three-point line. I jump up to block the ball and fail. The ball connects with the backboard and drops into the hoop.

"Uh, not much. She kicked me out because we didn't have any rubbers." I shrug, chasing after the ball and dribbling it back to the centre line.

"What? Dude, you should have come to Riley's room and grabbed my wallet." My face contorts in disgust at the idea of seeing Rhys mid-romp.

"Yeah, no thanks. It was better this way. We're going to be working together soon for her father's new expansion."

"Oh, so you completed the deal?"

"Well, we shook on it. So, it's as good as done. I'm just waiting on his assistant to send over the final documents to sign with the amendments," I reply flatly. Rhys tries to steal the ball from me, but I dodge him and make my way up to dunk.

"What are the amendments? Isn't it a straight business deal?" Rhys walks over with his hands on his hips, rolling his head from shoulder to shoulder.

"Not...exactly..." I'm not proud of it, but Rhys is my best friend. I know I have to be straight with him. He looks at me expectantly.

"He will only do the deal if...if I marry Elissa within a year," I mumble. Rhys stares at me, his eyes nearly bulging out of his head.

"Uh, what?" he says in disbelief. I shrug.

"What the fuck? And you accepted his conditions?"

"Er...that's not even the sketchiest part..."

"Oh, fuck. What the hell did you agree to, Brandt?"

I tell Rhys about the deal, and how Harold wants me to marry Elissa within a year, but it needs to seem natural because she will outright refuse an arranged marriage. This is his master plan to get someone to take full control of his company and not, as Harold puts it, "give it to his ungrateful daughter."

"Shit, dude. And you said yes? To all of it?" I press my lips into a thin line and nod slowly.

"There's...one more thing. I don't know if you remember...in fact, I'm pretty sure you don't, but back in high school? That freshman girl you always caught me staring at in senior year of high school and made fun of me for liking?" Rhys' brows furrow in confusion, but after a moment he nods.

"Yeah, I remember. Why?"

I clear my throat. "Well, that was her. That was Elissa Black. And I just got swept up in the fantasy of the infatuation that I had for her eight years ago." I pause. "Well...to be honest, the infatuation never really faded. It's always been her."

Rhys' mouth drops open and he pushes both hands roughly through his jet black strands, slicking them back with sweat.

"Duuuude," he drawls. "You not only hooked up with her, but now you're going to marry her?" he asks in disbelief. A small grin hitches up the left side of my mouth, like I just won a minor victory. We default to just taking turns tossing the ball into the hoop instead of playing one-on-one, and Rhys tries to further dissect this situation.

"How are you going to get her to settle down? Have you read up on her? She seems like she's pretty fucking wild and she clearly loves to party." I grimace.

"Yeah, I know. I've been kind of digitally stalking her over the past few years."

"No! Dude, that is so creepy!" Rhys exclaims and chucks the ball at my chest.

"Not like creepy stalking! More like...keeping tabs. Checking in on her social media accounts and stuff. Just seeing what she's up to." Rhys does not look convinced. "It's like you Insta-stalking your ex, but I've never dated Elissa."

"Yeah, no. It's still 200% creepy. You're just lucky I know you, and I know you're not a psycho. But, in all seriousness, good luck dude. I have a feeling you're really going to need it."

I drop my gym bag on the floor when I get back to my apartment. I see I have a new email from Harold, telling me that his assistant will send me the files to sign via courier in the next few days. He also included Elissa's cell phone number and email address so I could "start getting to know her." I would absolutely hate these circumstances were it anyone else. But...it's her. The girl I've always loved from a distance. The only one my cock decides he will rise for. I hope to hell she is worth it.

After I make dinner, I'm sitting at the kitchen table, debating on whether to text her. Instead, I message Rhys.

Me: *Harold sent me Elissa's number to "get to know her." Is it creepy if I just message her out of the blue?*

I receive a response a few minutes later.

Rhys: *Depends. You need a reason to actually message her.*

Shit, he has a point. Another message comes in a second later.

Rhys: *Maybe ask her when her official start date is and blame it on her dad for not giving you the info.*

Me: *Genius. Thanks, man.*

Rhys added a "thumbs-up" reaction to my response. I add Elissa's information to my contact list and click "new message" to start drafting a text.

Me: *Good evening Elissa. This is Brandt. Your father gave me your info, but he forgot to mention when you'd be officially* *starting at the office. Please let me know so I can coordinate my schedule.*

No answer, even hours later. However, I can see she read my message. *Shit. She left me on read.*

It's not until two days later that she responds to my message.

Elissa: *I start on Monday. Sorry for the late response. Still getting settled.*

Finally, a response. But she starts on Monday? *This* Monday? I grit my teeth, pissed that she is only giving me two days' notice.

Me: *I am a very busy man. I don't appreciate tardiness — in person or digitally. I now have limited time to make arrangements for the meetings I am supposed to be in on Monday. In the future, I expect a response within eight hours.*

The three dots appear and disappear on the screen, intermittently. Finally, about half an hour later, I receive a response.

Elissa: *I deeply apologize for my tardiness, sir. This will serve as a blanket apology for any future tardiness as well — in person or digitally. I didn't realize that you were such a busy man. You must be the only person who is busy, so busy you needed to make it known. I will try my best to endeavour all my responses within the eight-hour limit. Should I fail to follow those guidelines...you can kiss my ass. *kiss emoji* *peach emoji**

At first, I growl out loud at her mocking me, but then chuckle at her defiance and sarcasm. I send a quick reply.

Me: *I appreciate the consideration. I would rather bite that juicy ass.*

CHAPTER

SIXTEEN

RILEY

It's been almost a week since we've moved to Toronto. Our condo, the one Harold bought for Elissa, is in the centre of the Entertainment District. It's a perfect location for both of us. Elissa can walk a few blocks to work, and I have everything at my disposal for media content. Today, I've set up my streaming equipment on our wraparound corner balcony. It may be narrow, but there is enough space for me to do my yoga. And did I mention it wraps around the corner of the building? I press the record button on my remote.

"Good morning my lovelies!" I announce cheerfully to the camera. "Today we're going to do some yoga on this gorgeous balcony of my new pad!" I use the remote to pan the camera around, allowing the video to capture the expansive, beautiful Toronto horizon from my balcony before turning the device back toward me.

"I just love a good yoga session in the fresh air," I say, as I stretch my calves and lunge right to left, loosening up my hips before starting my yoga routine. Just as I am about to wrap up and sign off, the buzzer for the door goes off. I ignore it and do my sign off. But the incessant buzzer keeps droning on. The asshole at the door is obviously pressing it down repeatedly and consistently, as it moves from a pattern of annoying buzzes to a solid drone, and back again.

"For fuck's sakes!" I shout. I hit the record button again to stop the device from filming and stomp over to the front door to answer the buzzer.

"Yeah?" I'm so completely annoyed that I can't even fake a nice greeting.

"Baby, it's me. Let me in." A somewhat familiar, manly voice purrs into the intercom.

"It's me, who?"

"Riles, this isn't a knock-knock joke."

"And I still don't know who you are. Sorry buddy, not letting you in." The intercom is quiet for a moment, then a big sigh crackles through.

"Who else would call you baby and lives in Toronto? Also, I am a little offended you don't recognize my voice," the deep voice grumbles. But before I can say anything, the intercom goes dead and the person on the other end has given up. Racking my brain, I still cannot figure out who it could have been. I grab a water bottle from the kitchen and head back toward the balcony when there's a knock at the door.

I freeze briefly, wondering how this guy would have gotten into the building. I look through the peephole and there is Rhys. My heart swells and my fingers tingle. The door locks clunk as I unlock them, throw the door open, and toss my arms around Rhys' neck.

"So, it was you buzzing!" I squeal. He chuckles at my reaction. Suddenly, my body stiffens and I slide my hands down to his hard chest, anchor myself, and push off him.

"How did you get in?" I ask warily. "Wait, and how the hell do you know where we live?" A devilish grin appears on his face.

"I know people." When my face doesn't change from the cautionary look, he sighs.

"I knew you were rooming with Elissa; Brandt works with Elissa. I got your address from Brandt."

"Yeah…that doesn't make it any less creepy," I groan.

"Creepy, romantic. Yeah?" He wags his eyebrows at me and scoops me up into his arms. I wrap my legs around his waist and he crosses the threshold of the apartment. Kicking the door closed with his foot as he sucks my lips into his mouth, he mumbles, "Where's your room?"

My response comes out in heavy pants in between kisses. "Right…door." My arm gestures right behind me, as my room is right off the main entrance and across from the main washroom. His hands squeeze my ass as we enter my room and he slams the door shut. He throws me down on my double bed and looks around.

"Nice digs," he says, nodding approvingly. My room isn't the biggest, but I didn't pay for the place, so Elissa gets the primary bedroom. My room is cozy. It has floor-to-ceiling windows on one wall, and a big mirrored closet the length of the opposite wall, except for where the door is. My double bed fits between the windowed and closeted walls with enough room for two generously sized nightstands. Across from the bed on the fourth wall is my TV, mounted, with a six-drawer dresser that functions half as a dresser and half as an entertainment centre.

"I preferred our condo in Kingston, but beggars can't be choosers," I say with a shrug. "Now, get naked and help me christen my new room." I look at Rhys with my best smoulder as I strip for him like a courtesan. It doesn't take him another word to rip off his t-shirt and drop his pants. He's already firmly at attention, and I lick my lips as I crawl over to him. I press feather-light kisses on his tip and he sucks in a breath of anticipation. My tongue drags along the length of his shaft, and when my tongue finds a prominent vein, it flicks up over the vein while still travelling down his shaft.

His dick twitches, letting me know that he's enjoying it. I bobble my tongue back toward the tip, swirling it around for a moment before taking in his length. His thick eight inches bottoms out against the back of my throat.

"Fuck, Riles…" he moans as I deepthroat him. I grab his ass with both my hands, and when his tip is back at the entrance of my mouth, I tug his ass to me, slamming his dick to the back of my throat, almost making me gag. One of his hands snakes into my hair and grasps a fistful, bracing himself as his head falls back.

Repeating the hard thrusts a few more times, he uses both hands to grab my head and restarts the pace his way. I release my hands from his ass to find his balls and massage them. A shiver runs up his spine. He moans loudly. "Fuck. Yes. Just like that," he huffs.

"Riley…" I feel the tension in his balls build and I push his hips away from my face, not allowing him to come inside my mouth. A growl erupts from him.

"Fucking tease." I wipe my mouth, peering up at him through my lashes and giving him an evil grin. He pushes me and I flop back on the bed, giggling as I land softly on the pillows. He crawls overtop of me, but then, with a mischievous grin, he starts to move lower.

"Open. Now." I obey. My pussy reacts, allowing my wetness to seep out slightly at his gruff command. He dives in between my thighs and doesn't ease me into his touch. His teeth nibble on my clit, sending electric sparks shooting through my body. I buck my hips up, begging for something more. He slams my hips down with his large hand and pins me down. He rolls his tongue on my swollen nub as he dips one finger, then two, into my dripping pussy. A loud moan escapes me as my breathing grows more ragged. I beg for more.

"Please, Rhys. I need you." But he doesn't stop, only continues to give me just enough to bring me to the edge, but not push me over.

"No. You'll wait until I'm ready. Not so fun when you're the one being denied, huh?" he says darkly, taking a break from using his mouth as he watches me squirm while he thrusts his curved fingers in hard.

"You like how I play with you, don't you?" I moan at his question. "Use your words."

"Y-yes." I respond, and jolt when his tongue slides over my clit again.

"I can't hold it anymore. Please, Rhys." When he releases his mouth and says the word "come," I already am. He chuckles.

"Oh baby, couldn't hold it back anymore?" He dives between my legs again, licking up the mess he made with my juices. When he's done, he climbs on top of me, reaches over to my nightstand and grabs a foil packet. Once he's rolled on the latex, he positions himself at my entrance. He doesn't give me any notice and just rams his dick into me.

"Fuck, you feel good," he says, staying still to allow me to adjust to his size.

"God, I missed this pussy," Rhys whispers. I wrap my legs around his waist to allow him to enter deeper. I circle my arms around his neck and pull his head down toward me.

"I missed your dick," I whisper back to him as I pull him into a deep kiss. He thrusts with hard, deep strides. He hoists my legs over his shoulders, folding me in half, and gradually picks up speed. With the new position allowing him to enter me deeper, he can hit the spot that shoots fireworks off in my mind. And, just as we both find release... the front door slams and a gut-wrenching, high-pitched scream echoes through the apartment.

CHAPTER

SEVENTEEN

ELISSA

I slam the door shut behind me.

"Aaaaaahhhhhh!" A guttural scream escapes the confines of my throat. I step out of my black pumps, pick them up, and hurl them down the length of the hallway until they bounce off the wall at the end and skitter into the kitchen.

I follow the path of my pumps, stomping as I make my way to pick them up and put them away in my closet. The creak of a door behind me lets me know Riley is home. She follows me into my room and is wearing a satin housecoat, wrapped tightly around her size zero body, with her hair mussed and face flushed. She clearly was in the middle of something fun until my outburst.

"Hey hun.… Everything okay?" Riley rubs my shoulders from behind me. I relax into her a bit, feeling thankful once again that my best friend moved with me, but the feeling evaporates like ice on a hot summer day when I think about how I spent my last eight hours.

"Fuck no. Nothing is goddamn okay!" I snap in frustration. Riley sighs and walks me over to my bed, and we both plop down on it.

"My father is a fucking control freak. He spent eight hours telling me about starting tomorrow. What I need to wear, how to do my hair, how to do my makeup, and so on. He said if I couldn't handle it, he'd send a team over to do it for me. Send a fucking team. Like I'm a goddamn celebrity!" I shout.

"Babe, watch the language," Riley soothes. I roll my eyes; out of everything she's concerned about, the swearing couldn't be less of an issue. It's the "God" thing — as a Christian, she can't help but chastise me for the use of His name in vain.

"I just don't understand. I'm following the path that he wants. I'm working for his new division, I went through the program of his choice at university. Why does he think he can control my physical image? Is he trying to sell me off to someone?" I let out an exasperated breath. I know that, in the grand scheme of things, my *charmed* life probably seems like a good thing to most people. But my parents are equally as distant as they are demanding and overbearing. And it's not lovingly. If I were born with a dick between my legs, now that would have been a different story. I'd be the prodigal son; eternally loved. Like Hercules coming home to

Olympus. Instead, I am Persephone, tied to Hell for all eternity. Surrounded by loneliness even though I am not alone.

"Then quit. Leave. He can't stop you. You're more than capable of making it on your own."

I groan. "Yes, I know I can, Riles. I want to leave. I don't want to be a part of this fucked-up family anymore. But...I keep hoping one day, they'll be the parents I deserve." I cringe at my own words.

"I sound like a fucking prepubescent teenager. Fuck me." I cover my eyes with my arms and groan, biting back tears.

Suddenly, I hear the whoosh of the toilet flushing in the main bathroom. I jolt upright and look at Riley. She also sits up and her face goes red.

"So.... Uh, yeah. I have some company." I raise my eyebrows at her. She giggles.

"It's Rhys. He found me. Isn't it so romantic?" She stares off into space with a disgustingly dreamy face. I push her off my bed and toward the door, silently letting her know she's allowed to get back to her romp.

"Thanks, doll. And cheer up. Things will be better. Tonight, we'll plan your outfit, go for dinner and drinks, and then tomorrow I'll get up early and help with your makeup and hair." She blows me a kiss and drifts out of my room. I cross the room and slam my door shut. I dig through my purse until I find my AirPods, shove them in my ears, and blast some City and Colour while I scroll through Instagram.

A few hours later, after a two-hour run and an hour-long shower, I am in the kitchen, making a racket as I slam things around, trying to find where Riley stored the liquor. I hear murmuring and kissing noises, then the click of the main door shutting. Riley, now dressed in pajama shorts and a rosy pink tank top, floats into the kitchen like she's riding on a cloud. I can almost see the halo appear over her head and wings sprout from her back as the harps pick up in the background.

"All right, Riley. You can come back down to hell now," I say, breaking her out of her trance-like state. She sighs.

"Top righthand cupboard," she sighs, pointing to the spot where she's hidden my whisky. She's stashed it on the top shelf that is nine feet high, and the door slowly opens and closes vertically. I try to reach for the long, brushed nickel handle shining against the ultra-glossy chestnut cupboards.

"Stool is inside the cabinet."

I open the door directly in front of me and see the step stool. I pull it out, shake it open, and grab a tumbler and my whisky decanter.

One thing I seemed to inherit from my father, aside from his eventual fortune and company, is his love for whisky. It's also a flex when you're a woman in a man's world. Being able to drink them under the table, and with hard liquor at that, seems to impress them, but also intimidates the fuck out of them. Most of the men drink liquor to seem…I don't know. Powerful? Because that's what suits do in the movies. But most of them are pussies and only want or like beer. Me? I love the rich, strong taste. I live for the burn; it warms up my body as it slides down my throat and settles into my stomach. It's like feeling the warmth of the sun's rays bloom over you when you're at the beach, lying on your towel, and the sun peeks out from behind a cloud, creating goosebumps across your flesh. Making you shiver because the heat feels good.

I carefully pour the whisky into the crystal decanter, then pour myself two fingers of the warm amber liquid and slam it back. Normally, I like to sip and enjoy my whisky slowly. But right now, I need it. I pour another two fingers and slam it back. I plug the stem for the decanter back in, rinse my glass out, and place it upside down on the drying mat. Riley is chatting in the background about tomorrow and what she thinks will be a decent wardrobe choice for my first day at the office. But my mind is already on tomorrow at the office. I am dreading going to work tomorrow and don't want to see my father. I don't want to see Brandt. *But you do want to see Brandt.* My groin aches to remember him.

His body is tall and muscular, but limber. His golden-brown hair, perfectly styled, standing a few inches on top and then swooping neatly to one side, but clean and short on the sides of his head. His green eyes glimmering in the moonlight, growing darker as the heat cranks up in the room.... A hand waves in front of my face and I am dragged out of my reverie.

"Earth to Elissa..." Riley drones. "Where did ya go?" I shake my head, clearing the dirty thoughts.

"Uh, sorry. Was thinking about tomorrow and dreading it."

"Well, I think we should go into your room and pick out your outfit. I think I know exactly what you should wear, down to the purse and heels," she squeals excitedly, sprinting into my room and sliding open the tall mirrored door of my closet. "C'mon!" she yells back at me. I pour another two fingers of whisky and gulp it down.

• • •

My purple satin, open-toed Jimmy Choos with an eccentric emerald-green jewel on the forefoot clack across the charcoal marble tile. Flecks of gold sparkle in the tile from all the natural light that pours into the lobby of the Black & Wells Publishing and Press Tower. I secure my oversized business clutch, containing my laptop, notebook, and wallet, under my arm. Thanks to Riley's insistence, I'm wearing a light grey wrap dress that hugs my curves up top but is loose and flowy in the skirt. The dress is sleeveless, showing off my defined, slim arms.

I'm busy texting Riley as I head toward the elevators. I know this building like the back of my hand, so I don't need to watch where I am going. I'm approaching security, and I glance up briefly as I wave my freshly manicured hand, bedazzled with my white gold Michael Kors watch, at the guard. He nods and lets me through without question. My hair is down in loose curls, and I flip the curls over my right shoulder, exposing the left side of my neck.

My shoes never cease clacking as I stride to the elevators. I know I am nearing the elevator bay when I suddenly barrel into something hard, and it lurches forward. I stumble back and drop my phone on the tile floor, hearing my poor screen shatter. I kneel down to pick up my phone when I notice someone else is eye-level with me, also reaching out to help me pick up my shattered phone.

"Could be a lot worse," a deep, yet familiar, voice says quietly. The hair on my arms stands up and goosebumps prickle across my skin. "Could have been your purse with your laptop."

I look up at the person speaking, and my heart stutters. Familiar green eyes lock with my blue ones — Brandt Collins.

CHAPTER
EIGHTEEN

ELISSA

Brandt stands and extends a hand toward me. I accept his hand, allowing him to help me up. I smooth my skirt out and mumble out, "Thanks." He chuckles softly.

"I assume you're going to the twenty-second floor?" he asks as he presses the call button of the lift. I nod my head in affirmation — that's my father's floor for his office in the Black & Wells operation, after all.

"Figured as much."

I'm dreading the ride up to my father's floor, as we're the only two people to step into the elevator. The doors glide shut, and the tension in this small, confined space is palpable. My heart feels like it's beating like a cartoon character, pounding right out of my chest. I wonder if he can see my heartbeat ticking in my chest, or if he can hear the beating, because I sure can. Tidal waves of blood bash against my eardrums as heat rises from my core and travels up, lighting my skin and soul on fire. I don't dare risk a glance in Brandt's direction, but I can feel his eyes drilling into my soul.

We've only travelled three floors in the lift, but it feels like we've been travelling for hours. Finally, I can't stand it anymore and I turn my body to Brandt, to see if he's reacting the way I am. But I don't see much. In a blur of motion he rushes me, presses me against the elevator wall, cups my face with one hand, and snakes the other around my waist as his mouth devours mine. His chest is pressed firmly against mine and I notice the pounding of his heartbeat matches mine. I relax a little into his heated kiss, relieved to know I am not the only one feeling this exchange. His strong hand locks around the back of my neck, exposing the underside of my nape, as his mouth descends, pouring kisses down the length of my neck. The hand that was wrapped around my waist has now moved lower, gliding over the crest of my butt, and continuing lower until his fingers are trailing up the backside of my thighs, slightly pulling up the flowy skirt, the fabric bunching atop his wrist.

After what feels like an eternity, the lift dings and suddenly we're shooting away from each other to opposite ends of the car. The door slides open on the thirteenth floor. I spin around to face away from the people getting on, fumble to grab a compact mirror out of my clutch, and open it to check my lipstick. *Fuck*. It's smeared. I get a tissue out, dampen it with my saliva, and blot away the mussed lipstick. The elevator stops again at the twentieth floor and the elevator empties until it is just Brandt and I, alone again. Before he has a chance to say anything, I raise my hand and avoid looking at him.

"Let's just forget what happened. This is already awkward enough as it is. Yeah?"

He clears his throat and responds with a gravelly "Sure." When the lift reaches the top floor, I excuse myself from Brandt and speedwalk out of the elevator and down the corridor to find the ladies' room. When I am safely behind the door, I lean back against it, my knees bowing into each other. I allow myself to slide down until I reach the floor. With my legs still bent toward each other, I place my elbows on my knees and drop my face into my hands. I try to regulate my breathing and get my nerves under control. When I've finally settled a bit, I get my ass off the floor and carry myself toward the mirror. I brush out my dress, trying to smooth out the wrinkles. I fluff my bronze curls, arranging them neatly behind my shoulders, then grab my lipstick from my purse and reapply the crimson paint.

Feeling satisfied with the freshening, I pull my phone out of my purse and groan. The glass of my phone's screen has cracks spiderwebbed across it, and it's missing a few small chunks of glass in the bottom corner. I double-tap the screen to wake the phone, and thankfully, it still responds. I try to navigate to my text messages, but my phone isn't responding well to my touch. *Not exactly surprising.* Instead, I decide to use Siri to message Riley.

"Hey Siri. Message Riley."

Siri dings and responds, "What do you want it to say?"

"Dropped my phone at work. Will be home late. Broke my screen so I need to buy a new one. Can't text." Siri dings again and speaks.

"Sending: 'Dropped my phone at work. Will be home late. Broke my screen so I need to buy a new one. Can't text.' Would you like to send it now?"

"Yes." My phone makes the swooping noise that lets me know she sent the text to Riley.

I exit the washroom and I feel the hairs on the nape of my neck stand on end.

"Do you need a ride later to get your phone fixed?" My soul threatens to leave my body as the booming voice from beside me breaks the silence. I drop my phone again.

"For fuck's sakes!" I shout. Brandt has already bent down to grab my phone and hands it back to me. He chuckles.

"Sorry for startling you. Shall we?" He gestures forward, escorting me to my father's office. I follow his lead, making a mental note to pack my runners and a change of clothes from now on because if I'm going to deal with him and my father daily, I am going to need an escape.

My father has us move from his office to the conference room down the corridor. He connects his laptop to the giant monitor in the room and clicks open a presentation he's using for this meeting. I've seen most of this presentation before because I created most of it. There was a year-end business project in one of my university classes that had to do with a start-up company, so my father decided my project would be on the new division he was creating.

He got free labour and a free presentation, and all I received was an "A" on the project and no appreciation from my father for my hard work. Nope. Instead, he passed it off to investors and the board like it was all his hard work.

Seeing the slides again irritates me. Slowly, the anger rises in me, and my leg starts bouncing under the table as I try to soothe the fire burning through me. Brandt's head turns slightly and I can see him glancing at me through his periphery, cocking his eyebrow. He carefully places his hand on my bouncing knee and I immediately freeze. Sparks fly through me from the slightest touch of his hand on my knee.

The angry fire that was burning inside me moments ago now simmers deliciously inside me, warming my core. It melts away some of the frost around my heart and pools inside my underwear. I shift my leg away from his touch and readjust myself, squeezing my thighs together to quell the want. I clear my throat and my father looks at me questioningly.

"I am sure Mr. Collins —" Brandt interrupts me.

"Please, call me Brandt. No need for formalities." I give him a tight smile and return my stare to my father.

"I am sure *Brandt* has done more than his fair share of due diligence when it comes to reading this presentation. Otherwise, he wouldn't have invested in the new division." My father's face pinkens. "It would be a shame to waste time rehashing old details, especially when I created the business plan for the division."

My father tenses and narrows his eyes at me, clearly feeling disrespected by my intrusion into his meeting. It would seem he would rather me shut up and look pretty while the "men" do all the talking. I return my father's look with a soft smile, letting him know he can't get to me.

"Well, Brandt," my father speaks up. "If that is also fine with you, maybe we should go downstairs and look at the new division's office setup." He turns his gaze to me.

"Would that be okay with you, Elissa?" I smile triumphantly and nod, happy as hell to get out of the conference room and put some distance between me, my father, and Brandt.

When I get home, Riley and Rhys are on the couch, horizontal, full-on making out, teenager-style. I roll my eyes as I pass by them and slam my bedroom door shut. I place my clutch on my desk and walk into my en suite washroom. I pop open the medicine cabinet and swallow a couple of Advils down, exit the washroom, and make my way over to the dresser across my room, undressing as I go. I am just zipping up my sports bra when Riley enters my room.

"Oh, shit. Sorry," Riley seems surprised that I am in my room half-naked. "I was seeing if you wanted to go out for dinner with Rhys and I tonight?" I fish out a red tank top from my top drawer, yank it over my head, and bend down to find some black spandex shorts in my bottom drawer.

"I suppose so. When are you guys going?"

"We can wait until you're back from your run." I turn to her and raise my eyebrow.

"Really? And what if I take a two-hour run?" I ask. Riley gives me the most devious look.

"I'm sure I can think of something to occupy our time." She lets out an evil little laugh and closes the door softly behind her. I chuckle to myself as I sit on the edge of my bed, tying up my runners.

I wave to Riley and Rhys as I exit the apartment, shoving my AirPods into my ears. I swipe through the different playlists on Spotify I've created for running until I find the one labelled "Beats and Pace." It's really just a bunch of songs, of many genres, that all have wicked timing and bass guitar, things that really seem to motivate me to push myself as I run.

The first song that pops on when I hit the shuffle button is *Everybody Talks* by Neon Trees. For me, this is a perfect song to warm up to when I'm just starting my run. It has a steady beat right off the bat and picks up at the chorus, allowing me to run more intensely for about thirty seconds, then the pattern winds down more slowly again, allowing my body to recover momentarily.

I am jogging along, about half an hour in, when I see someone familiar flash by me running in the opposite direction. My head follows their direction for a split second, but I refocus and point my head forward, making sure I don't run into anyone or anything. Then, out of my side view, I notice someone is keeping pace with me. I look over to my left, shriek, and veer off, slowing down. I am doubled over, gasping for air, when Brandt turns around and jogs back to where I am panting.

"You scared the Christ out of me, Brandt!" I shout at him, though much louder than I expected to, thanks to the music blaring in my ears. He fucking smirks at me, and I pull out one of my earbuds.

"Yeah. Seems like I'm always sneaking up and scaring you," he chortles. "Guess you should pay more attention to your surroundings." He walks away for a moment and I double over again, panting heavily. He returns with a water bottle and passes it to me. I glare at him, but warily take the bottle.

"Thanks," I murmur, twisting off the lid and gulping half of it down.

CHAPTER

NINETEEN

BRANDT

I get a notification on my phone.

Rhys: *Dude, she's going out for a run. You should totally "bump" into her.*

Should I fake a bump-into scenario? I reply to Rhys' message with a thumbs-up emoji and quickly go to my bedroom and change into my workout gear. It takes me about half an hour of wandering to find out what route Elissa's taken. I am dripping sweat by the time I find her. She looks fucking gorgeous. She is also all sweaty, but she fucking glows. Her warm bronze hair is tied up in a high ponytail, and it swishes across her back in time to her strides. Her breasts are bouncing, and slightly squished together because of the sports bra she's wearing, but it gives her major cleavage. Her long, toned legs soak up the late afternoon sun and her pale thighs and calves are flexing as she takes hard, strong, purposeful strides.

Fuck. I need to look away before my shorts rise in the front. I focus on the distance I have until we're close. And, just as I am about to pass by her, I slow down, just a little. Enough for her to catch a glimpse of me, and enough for me to breathe in her sweet, yet salty, vanilla scent. Sure enough, it works. I can feel her head swivel to follow me briefly. When I notice she doesn't stop, I turn myself around and jog back toward her, keeping time with her until she notices me beside her.

She screams, jumps, and tries not to crash as she veers away and slows down. I try my hardest not to laugh out loud at her reaction. I slow down and turn back toward her. She's doubled over, hand on her chest, heaving in breaths. I chuckle to myself as I walk over to her with my hands on my hips. Her head tilts up slightly and her eyes linger on my legs.

"You scared the Christ out of me, Brandt!" she shouts at me, and I can't hold back the grin spreading across my face. I almost outright smile.

"Yeah. Seems like I'm always sneaking up and scaring you," I chuckle. "Guess you should pay more attention to your surroundings." She's still doubled over, panting. I guess I scared her well. I notice a street vendor a few feet away. I jog over, purchase two water bottles, and jog back to where Elissa is still bent over, huffing.

She suddenly stands up straight when I'm beside her

again. She gives me a skeptical look when I hold out a water bottle for her, but she accepts it, drinking half of it in one go.

"So, are you finished your run?" I ask her. She shakes her head.

"Not even close. I usually run for another hour and a half."

I nod and scratch my head. "Well, do you mind if I join you? I promise not to scare you again," I snicker. She playfully pushes my shoulder and looks at me with a glint in her eyes.

"Think you can keep up?"

I look at her incredulously and feign offense. "Wow. Full of yourself, aren't you?"

She smirks at my retort, shrugs, and waves at me to follow her. She plugs her earbud back into her ear, double-taps it, and takes off. I finish my water, toss it into a random blue bin on the sidewalk, and catch up to her.

We reach the front of her building an hour later. As she cools down, she stretches her limbs. I watch her bend over and elongate...everything. Thankfully, she isn't looking, so I can tuck my boner into my waistband. I grab the collar of my sleeveless shirt and pull it up over my head. As I yank the shirt up, I feel hot — and not from the heat of the mid-May sun. I feel a unique burning sensation, and I know Elissa is watching me as I strip off my shirt. I flex my abs as I swipe the shirt across my face and down my torso to mop up sweat.

I feel her eyes drifting over my body, from my wide shoulders down to my pecs, from my pecs to the glistening six-pack that cuts into a "V" shape at the top of my waistband, which is slung low over my hips. I laugh inwardly, knowing that if I were to look at Elissa right now, she would instantly blush crimson and look away, which would make it even more obvious that she was eye-fucking me. *No complaints here.*

I clear my throat, giving her a warning that I'm about to stop what I'm doing and look in her direction. I think she took the hint, because when I do look over at her, she turns away from me and starts stretching her arms above her head. She turns to me after a moment, takes out her earbuds, and places them back into their charging case.

"So, do you want to come up?" she asks. I look at her, one brow quirked inquisitively.

"I just mean, I think Rhys is still upstairs with Riley," she explains, rolling her eyes. I shrug and say "Okay," then follow her inside and up to her apartment. I let Elissa show me the way, trailing close behind her when the elevator stops at her floor. Instead of worrying about keys, her apartment door has a number pad as an alternative method of unlocking the door. She presses the code into keypad, and it emits one long beep before the gears inside grind open the lock. When we enter her apartment, Elissa toes off her shoes, and I do the same. She walks down the hallway and knocks on the door to her right.

"Riles! Get out here. Rhys has a guest." I can hear Rhys and Riley giggling behind the door, movement, and then what sounds like someone tripping. The door swings open and Rhys tumbles out, trying to pull his pants on.

"Yo, Collins," Rhys says, giving me a slick grin. "Whatcha doing here?"

"I ran into Elissa when I was on my run and when we

finished, she invited me up because she knew you were here, I guess." Rhys accepts my answer and winks at me.

"Well, now that Elissa is back," Rhys says slyly, "us three were going to go grab some dinner. I'd ask you to join, but you're all sweaty." I tense at his suggestion.

"I can go home and shower quickly and meet you guys at the restaurant. Text me what restaurant you decide on and I'll meet you there," I counter. Rhys looks over his shoulder. I presume he's looking for visual confirmation from Riley that it's okay that I just invited myself. When he looks back at me, he has a huge grin on his face and flashes me a thumbs-up. I release the tension I didn't realize I was holding, instantly relieved that Riley said I can join. I say my goodbyes and shove my damp socked feet back into my shoes, then head out.

On my way back to my apartment, which is approximately two blocks away, I think about how nice the run with Elissa was. Even though we didn't say much, just being beside her was thrilling and relaxing. I could feel every fibre of my being buzzing, but I also felt peaceful. I don't quite understand how I can feel both sensations at the same time. My body reacted to her being so close, but the entire world and my thoughts just melted away.

I'm so antsy at the thought of seeing her again that I don't wait for the elevator. Instead, I run up seven flights of stairs to my condo. I rush inside and strip as soon as I shut my front door, letting my clothes drop to the ground in a trail behind me as I make my way to the bathroom.

I brush my teeth quickly while the shower warms up. Once the water is hot enough, I jump into the shower and try to get in and out as fast as possible. After I towel off, I quickly run my fingers through my hair with a bit of gel before getting dressed in a rush. My phone lights up with a message from Rhys as I pull my shirt over my head.

Rhys: *We're heading down to Rhonnie's Pub. It's on Peter Street. We'll be there in about ten minutes.*

Me: *K. Meet you guys there. Just heading out now.*

When I finally near the pub, I take a moment to fix my hair using my reflection in the store window next door. I probably look like a vain asshole, but oh well. I walk into the pub and spot Elissa immediately. Riley and Rhys' backs are to me and they are attached at the lips. Elissa is fidgeting awkwardly and staring off into space, apparently in an attempt to avoid looking at her friend making out. I saunter over, and when Elissa realizes I'm there, we lock eyes for a moment before she drops her gaze and lets her eyes roam over my body. I'm wearing a black v-neck t-shirt that shows off my ropey biceps and broad chest. The shirt tapers nicely down my torso to meet my favourite pair of jeans, which show off my ass and my package perfectly.

Elissa clears her throat and widens her eyes at Riley, alerting her of my arrival. Riley jumps up and turns around.

"Over here, Brandt!" Riley waves me over. When I reach the table, Riley is now sitting beside Elissa, and Rhys is across from Riley, leaving the seat directly across from Elissa conveniently open. I slide into the booth beside Rhys and when the waitress comes over, we all place our drink orders. A few minutes later, the waitress returns with the drinks.

Riley and Rhys dominate the conversation, which is fine with me. I'm more of the "strong and silent" type, but I can definitely converse when needed. Elissa makes polite conversation with Rhys and Riley. I take a swig of my beer and level my eyes on Elissa. She squirms a bit and then realizes I'm staring at her. She glances back at me, then blushes and tries to look anywhere else. From what I've seen so far, she doesn't strike me as the type of person who would be shy or feel awkward. Suddenly, Elissa crosses her arms and huffs indignantly. *Did I say that last bit out loud? Oops.*

"Yeah, well. It's kind of awkward when your friend and her…whatever he is, are making out for twenty minutes in public. And the guy sitting across from you is someone you almost hooked up with."

Touché.

"Sorry, I didn't mean to make you uncomfortable," I say with a chuckle, taking another long pull of my beer. Elissa swirls her glass of whisky before taking a drink. She shrugs.

"It's fine. I guess we need to shake it off anyway. We'll have to see each other regularly now."

My insides vibrate with happiness when she mentions seeing each other on a regular basis. I knew we'd be in close proximity at the office already, but hearing those words come out of her mouth feels heaven-sent. I've spent too many years waiting for my chance to be in her orbit, to be able to talk to her. Elissa's eyes have been glued to me for the last few minutes.

"You know…you seem quite familiar," she mentions casually. I still, but force myself to relax.

"Hmm? How so?" I reply. She squints and stares at my face, trying to place where she might know me from.

She sighs.

"Honestly, I don't know. There's just something about you."

Rhys snorts, and Riley and Elissa turn to him with questioning looks. I turn my head to glare at him.

"What's so funny?" Riley asks Rhys. Rhys clears his throat and shakes his head before taking a sip of his beer. Elissa excuses herself to the washroom and Riley opts to go with her. I turn to Rhys, my eyes shooting daggers at him.

"What the fuck, Rhys?" I whisper-shout at him. He gives me a cocky grin.

"I'm sorry dude. You know I didn't do that on purpose. I'm not trying to blow your cover, I swear," he says, as he raises both of his hands up. I rub my face with one hand and bring my beer up to my mouth with the other, shaking my head before sipping.

CHAPTER TWENTY

ELISSA

"Girl, you need to loosen up," Riley says to me from the next stall over. I sigh. *Is it that obvious that I'm freaking out a little?*

"Shit," Riley whispers suddenly. I see her hand pop under the divider.

"Can I have some toilet paper? Apparently I'm out."

I pull at the paper, rattling the dispenser, and stuff a wad of rough, thin bathroom tissue into her hand.

"I want to loosen up. God, do you see how hot Brandt is?" I ask her. She makes some kind of disgusting slurping noise, letting me know she agrees with my assessment of him.

"But I work with him! I need to make sure things stay professional."

"What you need is to get laid. Your dad is stressing you the fuck out. You need to relax," she says. I can hear the grin in her voice.

"Okay. If not Brandt, what about Liam? I bet he'd be down for a hookup. I can get his number for you from Rhys." I hear Riley stand up, then the whoosh of the toilet flushing. I stand up and flush the toilet in my stall.

"I don't know…maybe. Liam is too sensitive. I mean, after one night, he thought we were exclusive or something. It was so strange." I walk out of the stall and over to the sink to wash my hands.

"I guess so. But he was so good-looking! And you said yourself that the sex was good," Riley counters.

"Yeah…" I say, as my thoughts drift back to a few weeks ago. I look into the mirror, dry my hands with some paper towel, and carefully reapply my lipstick.

"But still, it was strange. And considering that he lives in Toronto, and we lived in Kingston, even though he didn't know we were going to be moving soon, the fact that he acted as though we were an item so quickly creeped me out. It was almost like he was possessive of me or something." Riley laughs and rolls her eyes.

"You have some commitment issues. But also, like, you have this problem where almost every guy you hook up with seems to want more than just a hookup."

"Ugh, shut up, I know. It's like I tell them up front that I'm only looking for a hookup and they decide they need to prove they're boyfriend material." I stick my finger in my mouth, pretending to gag. Riley giggles and playfully bumps me with her shoulder.

"Let's convince the guys to go to a bar and get drunk and dance. I know you work tomorrow, but what the hell? You work for your dad. I'm sure he won't fire you." I groan at her suggestion but nod my head anyway. We head back to the table and Riley pauses when she sees two beautiful women talking to the guys. One of the women throws her head back and laughs as she places a well-manicured hand on Rhys' shoulder. I hear Riley's teeth grind together and she mutters, "No fucking way." She stomps over to the booth and hip checks one of the leggy blondes out of her way so she can slide into the booth across from Rhys.

"Hey babe, we're back," she says to Rhys before turning a hardened stare to the women. I hear Rhys chuckle, and I notice Brandt looks bored as I get closer to the table. The two women scowl at me and give me an obvious once-over. I roll my eyes and plop into the booth beside Riley.

"Hey ladies, if you want to join us, you're more than welcome to. But you're grabbing the next round. And I drink expensive whisky," I say to the women. They look offended, and when it becomes clear the guys aren't going to ask them to stay, they scoff and walk away. I chuckle to myself as my eyes meet Brandt's. His eyes are bright, and his lips are quirked in amusement. Riley breaks the momentary silence.

"So, Liss and I were talking in the bathroom and we're going dancing and drinking." She raises a hand to stop anyone from protesting. "I know it is a workday tomorrow, but it's one night, and Elissa had the day from hell with her father today."

Rhys and Brandt look at each other and, after a beat, shrug simultaneously.

"Yeah, that's cool with us," says Rhys.

"Excellent. Let's go!" Riley exclaims. She bounces to her feet and scurries off to the barmaid to settle the bill. She comes back, links her arm with mine, and leads us out of the restaurant and down the street to the nearest bar.

For a Tuesday night, it is ridiculously busy. I guess now that I'm working and no longer in school, I forget that it's summer break and the college students are out partying in full force. The four of us head over to the bar after paying our cover fee and order a round of drinks. Riley also orders us two rounds of shots.

"Porn stars, baby!" She exclaims as she hands out two shots each. We clink our glasses in cheers, and I shoot both of mine back immediately. The boys haven't caught on to our drinking ways yet, but they'll learn. Especially if Rhys dates Riley for real — the boys will have to keep up with us. I grab my whisky off the bar, throw it back, and order another one. I catch Brandt looking at me with approval in his eyes and I shift my weight, feeling a bit uneasy. I'm not sure if it's because his stare is making me uncomfortable, or because I feel my heart glow from the way he's looking at me.

I shake it off and watch Riley pull Rhys to the dance floor. Instead of going to the dance floor right away, I finish my drink and order another two Johnnie Walkers. Brandt is finally finished his first beer and before he can order another one, I pass him one of the whiskies I ordered.

"Here," I say. "You need to try something other than beer." He shoots me a confused look. I lean in closer so he can hear me over all the noise and music.

"The last time we went out, it looked like you only really ever drink beer." Brandt shrugs.

"Well, here. Have a whisky. Loosen up, then we'll dance." I take another sip from my glass and feel the warmth of the whisky seep into my core, unravelling me just a bit. Brandt accepts the drink and gulps back half of it. His face screws up as he holds back a gag, and I lose it. I laugh so hard that my eyes tear up, but my laughter is swallowed by all the noise in the club. *Yep. He's definitely a beer guy.* His eyes light up, even though I'm laughing at him. I grab his hand and bring him over to where Rhys and Riley are on the dance floor.

Riley breaks away from Rhys and starts grinding with me. I indulge her and reciprocate. As we sway and grind together, the guys bob to the beat and watch the show Riley and I are putting on. I'm not sure how long we dance like that for, but Rhys eventually cuts in to dance with Riley. I look to Brandt and nod my head toward the bar. He reaches out to place his hand at the small of my back and we walk to the bar together.

I order another whisky for me and a beer for Brandt. When his drink arrives, he looks at me gratefully. I smile softly and hold my glass up. He clinks his glass to mine and we each take a sip. We start to head back to where Riley and Rhys are basically humping on the dance floor, but after glancing at each other, our eyes seem to silently say the same thing: "Let's just stay here." We laugh and, as the song changes, we start dancing together.

When the songs start to blur together, I know the alcohol has done its job and gotten me tipsy. My worries slowly wash away, the way a wave retreating back into the ocean washes away a footprint in the sand. I know I'm tipsy because of the way my body gravitates toward Brandt, like he is the sun, and I am the earth. My body hums with energy, the humming growing louder the closer I get to him.

Our bodies are finally pressing against each other, and we dance together as one. It's like our bodies naturally understand one another and we're completely in sync. Brandt leans down and rests his forehead on mine, his hands gripping my hips. I sling my arms around his neck, lock my hands together, and pull him down until his lips are hovering over mine.

I can feel his pants growing hard as our lips touch, but I don't engage. I pull away slightly and rest my lips against his ears to ask, "Wanna get out of here?" Even as I hear myself say these words, I can't stop them from tumbling out of my mouth. Brandt grabs my hands, pulls them away from his neck, and laces his fingers through mine. He tugs me along, leading me out of the bar.

He flags down a cab, and when we climb in he tells the cab driver where to drop us off. His hand is still wrapped around mine, gripping it tightly. He stares ahead, not making eye contact with me, almost like he's nervous. I, however, cannot tear my eyes away from his lips. I instinctively press my thighs together because looking at his lips triggers flashbacks to yesterday in the elevator, and the cab can't seem to drive fast enough.

It's only a short five-minute drive from the bar to my condo, but it feels like it's taking an hour. My body is screaming for Brandt to touch me, to cover my skin in kisses. I want to feel his smooth, wet tongue glide between the valley of my breasts and down to my navel. We finally reach my building and I throw three twenties at the driver and pull Brandt out of the cab.

We dart through the lobby until we reach the elevators. I crush the button that calls the lift. Once the doors slide open, we rush inside, and I tap my key fob to the sensor to take us to my floor. When the doors clang shut, Brandt yanks me into an embrace and winds my hair around his wrist, pulling slightly to expose my neck. Instead of kissing my lips first, he aggressively kisses down the length of my neck and alternates with passionate sucking every few kisses. I moan softly as my arms wrap around his waist, and I drag my hands down his back and slip my hands into the back pockets of his jeans.

Brandt's mouth travels lower, kissing and sucking down to my clavicle and then to the swell of my breasts.

"Brandt…" I moan. He trails his kisses upward until he's placing light kisses on the corner of my mouth, building the tension before he starts devouring my lips. His tongue swipes against my lips and I obey, opening eagerly so our tongues can touch. As our tongues dance together, the lift finally slows and dings as it stops at my floor. When the doors open, Brant palms my ass and lifts me while I wrap my legs around his waist, locking my ankles together.

He doesn't stop kissing me as he carries me toward my apartment. When we reach the door, he sets me down, pushes me against my door, and cups my face. He breaks our kiss, staring deeply into my eyes. I can see a hint of darkness behind his gaze.

"Open the door," he demands in a low, firm voice, and it reverberates through my entire body.

CHAPTER TWENTY-ONE

ELISSA

Once we pass the threshold of my apartment, Brandt kicks the door closed. He presses his body against mine, forcing me back against the wall behind me. His hands slide into my hair, his tongue forces my lips open as he explores every millimetre of my mouth. All I can hear is us panting, moaning, and the blood pounding in my ears. I slide my hands up and down his hard chest, feeling every ridge of his muscles.

Brandt paws at my chest with one of his large hands and presses his pelvis into my stomach. I can feel his thick, hard member throbbing, and the sensation excites all the molecules in my body, making them vibrate with intensity. The way his mouth is suctioning over mine allows him to steal my breath. I'm breathing so deeply through my nose, struggling for air to keep the intensity of this kiss up, but I start to feel lightheaded.

In order to regain some oxygen, I pull Brandt's t-shirt over his head, momentarily forcing us to break the kiss. His chest is rising and falling hard. He looks down at me with a dangerous dark glimmer in his eyes as his jaw tenses. He's standing half-naked in front of me, just staring, breathing hard. His eyes find mine and I can't look away. Time seems to slow, and then freeze. It's only us, the only two people in the world. I break his gaze for a moment as I drag my tank top over my head and let it drop to the floor, so that I'm standing in front of him in my black lacy bra and jeans. He sucks in his bottom lip and sinks his teeth into it as his eyes flutter shut for a moment. I assume he's trying to keep his composure.

I grab his hand and tug, pulling him behind me to my bedroom. I shut the door behind us, then fold my arms behind my back and lean against the door. We're a couple of feet apart for a moment until Brandt closes the gap and hoists me up. I wrap my arms and legs around him. He claims my lips and walks us over to my bed, carefully laying me down as he lowers himself over me. I press my chest up, lifting my back off the bed, and his hand slides underneath to unclasp the hooks of my bra. I lift my arms out of the straps and fling it across the room. His eyes wander from my eyes down to my bosom. My dusty pink nipples are tight and Brandt bends down, licking the valley between my breasts. He trails his tongue up to the peak of one breast and, with his hand, squeezes the other gently.

He sucks in my nipple, tugging gently as his hand massages my other breast. My head tips back and my mouth falls open as I moan.

"Brandt," I whisper, as my fingers rake through his hair. He moves his mouth to pay attention to the other breast. He shifts his body and instead of handling my free breast, he trails his knuckles lightly down my tight stomach. My tummy jolts from the ticklish sensation, and Brandt's mouth tightens into a smile around my nipple at my reaction. His hand lands at the top of my jeans and makes quick work of undoing the button and zipper. His mouth finds mine again as I move my hands to help him remove his pants. I lift my hips toward him as he tugs down my jeans and use my foot to push his pants down to around his knees, where he finishes kicking them off himself. The weight of his lower extremities presses down on me as he holds his torso up with his left arm. He grinds his erection against my soaked panties, stirring my arousal further.

His right hand glides down my belly and stops when it reaches the top of my panties. He teases me as his fingers hover just inside the waistband, stroking back and forth. I thrust my hips toward him, my body begging for Brandt to touch me. There's a slight tremble to his hand as he sinks it further into my underwear, finally reaching my hot spot. His middle finger traces gentle circles on the sensitive little nub. I writhe under him, signalling to him that I need more. He runs two fingers along the opening of my lips.

"Fuck, you're so wet," Brandt mumbles through a giant exhale of breath. He plunges two of his fingers inside my hole and hooks his fingers, finding the spongy spot that makes my toes curl. As he uses his fingers to thrust into me, it still isn't enough. I continuously roll my lower back, riding the heel of his palm, stimulating my clit at the same time he's driving his fingers into me. It doesn't take long before I am ready to let go. I know he can sense the tension building inside me because I can feel a proud smile creeping across his face as his tongue continues to explore my mouth.

I moan louder as I'm getting closer, and Brandt mumbles against my lips, "Come on my fingers, baby." That's all the encouragement I need, and I let myself release. My pussy clenches around his fingers, convulsing in ecstasy.

"Oh, Brandt…" I whisper, trying to catch my breath. Once my breathing regulates a bit, I roll him over, so I am on top of him. I scoot back so I can pull off his black boxers. Once they're off, I lick my palm and fist his impressively large dick, slowly pumping him. I look him in the eyes through my lashes as I pump him. He brings a hand to my cheek and strokes his thumb across it. I pause for the briefest of moments at the weirdly intimate gesture, then blink the thought away and use the pause as an opportunity to switch gears. I flip my hair over one shoulder, lean down, and place kisses along the length of his dick. It twitches, hard. I run my wet tongue along the underside of the shaft and when I reach the tip, I swirl my tongue around it before pulling it in and sucking.

Brandt groans loudly, and his hands twist into my hair and tug my face down, pushing himself further into my mouth. I let him guide my head and set the pace for how he likes it. It only takes a few minutes before he is sighing loudly and his balls are tensing. I break the seal my mouth has around his cock.

"I'll swallow," I say breathlessly. I barely have my lips wrapped around him again before his cock is shooting hot, white strands of come into the back of my mouth. I take it all, swallow it down, and lick the tip of his dick a few times like an ice cream cone before I reach over to my nightstand and grab a condom out.

I kiss down his torso as I rip the foil packet open and roll it down the length of his cock. I trail my kisses back up to his mouth and wriggle out of my panties before hovering my pussy over the tip of his cock. I pause to bend down and kiss him, extending the anticipation of contact.

CHAPTER
TWENTY-TWO

BRANDT

Elissa's straddling me and hovering her pussy over my dick. The way she is making me wait is driving me crazy. *I need to bury my dick inside her. Now.* My hands dig into her hips, and I roll her over so I can take control. I open her legs, line myself up with her entrance, and plunge my hard cock inside her. I stop once I'm fully sheathed.

"Fuck," I grunt. I've never felt anything like this. Her perfect, tight pussy is wet and warm and fits like it was made for me. I'm about to come from the intensity of being in a pussy. I can't believe I waited this long, but holy fuck is Elissa worth it. She's the only one who's ever been able to get my dick hard. I wait a few moments, soaking in the feeling of her pussy and trying to clear my mind so I don't cream immediately.

I start to thrust into her, moving slowly at first and adjusting my position to find the way I connect with her the best.

"Shit, Brandt," she moans. She moves her body, riding me from below. She anchors her legs around my waist and locks her hands around my neck, pulling me down to kiss her. I sink a hell of a lot deeper into her with her legs wrapped around me. *Fuck. This feels unreal.* I pick up the pace and as I thrust deeper, Elissa's moans grow louder. I kiss and nibble behind the lobe of her ear and a delicious shiver runs down her spine. I'm close to losing it from her reactions alone. The way she drags her nails down my back makes my skin break out in goosebumps.

I ramp up the pace, getting closer to finishing. Her thighs squeeze my waist, and I can tell she's close. I tell her to come, and she screams my name, her pussy milking the shit out of my cock. Every atom in my body vibrates like something has electrocuted me as I explode in the condom.

"Fuck, Elissa!" I shout. Panting profusely, I collapse beside her. I take in the view of her post-orgasm, and she is glowing like a Greek goddess. Her chest is rising and falling, jiggling her tits, and my cock twitches, raring to go again. Elissa rolls off the bed and heads to the washroom. I give her a minute, then pull off the condom, tie it up, and follow her to the washroom to throw it in the garbage. She flushes the toilet and turns on the shower, then looks over her shoulder at me.

"Gonna join? Grab another rubber if you do."

I don't need a second invitation. I go and grab another condom out of the nightstand, put it on, and walk into the shower. She jumps into my arms and wraps her legs around my waist. I grab her ass and she sinks onto my cock, all in one swift motion. Her head drops back, and I suck and bite at her neck while I slide her up and down my shaft. Elissa's hands tangle into my golden hair and pull, leveraging herself to allow my dick to go deeper and faster. Her legs tense up and she digs her nails into my back as she tightens around me. A few more hard pumps and I am groaning as I fill the condom. I gently place Elissa on the shower floor and grab the body wash and loofah. I lather up the loofah and glide it across her shoulders, then down to her tits, giving each one a thorough cleaning.

After the shower, we head back to her room. I'm pulling on my boxers when the front door slams shut. Elissa pops her head out of the door and laughs to herself.

"Well, looks like Rhys and Riley are finally back," she says, bending down to pick up my pants and tossing them to me. Clearly she's letting me know that it's time to go. I tug on my jeans and walk out of her room to the hallway to find my shirt.

"So, I guess I'll see you tomorrow morning at work."

"Yep," she says and pops the "p." We stand at her door in that awkward *do we or don't we hug or kiss goodbye?* limbo. I decide to give her a peck on the forehead. Nothing super intimate, but something more than a casual cheek kiss. When I take a last look before leaving, I notice a blush blooming across her face and neck.

The next morning, I groan as I get up at 5 AM to start my usual morning routine. I definitely drank too much last night. I wasn't drunk, but I wasn't exactly sober either. If I'd only had beer, I probably could have drank quite a bit, but damn Elissa and her stupid whisky. What girl drinks hard liquor like that? Although, it's pretty fucking hot that she can handle her alcohol.

I pop out of bed and throw on some running shorts and socks, then hunt down my runners. I grab a water bottle and sling a towel over my shoulder, then make my way down to my building's private gym. I start my workout by running five kilometres, then cooling down with a light jog for ten minutes. *This is about the time when...and there she is. Right on time.* A woman in the building who has been trying to get with me for a while enters the gym. The tall, leggy blonde sashays into the room, kitted out in spandex micro shorts and a sports bra that strains to cover her enormous breasts. She somehow seems to always time her entrance so that she can get on the treadmill just as I'm cooling down, so we can make conversation — and so she can ask me out for the umpteenth time. I'm not blind, she's a very attractive woman — she just doesn't do it for me.

"Hey, Brandt," she purrs, her syrupy voice hanging in the air. "Lookin' good today."

Her eyes land on my chest and roam down, following my dirty blonde happy trail. She ties up her hair as she climbs onto the treadmill. When she starts to walk, her golden hair swishes as she moves, and I get a whiff of her strawberry shampoo.

"Hey, Lexi," I murmur. She flashes me a bright smile.

"Any plans for this coming weekend?" She's already stepping into her regular routine of laying the groundwork to ask me out. I have to hand it to her, she's nothing if not determined. Three days a week she's in here at the same time as me in the mornings, and every time she asks me out.

I shake my head. "Nope. Probably just doing some more work things to get ahead for the coming week. Boring like normal." Lexi smirks; she knew that was going to be my answer. I honestly think our little gimmick here is more entertaining to her now, rather than her being seriously interested in going out with me.

"Oh, well, that's too bad. I actually have a date this weekend," she replies. That's new. Normally, she doesn't volunteer this kind of information; I assume because she wants to seem available to me. She keeps her focus on my face, clearly hoping to get a reaction from me, but my face remains neutral. Her smile drops a bit when she realizes that I'm not going to give her the reaction she's looking for.

"Oh, really? You must be excited," I say placidly. Her face twists for a second, then she plasters a smile back on her face.

"Definitely. He's *gorgeous*, too. Careful, Brandt. You'll miss your chance if you keep saying no to me," she singsongs, then pouts her puffy bottom lip out. A wholesome chuckle rumbles from the depths of my throat and her smile widens with pleasure that she has made me laugh. I punch the stop button on the treadmill.

"Well, that's it for me. See you later, Lexi." She gives me a halfhearted wave and watches me walk over to the weight area through the wall-length mirror.

• • •

When I arrive at the office, I go directly to the twenty-first floor and head for my office. Only yesterday did Elissa and I decide who was going to take what office. I decided that since she'd be here more often than I would, she should get the largest office with the attached balcony. She seemed to accept my suggestion gracefully, but I have a feeling that was just because her father was present. I'm sure she couldn't care less about which office was hers.

Once I shut the door behind me, I make a note for my assistant, Selena, to grab a few things to liven up the place. A few plants, a coat rack, and maybe a wardrobe, to store an extra set of clothes and my workout gear when needed. I pull my laptop out of my leather messenger bag and set it up on my desk, plugging it into the HDMI cord that allows my screen to mirror on the fifty-five-inch monitor beside my desk. My desk faces the door and my back is to the window, which I prefer.

It's around 8 AM when Elissa arrives. She rushes from the elevator to her office and shuts the door behind her. She's clearly not a morning person, and I find it amusing. Selena gently taps on my door.

"Good morning, Mr. Collins," she purrs, her eyes roaming over my face and taking in my wide shoulders. "Would you like a coffee?"

"Sure. Black, please." She nods, and her heels click away toward the break room. I watch her walk away and she swivels her hips a bit more than she normally would, probably hoping I would notice and watch. Well, it worked. I watched and…nothing. She's got a nice round ass that looks great in her tight pencil skirt, but it just doesn't ignite anything inside me. From the other side of my wall, I hear the sound of grumbling and cussing. I push my chair out from my desk with a chuckle, walk over to Elissa's door, and knock.

"Come in," she coos. When I open the door, her face falls.

"Oh, it's just you," she deadpans. I clutch my hand over my heart and pretend to be hurt.

"Ouch, you wound me." She chuckles at my remark, and my heart skips a beat. *God, she's perfect.*

"Heard you grumbling. Anything I can help with?" She rolls her eyes, as if to say she doesn't need a man and can figure things out on her own.

"No, I'm fine. Just grumbling because I do not want to be here." *Huh. That's a new one.* I cock an eyebrow at her. She sighs and continues.

"Let's just say this was not my first choice. I'm being forced into this position." Of course, I already know this, but I will not let her know that. I play along.

"So tell your dad that you want to do something else."

"My *father*," she corrects me, "won't tolerate me not taking over this position. Trust me. I've tried for years to get out from under his thumb. The closest I got was when I left for university."

"Ah, I see." Just then, Selena walks over and runs her hand down my bicep. Elissa's jaw tenses and her brows furrow.

"Sir," Selena interrupts, "I placed your coffee on your desk." She gives Elissa a cool once-over, then looks back at me with a sultry smile. I clear my throat.

"Yes, thank you." Selena takes off back to her desk. I turn back to Elissa.

"Well, see you in a bit." Elissa nods and turns her attention to her computer as I swing the door shut.

CHAPTER
TWENTY-THREE

ELISSA

Who the hell hired these flirty bimbos? Ugh. *Selena* is so unprofessional, hitting on Brandt. At work, no less! And how dare she give me that *look*, as though she thinks I'm less than her? Fuck her. Even my assistant, Lori, seems more eager to help Brandt than me. I've had to fetch my own coffee twice already; not once was I asked. *Bitches*. No. I'm not jealous. I don't get jealous...*I can't be jealous.*

I have a feeling my father hired these two specifically because he thinks they're hot and will hop on his dick because he owns the company. He's such a pig. My mom knows all about his affairs, but she has her own roster of men waiting on the sidelines for when my father isn't around. She's probably copulating with the pool boy as I speak — she's a total cliché, and she doesn't even have a pool.

But to be honest, I feel like more of a cliché right now. The man I just slept with is next door because I work with him. I'm like every romance novel with a workplace romance trope. *Just kill me now.* I will say, though, that Brandt was great in bed. He definitely paid attention to me before he finished. I'll need to find time to speak to him later, in private, to let him know it was a one-time thing. Cannot happen again. Nope.

Except...there's this raw magnetism pulling me toward him. I can feel his presence everywhere, and working beside him every day is going to be a struggle. Especially when I can't stop thinking about the way he grabbed and squeezed my ass as he lifted me up and down on his cock. Shit, that was some of the best shower sex I've ever had. And he was so thoughtful after, taking the time to wash my body for me. Normally, that would have been too intimate an interaction with one of my hook-ups, but it...felt natural with him. Like he didn't know any other way.

My assistant knocks on my door. I don't answer right away because I have a closed-door policy — meaning it's closed all the time. I don't really want to bother with being nice or getting to know people. Lori raps on my door again and I reluctantly say, "Come in."

Lori swings the door open. She's a small, but feisty, blonde, for sure. She definitely turns all the boys' heads when she goes out, with her shiny blonde hair and chocolatey doe eyes. She lingers in the doorway, waiting for me to acknowledge her.

"Yes?" I ask her pointedly. Lori shifts her weight to jut out her hip as she folds her arms across her ample chest.

"Is there anything else you need before I head out for the day?" she snips.

She realizes I'm her boss, yes? And I can fire her ass for copping an attitude? The arrogance of some people, I swear. I take a moment to register her words and look up at the clock on my wall. It's 5:08 PM. When the hell did the day finish? Did I even take a lunch?

"No, that's all…" I say hesitantly. She moves to turn away, but I'm not done.

"Lori." She turns back around.

"It would be best if, when you come in tomorrow, this attitude is gone."

A splash of crimson colours her face. She bows her head slightly and says, "Good night, miss," as she exits my office.

Around 6:30 PM I pack up my laptop and notice there is still a light shining in the office. To no one's surprise, the glow of light is coming from the door next to mine — Brandt. I stroll over to the door, flicking off the overhead lights as I pass the switch, and knock lightly on Brandt's open door.

"Well, I'm out for the night," I exhale, thoroughly drained from today. I can't wait until I can dive into my bed with some greasy-ass food and have a Netflix marathon. Brandt stands up and starts collecting his things, placing them in his dark brown leather messenger bag. When he's finished, he looks up. His eyes find mine and a small smile appears on his face. I notice again that the left corner of his mouth tugs higher than the rest of his smile. I nod and start to turn away, but before I can, Brandt asks me if I want to go to the pub down the road and grab some dinner. I'm too stunned to say anything, so I just nod my head and place a polite smile on my face.

He struts around his desk as he slings his messenger bag over his shoulder and leads the way out of the building. Brandt takes long, purposeful strides, and his ass looks fantastic in his slim-fit khakis — perfectly round and firm and, I imagine, delicious to sink my teeth into. I press my thighs together a little tighter as I walk, trying to sate the desire pooling in my panties.

Through every door we pass, he is a consistent gentleman, holding the door for me. Brandt's hands are large and strong, and I can't help but think of them caressing my body every time he grasps a handle to open a door. I need to get these thoughts out of my head if I'm going to work with him. I desperately need to go out with Riley and find another hook-up — and fast — so I can screw him out of my system. Brandt is the definition of sex. He knows how to appreciate his lover; he knows how to use his body to make everything feel amazing.

We slide into a booth and he unbuttons his jacket, takes it off, and rolls up the sleeves of his well-fitted button-down, revealing thick, tanned, corded forearms. He picks up a menu and my eyes dart down to watch his hands move with ease. Suddenly, everything moves in slow motion as I watch the scene unfold. I can see every one of his muscles flex, then Brandt's hand lifts to his forehead as he slowly twists his head and runs his hand through his golden locks. His eyes flutter shut, like one of those slow-motion scenes in a movie.

I'm staring him down and biting my lip, desperately holding back the urge to reach out and stroke his medieval knight-like forearms. Someone clears their throat loudly, pulling me from my reverie. I shake the cobwebs from my mind and notice the waitress has appeared next to me. Her hip is cocked to one side with her hand on it, and she's smacking the gum in her mouth, clearly waiting for me to answer. My eyes dart between the waitress and Brandt, who has a shit-eating grin on his face.

"I'm sorry, I...zoned out," I say distractedly. The waitress rolls her eyes and asks me what I want to order. Brandt passes the waitress the menus as I order a BLT and black coffee. The waitress, whose name is Isabelle, according to her name tag, gives Brandt a flirtatious smile and stalks away, shaking her ass, obviously hoping Brandt is watching. But he's not. His focus is on me.

After we finish our meals and share some work-related chatting, Brandt walks me home from the pub. It's a cool evening, and I stupidly chose not to bring a jacket or cardigan to work. He must have noticed I have goosebumps, because he drapes his blazer over my shoulders. Immediately I'm enveloped in a cloud of clean-smelling sandalwood. My face flushes from the intimate gesture and I whisper a thank you. A couple of blocks later, we're standing in front of my building on John Street. The tall skyscraper seems endless when you're standing directly in front of it, looking up.

"Well, this is me," I say, doing that awkward goodbye dance. I remove the jacket and hand it back to Brandt. "Thanks again for dinner and your jacket. It was very kind." Brandt's face tinges a light pink and he shrugs, as if it's what anyone would do.

"Brandt," I say hesitantly. His eyes lock onto mine the moment his name leaves my lips.

"I know we have this weird attraction thing going on, but that's all it can be. We work together and I don't get involved with people. I'd like to be friends. I don't want to complicate our working relationship any further than it already is." His expression falters momentarily, but he recovers quickly and adopts an understanding smile.

"Of course," he says, stepping in closer to me and placing a soft kiss on my cheek. "Have a good night, Elissa."

"You too, Brandt." He pivots and stalks a few feet down the sidewalk before flagging down a cab. A sigh escapes me as I watch him leave, waving to him as the cab rushes past me. After a few moments, I take my leave, heading into my building and up to my apartment on the eleventh floor, where I plan on hibernating for the rest of the night. However, Riley has other ideas for me.

She rushes to me the moment I cross the apartment's entrance, eyes wide and focused.

"So?!" she questions me. I look at her, bewildered.

"How was it working with Brandt today?"

Ah, I see. She knows we hooked up last night and wants to gossip about whether or not the hookup has affected our work. I bobble my head in a nondescript way that leaves her looking puzzled until I cave and groan, telling her everything was fine.

"Professional, even. He asked me to grab dinner with him and then he walked me home." Riley's eyes shoot up into her hairline.

"Oh. My. God. You had a date! An actual date!" Riley shrieks. My upper lip curls while I scrunch my nose.

"Uh, no. It was a business dinner. Two people who left work at the same time and were hungry. I even took the receipt to write it off and reimburse him."

Now it's Riley's turn to grimace. "How romantic…"

I laugh at her reaction. She knows I don't date, so it's unclear why she thinks I'd suddenly start now…and sure enough, as someone who has known me my entire life, she's read my mind.

"I know, I know, you don't date. But have you *seen* Brandt? He's like a tall, muscular mountain. He's got a nicer body than Rhys — and I love Rhys' body. But you know Brandt will not stay single for long." I roll my eyes because it shouldn't matter to me whether Brandt is single. He's probably fucked his way through half of Toronto by now, and the only reason we haven't crossed paths yet is because I've been in Kingston for the last four years.

"To be fair, though," I interject, "he's been photographed with a variety of women, but never with the same woman, and he's never outright said he dates."

Riley doesn't seem to entertain my objection. If I'm honest with myself, I reject the idea of something more with Brandt because of the powerful chemical connection we already have. It's like I can't think straight around him, as much as I try. Whenever he's in my vicinity it's as though my body's being propelled toward him of its own accord. There's something to be said about how comfortable I am with the intimate gestures he's made toward me, like the kiss on the forehead, or cleaning me up after sex. It's strange, but comforting, and normally it'd be a big "Hell no" if anyone else were to try it. Riley's resolve falters when she notices I've retreated into my thoughts.

"I think you need to really think about it. Because he actually seems like he might be good for you." I roll my eyes at her and stick my tongue out.

"You only say that because you're practically in love with Rhys and are worried my relationship, or lack thereof, with Brandt may affect you. Trust me, it won't. Rhys and you are inseparable already. I'm surprised you're here with me and not with him."

A blush creeps across Riley's face, telling me all I need to know. First, she has, in fact, fallen hard for this guy. Second, she reluctantly rejected hanging out with him today in order to get the scoop on me. Traitor, on both accounts. I jab my finger into Riley's shoulder.

"You better not tell Rhys anything I said tonight." Riley giggles, crosses her heart, and pretends to choke herself. *Good girl.*

Before I end my night, I change into my running gear and head to the building's gym. I hop on the treadmill and start running, queuing up a Taking Back Sunday playlist, because I am not comfortable going for a jog at night in downtown Toronto. I think about what Riley said and wonder if I'm making a mistake with Brandt. The turmoil inside my body is eating at me. My heart (and more enthusiastically, my vagina) says take a chance, but my mind knows it won't end well and cautions me to keep my distance. For the sake of my heart and the business, I steel my resolve and decide I need to keep it platonic.

CHAPTER TWENTY-FOUR

ELISSA

Over the next few weeks, it becomes increasingly hotter outside as the summery weather of June takes hold. At work I've kept a low profile and only conversed with Brandt when absolutely necessary, as I couldn't even blame the weather for all the cold showers I've been taking lately. Even when I was keeping my distance, something constantly drew me to him. I wish like hell I wasn't the girl that purposely lingers at the coffee station or photocopier, or hell, even looking up every time someone passes my door. But guess what? I am. I tell myself I need to get under another guy, get Brandt out of my system. My goal is to do that exactly.

Me: *Lady, ditch the dick and come out with me tonight. Don't even need to drink, since it's a work night. I just need to fuck something.*

I don't get a response from Riley right away, but an hour later I receive an answer.

Riles: *Fuck the guy next door to you. ;)*

Me: *Ew. Please tell me you're not talking about Henry. Not the guy in 1102. Yeah, he's kinda hot, but such a douche.*

Riles: *No, lady. The guy in the next office.*

I groan inwardly. Her suggestion is utterly ridiculous. I don't even dignify her message with a response, because it's been three weeks since I last hooked up and I need some action. I'm going to get some, whether or not I go out with Riley. Apps exist for just these reasons. I open Tinder and swipe right on a few guys, but their chats are lacklustre. Not that I'm looking for something to pique my interest, but the guy has to have at least one small redeeming quality, though I'm not really wanting someone for pillow talk.

The end of the day arrives, and I've successfully lined up a Tinder hookup for tonight. He's some suit in the business district and does something with finance — I don't really remember. I could reread through the messages, but I truly only cared about his body, face, and name (in no particular order). Jesse is a dark fountain of lust, and his abs virtually rippled on my screen as I scrolled through his photos. The one photo was either post-sex or post-workout, I don't know. But the beads of sweat were glistening, and I wanted to slide my tongue all over his ridges and drink him up, taste him.

Jesse was thoughtful enough to send me an Uber to bring me to his place. When I exit the elevator into the lobby, my eyes are on my phone. Suddenly I bump into someone, and I clutch my phone for dear life because this one is still new from the last time I shattered it. I mumble an apology and the person turns around.

"You and your phone," a deep, gravelly voice murmurs. My body stiffens, the hairs on my nape stand, and my heart thumps.

"We really need to stop meeting like this," Brandt chuckles. I feel a crimson blush bloom across my face, and suddenly the early June air feels like an insufferable August night. I try my best to laugh it off confidently, but I don't quite succeed, and my laugh comes out more like that of a nervous little schoolgirl who got caught for lying. Mumbling a goodbye, I head out of the building and toward the Uber waiting for me at the curb. As I yank on the handle, a warm, rough hand wraps around mine and takes over.

"Not walking home tonight?" Brandt inquires. I shake my head, trying to decide if I should divulge more information.

"No. A…friend…sent the car, so I am not exactly heading home just yet." The word "friend" sounds more like a question than a statement, and Brandt's body freezes. His gaze shutters and his expression turns to ice. God, I am horrible at this, and there is no reason to feel guilty!

Then why do I feel guilty? Fucking valid point.

Brandt releases the car handle and I slide into the back seat. He shuts the door softly and taps on the roof, and I watch him shrink into the distance as the car pulls away and my heart hurtles into my stomach.

The next morning sees me hobbling out of my room, with one black pump on and the other in my hand, cell phone clenched between my teeth, and my laptop and chargers tucked under my arm. Riley is leaning against the stainless steel and white marble island holding a bowl of cereal to her chin. She shoves heaping spoonfuls into her mouth, making her slurp. Her usual glossy, inky hair looks dull and matted as it peacocks out of the top of her head. She's wearing a grubby scoop-neck t-shirt that shows off half her stomach. She's had the damn shirt since high school, and if she were to lift her arms any higher, her breasts would pop out, which I'm sure Rhys loves. Her boy short undies are pink with little black cats on them. Her eyes rake over me, taking in the glory of the hot mess I currently am.

"Don't," I say, before she can say anything. I shout, "Have a good day!" over my shoulder, grab my keys and briefcase, and stuff my laptop inside. I make my way out of the apartment and into the lift when my phone starts beeping at me incessantly.

Riles: *You gonna tell me any deets? Inquiring minds would like to know.*

Riles: *Was the sex at least hot?*

Riles: *Girl, I need to know. I bet Brandt was happy.*

Riles: *You didn't get home until 3 AM!*

She exasperates me. I finally respond.

Me: *Wasn't Brandt. Met up with a guy from Tinder.*

Riles: *No way. Why didn't you fuck Brandt?*

Me: *Because I work with him. We've had this convo. Besides, Jesse was H.O.T.*

I had a feeling Jesse would catch her attention. She can't resist a good gossip session, especially when it comes to the guys I hook up with.

Riles: *How hot?*

I try to think of an appropriate description of Jesse and a certain gorgeous NBA player comes to mind.

Me: *Terry Rozier *drool emoji**

I don't hear back from Riley, but I assume it's because she's waiting to dissect the events after work. Instead of walking to work today, I flag down a cab for the four blocks it takes to get there. I hop out of the cab, smooth my black pencil skirt, and adjust my tucked-in blush pink blouse. With a toss of my head I shake my straight, sleek copper hair over my shoulders. I stroll into the building and wave to the security guy behind the desk as my other hand slides my sunglasses into my hair to rest on my head.

My black pumps click on the marble floor on my way to the elevator. As I approach, I hear giggling, and when I look up, I notice Selena and Lori hovering next to Brandt, touching and fawning over him. Bile rises in my throat and my stomach churns. I accidentally let out an audible scoff and the women whip their heads in my direction. When they see me, they give me a glare, and I suppress the urge to roll my eyes. Brandt spins around, but his face hardens when he sees me. I mumble a shaky "Good morning" and walk onto the elevator as soon as the door opens. The ride up to our floor is awkward, as Selena and Lori continue to flirt openly with Brandt. I clear my throat and scowl at the women, trying to convey that their actions are inappropriate.

I disappear into my office and slam the door shut, trying to block out the irritating sounds of cackling. Brandt wasn't very talkative, but these girls are like a pack of hyenas. I send Lori an instant message asking her to bring me a large black coffee along with my messages. Twenty minutes go by, and my message is still unread. I snort, stomp over to my door, and throw it open. To my right, both Lori and Selena are sitting in Brandt's office, rambling. He doesn't even pay them any attention; his focus is on his laptop. I clear my throat noisily and the assistants jump and twist their bodies in my direction.

"Lori," I say, "I messaged you over twenty minutes ago and you have not responded to, or even read, my messages. Instead, you seem more interested in flirting with one of your bosses."

Lori's smile disappears and her face reddens as Brandt gives me an unidentifiable stare. I settle my eyes on Lori and tell her to get her ass moving. When she scurries off, I give Selena a look that says the same, and she jumps up and chases after Lori. Brandt doesn't look happy that I ran off his adoring fans, but this is a workplace, not a bar.

"Was that really necessary?" he asks me. I shrug.

"Sorry, didn't realize you were enjoying your little fan club. I would've thought they were annoying you while you were trying to work." Brandt smirks.

"Someone sounds jealous." I scoff loudly.

"Yeah, I don't think so. I just prefer paying my assistants to work, not flirt with their boss."

He can't be serious. I am so not jealous. I'm just not a morning person, and I haven't had my coffee yet, and I tell him as much, but Brandt doesn't seem overly convinced. Instead of arguing the point further, I retrace my steps back to my office and slam my door shut, only for it to open a few minutes later to reveal Lori holding my coffee. *Fucking finally.*

The rest of the day is uneventful, mostly just emails back and forth to Brandt about the upcoming launch of our services. There's going to be a launch party with the press in a few months, and my father has left it up to Brandt and I to plan the event. Brandt's already agreed to hire Riley to do most of the planning so we can focus on the actual details of setting up the department efficiently.

I message Riley to see if she wants to meet up with us for a working dinner. She only agrees if she can bring Rhys, because she "doesn't want to be a third wheel." I have a feeling it's less to do with third-wheeling and more to do with trying to hook me up with Brandt.

We decide we're going to meet at Jack Astor's for dinner, and our assistants sulk when Brandt tells them they are relieved for the day. I gather up my things and perch on the leather couch inside my office, waiting for Brandt. He materializes in the doorway, typing on his phone, not really paying attention to me.

"Ready to go?" he asks. I nod, stand up, and wait for him to leave my office so I can lock the door behind me.

He doesn't wait for me, and I catch up to him at the elevator, where he's at least holding the doors open for me as I step in. The doors close behind me, and I'm reminded of the last time we were alone in an elevator. There's a hum in the air, and I'm not totally convinced it's the elevator making the noise. No. It feels like the humming is the raw electricity that is generating between Brandt and me. If there were any gas in the air, I'd be worried we'd cause an explosion. The tension is palpable, and I'm certain that he feels it too. There's no way this is only in my head.

Thankfully, the elevator arrives on the ground floor quickly, and when the doors open, Brandt is behind me with his hand on the small of my back. When his hand connects with my body, there's a spark, and I swear all the lights in the lobby flickered at the same time. I search Brandt's face for any sign he noticed the same thing, but he seems unfazed.

Jack Astor's is loud and packed, and we're lucky that Riley called ahead to secure us a table. Riley takes charge and tells the hostess our party's name, and we're immediately taken to a table. Once we're settled, the waitress returns. She rattles off the specials and takes our drink orders before disappearing again. I excuse myself and head for the bathroom, with Riley close behind. We each pick a stall and swing the doors shut.

"Has it been awkward at all?" she asks from the stall next to me. *Awkward? Yes. Will I admit it? No.*

"Not really. He's pleasant, and I'm pleasant enough. We keep our conversations on work." I say. I can tell by the small huff from Riley's stall that she's unconvinced. The locks on the stalls click open and we head over to the sink to wash our hands.

"I don't know what to tell you. I clarified with him that it was best we keep things platonic." Riley just shakes her head and laughs to herself.

CHAPTER
TWENTY-FIVE

RILEY

I really don't know who Elissa is trying to convince, but it sure isn't me. We leave the washroom and wind through the busy restaurant. When we near our table, Elissa stops dead in her tracks. I look at Elissa and her face is white; I fix my stare in the direction she's looking.

A leggy blonde is standing at our table. She's wearing a shimmery gold dress that cuts off right under her round, tight ass. She's slightly bending over the table, with one leg bent while the other juts out, creating a spectacle of her perfect curves. My eyes dart between the scene in front of us and Elissa. I can almost see the smoke steaming out of Elissa's ears, and when I glance back at the table, I know why. The blonde is now running her hand down the length of Brandt's arm. She hooks her pinky with his as his hand rests on his thigh.

I nudge Elissa and we continue to our table. I take my seat beside Rhys and Elissa walks around to her spot beside Brandt. Rhys has a smirk on his face as he watches the scene unfold. Elissa clears her throat, and Brandt introduces us to his new friend.

"Lexi, these are my friends. Rhys, Riley, and Elissa, this is Lexi, a friend from my building."

Lexi beams at Brandt, her icy eyes sparkling in the moody lighting of the restaurant. She bends lower to whisper something in his ear, and her enormous chest is now on full display. She's not wearing a bra, and I assume from Brandt's angle he can see her nipples, but it's hard to tell if he's even looking. He grins like a schoolboy at whatever she said, and my eyes dart to Elissa. She's staring down at the napkin in her hand, which she is methodically and aggressively ripping apart.

"Well, it was nice seeing you, Brandt," Lexi purrs. "And it was nice meeting you, everyone. Brandt, I'll see you Saturday, then?"

Brandt nods and gives her a genuine smile as she places a kiss on his cheek, then she saunters away. Elissa is fuming, and in this moment, I am grateful there is only a butter knife at the table. Had there been a steak knife, Lexi would have been dinner. Rhys notices Elissa's reaction because he elbows my ribs and juts his chin toward her. He smirks and chuckles to himself. I feel some sympathy for Elissa; her parents fucked her up so badly that she's entirely closed off and refuses to let anyone significant in. It's so clear that she has feelings for Brandt, but she absolutely will not let herself explore them.

The rest of the evening was tense, but we did end up accomplishing a lot. We nailed down decorations, a guest list, caterers, and even music (playlist, no band or DJ). Elissa barely glanced at Brandt or spoke directly to him. For someone who says she isn't into him, she sure is acting quite jealous. I've never seen her this way before. I snicker under my breath, but I guess not quietly enough, as Elissa shoots me a death glare. When our bill comes, Elissa tosses her company card on the table and asks for the receipt. The guys offer to walk us home, which is incredibly nice. My hand laces through Rhys' as we walk ahead of Brandt and Elissa.

"Did you see Elissa's reaction?" Rhys whispers. I chuckle and nod my head. "She told Brandt she wanted to keep it profesh, but she's acting like a jealous girlfriend." I don't disagree with his observation.

"Yeah, she told me the same thing." Rhys' eyebrows furrow and his lips press together tightly.

"What? You think I'm lying?"

"I didn't say that."

"You didn't have to! It's written all over your face," I retort. He shrugs and continues to walk in silence. "Seriously, Rhys. What she's told me so far is what I told you already."

"Okay, then. Let's just get back to your place. It's really none of our business, anyway." The rest of the walk was silent, other than Brandt and Elissa chatting politely, but they spoke too quietly for us to hear anything.

Back at the apartment, I ask if they want to watch something or play a game. A movie won out, so we ended up finding a random movie on Netflix. Twenty minutes into the movie and I'm on Rhys' lap, making out, not even paying attention. Rhys gets into some heavy petting, sliding his hands up my shirt and squeezing my tit, and I allow it. Heat pools in my core and my panties dampen. I need Rhys. Right now.

We quietly announce we are tired and move to slink away. Elissa whips her head around and gives me a death stare. I know she's silently asking me, *What the fuck? Don't leave me here alone with him.* I flash an innocent smile and allow Rhys to pick me up and throw me over his shoulder.

Elissa

That bitch. That selfish bitch. It wasn't awkward enough with her making out with Rhys on the couch, but to ditch me and leave me alone with Brandt? That was a dick move. Brandt nervously shifts his glance to me and then back to the movie. I can't stand the awkwardness any longer, so I say what's been on my mind since dinner.

"So…who was the pretty blonde?" I can feel my face tint pink and I hope like hell the glow from the TV gives nothing away. I can see him quirking his eyebrow out of the corner of my eye. "You know, the one at dinner?"

A small smile spreads across Brandt's face. He says nothing for a few moments, and it irks me. He finally answers, explaining that she's someone he knows from his building, and they're apparently going out on Saturday.

"She's been asking me out every week for a year," he sighs. "I guess I finally relented. Hard to keep ignoring someone, you know?" *Shit, he's going on a date?* That means Riley was right, he really wouldn't be single for long. But I don't want a relationship...right? Still, I can't just ignore the electricity that is between us.

"Brandt..." He turns his head to me, his green eyes piercing mine. "I don't do...relationships. But I can't ignore whatever this is between us. What if we were casual? I think I could do casual, no strings. We can't let this jeopardize work, but I just have this carnal urge to bury you deep inside me, and the smallest touch from you sets my body on fire. I don't get it. I've never experienced this before."

Brandt is quiet, seemingly mulling over my proposal. His hand reaches for mine, takes it. Then, he yanks on it, pulling me into his lap so that I am straddling him. My skirt rides up to my waist and his aggressiveness opens the floodgates below. He cups my face and touches our foreheads together, his chest rising and falling heavily, and I feel the front of his slacks grow hard. Brandt whispers a barely audible "Yes" before his lips crash down on mine, spiking a fever in my body.

His hand fumbles with my breasts for a few moments before he unclasps my bra through my blouse. Big, strong, masculine hands tear open my blouse in one swift movement, and my bra quicky follows, leaving me naked, my tits glowing from the light of the television. Brandt's eyes darken and his cock twitches under me as he takes in the view of my breasts. He leisurely massages my breasts in circles, rubbing his thumbs across my nipples. I let my head fall back, grinding my pussy against his hard crotch, coiling my fingers in his golden hair while he sucks and nips at my neck. He palms my ass, grips it tight, and lifts us off the couch, carrying me to my bedroom and tossing me onto my bed.

I sit up and rip my remaining clothing off while I watch him undress himself. I'm kneeling on the bed, and he crawls closer to me, then abruptly flips me over. He keeps my ass in the air and his calloused hand presses down on my neck, sinking my upper body into the bed. He reaches over into my nightstand and extricates a foil packet, ripping it open with his teeth. He pumps his cock a few times, priming it before he rolls the rubber down his thick, throbbing dick. I stay in position, wetness dripping down my thighs just from thinking of having Brandt enter me again.

He positions himself at my entrance, grasps my hips, and sinks into me in one thrust, his balls slapping against my clit. I groan in delight at the sudden filling of my chamber. He starts moving, gradually picking up speed; his balls tap against me, and our grunts fill the air. He leans forward and bites my shoulder hard enough to trigger a different sensation of pleasure within me. I arch my back lower and rock into him, trying to get him deeper. He reaches forward and pinches my sensitive, swollen spot before circling his finger around it. Brandt rolls his hips, crushing his dick into me harder, getting deep enough to brush against my cervix.

"Fuck, Elissa. Your pussy feels so good," he growls through ragged breaths, pushing himself harder and faster.

"I...I'm coming," I pant. He bucks into me wildly, rubbing my clit until I see stars and my come is running down my leg. Brandt's hand moves from my clit to gather the come running down my leg and continues massaging my clit with my wetness. It sends me over the edge again as I crash into another orgasm, my pussy clenching around his cock.

"Elissa," he moans as my convulsing opening milks his seed, filling the condom inside me. With a final buck, he collapses on top of me, catching his breath. A few moments later, he removes himself from me, and my body instantly aches from the emptiness. He cleans up the condom, gently flips me over, and settles his head between my thighs, using his mouth to clean me up before he sucks another orgasm out of me.

CHAPTER
TWENTY-SIX

BRANDT

About a month after Elissa and I started working together, Harold randomly calls me to his office. I pick up my cell phone off my desk and shove it into my pocket, about to head out, when Elissa appears in my doorway and lightly taps on the door.

"Want to head out to lunch with me?" Elissa asks tentatively. My heart plummets and glows simultaneously. Go figure that the first time she reaches out to me, and I can't go with her. *For fuck's sake.* I heave out a deep sigh.

"I'm sorry, I can't. I have a meeting with your father right now. He called me for a last-minute meeting."

Elissa's eyes dim momentarily, and the corners of her mouth soften.

"All right. See you later, then," she says in a dulcet tone. She spins on the balls of her feet and saunters away down the hallway, her pumps clicking on the floor as she disappears into the elevator. My heart sags, and my lungs feel like they've had all the air sucked out of them. She asked *me* to get lunch with her. This is the first time she's initiated any kind of plans together. Fucking Harold for ruining what could have been a perfectly pleasant lunch.

Ten minutes later I am storming into Harold's office like a hurricane in Florida. Harold is sitting behind his desk, a smug look etched on his face. His forefingers are steepled together as he leans forward onto his elbows. My stiff upper lip quakes slightly.

"To what do I owe this last-minute meeting?" I sneer. "I was about to take a working lunch with Elissa." Harold's grin widens like the Cheshire cat.

"That's precisely why I wanted to talk to you. I wanted to see how it was going from your perspective. I, of course, already know that you have been moving forward with Elissa. It certainly seems like you've made it into her bed," Harold gloats. I have no idea how or why he knows this information, but my cool exterior gives nothing away.

"It's been amicable; we work well together. And as for the other…part…I fail to see how any of that is your business. What Elissa and I chose to do together is strictly between us. I also do not appreciate you checking in on me and seeing how things are going," I say firmly. Harold seems a bit taken aback by my clipped tone. He shrugs it off as his eyes level with mine.

"Well, it can't be going that well if she's sleeping with other people still."

My heart stutters, and a sick, sinking feeling washes over me. At the same time, a slow, percolating burn sears through my veins and my hands curl into fists. I take a deep, cleansing breath and relax my hands.

"I'm not sure what you mean, but it hardly means anything. It does seem a little weird, however, that you know so much about her intimate life, something that should be private for anyone and everyone," I say, keeping my expression neutral. Harold's face pinkens and his grin falters.

"Yes…well. When your daughter is repeatedly caught on camera with a new man every night and all-too-frequently doing the walk of shame, there's a need for it. I have a reputation to uphold, and it would be easier to do so if Elissa were committed to one person. I can't tell you how many stories I have buried to avoid creating a scandal. It's one thing for a man in this world to have a reputation for sleeping around, but it means something entirely different when a woman does it." I'm stunned. For a second, it actually sounds like Harold cares about Elissa, in his own twisted way.

"If it didn't affect me and my business, and everything I worked so hard on building, then I wouldn't need to worry about what my slutty daughter does," Harold grumbles.

The hair on the back of my neck rises and my blood boils. I'm slowly starting to understand why Elissa is the way she is; every interaction I have with Harold makes it even clearer. If I had to define perfection, it would be Elissa in every way. All the achievements she's accomplished this far in life are astounding. Her parents should be proud of her, not tearing her down and snubbing her efforts at every opportunity. Elissa is beautiful, intelligent, witty, and yes, a little reckless, but that's what makes her unique.

Harold drones on about Elissa's shortcomings, but I'm hardly paying attention; I only hear the occasional abhorrent word — "selfish," "spineless," "needy," and so on. Finally, something inside me snaps. How dare he sit here in front of me and say these awful things about Elissa? I mean, aside from her being his daughter, the fact that he wants me to enter into a marriage with her but expects me to tolerate, or worse, agree with, these comments, is ludicrous. My anger gets the better of me and I spill everything I've been holding back.

"Harold, that is enough. She is your daughter. How can you say these things about her? If it were behind closed doors and to someone you're close with, it would still be wrong, but to sit here and speak in such a way about Elissa to a business partner? It's outrageous! She's not even here to defend herself. What kind of father — no, what kind of man — are you?"

Harold has turned about thirty different shades of red in the short time it took for me to finish my spiel. He started with an embarrassed pink and ended with a fiery red. As I spoke, his face morphed from one look to the next: appalled to enraged. And, if I were being honest with myself, I was fucking proud. I shut that sonofabitch down. No one, and I mean *no one*, deserves to be treated the way that Elissa has.

I'd done a little digging on my end before I accepted the agreement of convincing her to marry me in order to invest in the company. Harold was never home, and Elissa's mother was just as absent, even when she was around. Her father was off building his media empire while Elissa was being ignored and raised by the family's housekeeper. Her mother was often either drunk or out at some salacious rendezvous. Elissa was forgotten. Her parents rarely showed up to any of her award ceremonies or special occasions; they only attended the ones that would create media buzz and bolster their reputation.

After learning all this, part of me thought I must be crazy to enter into an arrangement like this; being dealt such an ultimatum — albeit an intriguing one. I should have run for the hills when Harold suggested the secret arranged marriage. On principle I should have walked away, said no. But the part that eventually won out said yes. The part of me that has been enamored with Elissa since I was eighteen years old wanted the girl, but the Brandt I am today? Well, that part wants to rescue her; wants to relieve her of the heavy burden her family has placed on her.

Harold sits in front of me, fuming, burning, spiralling. And me? I'm fucking done. I give him my best shit-eating grin.

"Are we done here?" I ask, but I don't wait for a response. I turn my back on Harold and strut out of his office. If I'm fast enough, maybe I can still catch up with Elissa and have lunch with her.

CHAPTER
TWENTY-SEVEN

ELISSA

The server sets my sandwich and coffee on the table at
Grounds Café, a cute little coffee shop across the road
from the office building. I look up to thank him when I
see a broad, domineering, tall man rush in. A few of the
servers pause what they're doing as the bell over the matte
black door rings madly, and a few of their faces flush as the
bronzed god walks over to my booth. My heart thumps
loudly and I wonder if anyone else can hear it.

A few of the female servers give me some side-eye —
I expect they're jealous that this beautiful man is sitting
down across from me. Brandt collapses into the booth and
leans forward slightly to pluck the pickle off the side of my

plate, giving me a wicked grin as he does so. A swirl of heat settles in my chest and stomach as he brings the pickle to his mouth and bites down oh-so-slowly.

"Sorry I'm late," he mumbles. My jaw slackens and I'm left a little speechless. After a second of sitting there like an idiot, I collect myself and wave Brandt off.

"No, it's fine. I didn't think you could make it. I thought you had lunch with my father."

"Er, I did. But our discussion ended quickly before even leaving his office, so I came down here to see if I could catch you," he replies, trying to act nonchalant. But I know the truth. His face is lightly flushed, his chest is rising and falling quickly but he's controlling his breathing, or at least trying to, in order to seem like he merely strolled down here. There's a faint salty musk that wafts over to me when he moves, and a small bead of perspiration rolls down his forehead to his brow line. There's no doubt in my mind that this man ran here. I chuckle to myself and give him a knowing look. Something in my body flips when he meets my eyes and it startles me. I press my hand to my chest for a moment, but it feels like my lungs are empty.

"Elissa?" Brandt's voice breaks through my haze, and I shake it off. I look into his eyes, and just like that, I'm lost again. *What is wrong with me?* I try to focus on what Brandt is saying, but I hear nothing. I'm too focused on the way his lips move; so elegant, so effortless. The way his tongue peeks through his teeth as it slides over the "s" sounds of the words. That left corner of his mouth is always slightly higher, and I just want to kiss it, maybe even lick it, it's so darn attractive. His full lips purse as he says "work" and something else, but there's a warmth settling in my core that takes all my attention, and I need to squeeze my thighs together.

"Elissa?" Brandt says again. I physically shake my head this time to get out of this trance.

"Did you hear anything I said?" he asks, a smirk painted on his face. I almost think I see a twinkle in his eyes. I give him my best mocking smile.

Brandt flags down a waitress. A busty brunette saunters over with a little skip in her step, and sets her sparkling grey eyes on Brandt. She licks her lips as she nears our booth, and the corners of her mouth turn up flirtatiously. She flicks her hair over her shoulder in one smooth movement, and the hair neatly flips around to rest over one shoulder, showing off her elongated, kissable neck. An acidic green sludge oozes through my body, poisoning and twisting my insides.

Brandt is looking up at the waitress during what seems to be a heavy discussion of what he should have for lunch when I can't take the way she's looking at him anymore. Her eyes roam all over his face, down his neck, and across his shoulders; devouring him little by little. Suddenly, my hand shoots out from under the table and lightly rests on Brandt's hand, winning his attention. I don't even recognize my voice as it pours out like liquid sugar.

"What were you saying about the meeting with my father, again?" I ask as I trail my fingers along the backside of his hand. The waitress catches this movement, and her stature shrinks as her smile falters. Brandt quirks his eyebrow at me, turns back to the server, and mutters an apology before placing his order. She gives a polite nod and walks away, scurrying off to the kitchen. A small quiver tickles the edges of Brandt's mouth, as though he's holding back a laugh. My head dips.

"What?" I ask, feigning innocence. His hand scrubs over the lower half of his face, concealing an all too obvious smile.

On our way back to the office, I realize I never found out what the meeting was about between Brandt and my father. I assume it was business stuff regarding the merger, but regardless, I decide to ask.

"Oh…" Brandt says slowly. "Well, it was nothing really. He just wanted to check in and see how things were going." *That's oddly vague.* "You know, with the merger, working with you, how the department is coming along…"

"My father talked about me?" I scoff, "Oh geeze, what did he say about me? How useless I am, and how he only gave me this department to give me something to do?" I say, half-jokingly. An uneasy, strangled silence falls over us. I stop walking and stare at him, waiting for him to say something. When he notices I'm no longer beside him, he turns around and paces back toward me.

"What did he say, Brandt?" His shoulders sag and he exhales heavily.

"Nothing, really. He's just an egotistical man and he said he didn't know if you were capable of being up to the challenge because of the way you partied in university." Brandt has his hands shoved deep into the pockets of his pants and he's staring pointedly down at his shoes. He looks like a puppy with his tail between his legs, scared to upset his master. My heart squeezes for him.

"Well, nothing new there. He forgets that I graduated top of my class. Hell, I was valedictorian. Fucking prick," I huff. I stomp the rest of the way to the building and don't let up my pace until we reach the elevator. Brandt doesn't struggle to keep up; his long legs seem to cover three of my steps. He's perfectly in pace with me, like he'd been holding back his actual pace before. I peer over at him, and his dark green eyes seem forlorn. Suddenly I'm mad at my father, which is nothing new, but this time, I'm mad at him for making Brandt feel like this, for putting him in the middle of whatever is going on, for treating him like a babysitter.

When the elevator doors slide open, we both step in; Brandt still seems sulky. I don't know what comes over me, but when the doors close and the elevator starts to move, I press the button for the emergency brake. Brandt gives me a questioning stare, and I don't overthink it. I step toward him and lace my arms around his neck, pulling him down to me, driving his lips to mine. His body is rigid for a moment but quickly loosens as his hands slide around my waist, tugging me closer to him. His mouth opens against mine and I press my tongue into his mouth, licking his tongue and running mine along the inside of his teeth. He sucks on my tongue, rendering mine useless. I thread and wind my fingers through his soft hair, making a mess of his perfectly sculpted golden waves.

His hands slide down my hips and over the crest of my ass, grabbing a handful and squeezing so much it lifts me off my heels ever so slightly. Our lips clash again and again, the kiss gradually becoming more heated and urgent. His fingers tease and tickle my skin around the hem of my skirt and my body itches for his hands to travel further, to sink his long, thick fingers deep within me. His lips trail over to the corner of my mouth, down my chin to my jaw, and land on the spot behind my ear.

"Oh," I moan. Heat simmers inside of me and pools in my panties. His tongue caresses the shell of my ear and he sucks on my lobe. One large hand gently slides up my body and the other hand palms my breast before sliding into my deeply cut burgundy blouse, rolling a finger over my nipple.

"Um, is everything okay in there?"

A crackling voice comes from the PA system, and we're instantly doused in cold water. When we pull apart, I am burning from head to toe. Every inch of me is blooming bright red like a rose. We straighten our clothes and I tuck my hair behind my ears. Brandt clears his throat.

"All good," he says roughly. He steps forward and disengages the emergency stop, and the car jolts upward in motion again. We reach our floor, and we walk in awkward silence, each of us stealing glances at the other, trying to figure out some way to thaw the glacier but to no avail. We reach the spot where we split to go to our respective offices, but we both just stand there, lingering in this weird tension, until suddenly Brandt chuckles.

"So, you *were* jealous, I take it?"

That's it. And he leaves me standing there as he walks into his office, loosening his tie.

CHAPTER
TWENTY-EIGHT

BRANDT

A ping sounds from my computer. I look up at the instant message.

Elissa Black: *I was not jealous.*

A chuckle rumbles in my throat. I close the messaging app and decide to let her stew in her not-jealous state a little longer. Instead, I open the presentation and files that Elissa put together for the plan of rolling out this new digital media division. I'm thoroughly impressed. She has done a fantastic job getting the stats on all similar media companies within Ontario, and has even done some preliminary head-hunting, looking into coders we might bring on board to build the platform we'd need to optimize systems for all the old archives Harold wants recorded.

I'm dreading the day when my role here in this division is over and I return to my company. I'm trying not to think about it too much because spending all this time with Elissa has been amazing, and it's going to suck when I don't see her every day. I've become addicted to her in the few short weeks we've been working together — her smell, her smile, her laugh. Even if I could be around her every day, it would never be enough.

Twenty minutes later, another ping.

Elissa Black: *I swear I wasn't jealous.*

Another chuckle rumbles inside me, and I finally respond.

Brandt Collins: *Sure you weren't.*

Elissa Black: *Seriously. Just friends. Right?*

Friends. Just friends. *Then what the fuck was that in the elevator after lunch?* "Just friends" don't kiss like that. They don't feel each other up in the elevator at work. But I don't want to say anything or bring up what happened because I don't want to be shut down again. I don't want to hear about being just friends again.

I shut my laptop and tuck it into my bag as I get ready to leave for the day. I notice that Elissa's light is still on in her office, so I walk to her door and knock lightly before entering. She's standing and packing up her things for the end of the day too. Her burgundy blouse is untucked from her skirt, her hair is slightly ruffled, and she looks drained, but her cerulean eyes glimmer like sunlight on the ocean when she looks over at me.

"What's up?" she asks lazily.

"Just wondering if you wanted to grab dinner tonight with me? I'm heading out now, but I can meet you somewhere in an hour if you want." She nibbles on her lips, contemplating, and how I yearn for it to be my lips she's nibbling on. How I want to feel her fingers tangle in my hair, gripping me.

"Sure," she replies in a hushed tone. "I'll go home and change quickly and meet you at Jerry's Pub?" I give her a curt nod and walk away before she can change her mind. I don't know if she knows, but she kind of just agreed to a date. With me.

• • •

An hour later, I'm walking into Jerry's Pub. Instead of business casual, I opted for some dark jeans and a black T-shirt that hugs my biceps and tapers my form nicely. I sense a few pairs of eyes on me as I walk through the pub to find the table where Elissa is sitting, but there's only one heated gaze that I'm focused on.

Elissa is sitting with her legs crossed under the table, her creamy skin exposed with jean shorts, and her hand wrapped tightly around a tumbler of golden liquid. She's watching me intently as I near the table, and she brings her glass up to hover near her lips for a moment before taking a sip. A sly grin is all I see behind the glass, and something dark flickers behind her eyes. I flag down the waitress as I take the seat opposite her at the table.

"Glad you decided to join me," I say in a husky voice, and I swear I see her shiver. Her plump bottom lip rolls into her mouth as a smile tugs at her lips. Her long auburn waves are pulled back into a loose, messy ponytail. Little tendrils of hair hang out of the updo, making it look tidy yet messy at the same time — thrown together, but you know she spent time making it look effortless. Her makeup looks fresh, with rosy cheeks and a playful palette of greens smudged on her eyelids, complementing her hair colour but also making her eyes magnetic.

"You look beautiful," I say, leaning forward a tick so my voice can drop an octave lower.

A blush creeps across her face and neck, and she looks stunning wearing the blush I created. The wash of pink cascades down to her chest, probably lower, but her plunging corset-style top hides the rest. What I wouldn't give to strip her down and see just how far it goes; to see if the flush meets the pink of her nipples, and if it's the same shade. Or to see if I can make them darken, deepen to a pomegranate red by kissing and licking the exposed skin raw. My need for her only grows right now and thickens against the zipper of my jeans. I shift and try to readjust myself covertly.

The server comes back with my drink, and we place our orders when Elissa slams back the rest of her drink and orders another round, for both of us. She gives me a sly smile and says, "Tonight, you're learning to drink like a real businessman."

By the time the waitress comes back, the pub has begun to get busier. Rowdy patrons are laughing and yelling, some are standing around the bar, a few of them are in the far corner, huddled around the pool tables. A sweet, smoky aroma floats through the air as the waitress arrives and places a pile of steaming hot wings in front of us.

"Dig in," Elissa says with syrupy sweetness. "You're going to need all the sustenance available to keep up with me." She gives me a wink and takes another long pull of her drink. My mouth quivers as I hold back a smile and I raise my glass to her before downing the contents in one swift gulp.

I walk Elissa home after we finish at the pub. Six drinks and three plates of chicken wings later, and we were ready to leave. Or, at least, I was. It was getting increasingly harder for me to be around this woman without being with her. She is literally perfection. My hands itch to reach out and hold hers in mine, to wrap my arm around her shoulders and snuggle her in close as we walk. To know what it feels like for her head to rest lovingly on my shoulder.

When we finally reach Elissa's condo building, she lingers, her eyes shifting between me and the building's lobby. Her lips slowly part and she mumbles something unintelligible.

"Sorry, what was that?" I ask. Her eyes find her feet and she takes a deep breath.

"Would you like to come up?" she asks, in a clearer, but still soft, voice. I feel my Adam's apple bob as I swallow hard. Her eyes are dark, urgent, and waiting for an answer. I step closer, taking her hand in mine and letting her lead the way into her building. She grips my hand tightly, but her hands are trembling. Like she's scared, or nervous.

"I can go, if you want," I whisper into her ear. Her breathing picks up, but she doesn't answer; she just squeezes my hand tighter. I follow her toward the elevator and as soon as the doors close behind us, we pick up from where we left off at work. I grip her ass and lift her, and she locks her legs around my waist. I press her into the wall and take both of her hands in one of mine, pinning them above her head. My lips feast on her neck as she moans, and I feel her groin getting warm against my abs.

"Brandt, we shouldn't," she moans in my ear, but I'm not listening. I can't pull back now. I have to have her. She moans again as I rake my teeth against her earlobe. Her breasts push against my chest as she writhes and grinds against me, panting hard. Her hands break free from my grasp and her nails clamp down on my shoulders as I bring my kisses down to her cleavage. Sucking hard, I mark her as mine, so she knows we're more than just friends. So she knows this game of hot and cold is over.

The elevator dings when it reaches her floor and I lower her back to the ground. Elissa tugs me down the hallway in urgency, wanting this just as much as me. When she unlocks her door, she flings off her shoes and pulls me down the hallway by the collar of my t-shirt.

CHAPTER TWENTY-NINE

BRANDT

Elissa drags me down the long hallway into the open concept kitchen and living room, where Rhys and Riley are making out on the couch. Rhys and Riley break their kiss to look over their shoulders at us, brows raised.

"Never mind us," Elissa sing-songs. She drags me past them and into her bedroom, then shuts the door behind us and starts removing her shirt, untying the corset-like strings at the front, loosening the shirt before pulling it up and over her head. Her hands travel down, dragging out the anticipation as she unbuttons her shorts and lets them drop to the floor. She steps out of them, hooks them on the tip of her foot, and flicks them toward me. She stares at me, waiting. My arms cross over my waist, tugging my black t-shirt over my head and exposing my rigid abs.

Elissa sashays over to where I am standing and drops to her knees, placing gentle kisses on each of the hard muscles, then down the happy trail of hair. The zipper grinds open slowly, the only sound filling the room other than our breathing. Elissa looks up at me through thick, long lashes, and her tongue slides across her lips slowly before she sinks her teeth into her puffy lower lip. Her rainbow-French manicured fingers grip my pants and boxers and tug them down, exposing my throbbing nine inches.

She sighs gently, rubbing her hands up and down my thighs. I am towering over her, muscles flexing with power, dick aching to be inside her. Both of her hands wrap around my cock and she pumps me; slow to start, but gradually gathering speed until she's at a steady pace. Her head tilts forward and her tongue slips out of her mouth, teasing and tasting my tip while her hands work in tandem. A guttural noise growls out of me and I grasp her shoulders and pull her up so she's standing in front of me. I pull her in, crashing my mouth down on hers, pressing my swollen member into her stomach. My hand sneaks between our warm bodies and plunges into her undies, seeking her sensitive area. Using my middle finger, it's a whisper of a stroke, teasing her like she did me.

She moans, "Please, Brandt," and I comply. I turn us around and lay her gently on the plush, floral duvet-covered bed. I kiss her lips, chin, neck, collarbone, and continue lower. My lips brush against her skin and my hot breath tickles her. She shivers from the contrast of hot and cold. My mouth lingers on her hip bone, sucking at her sweet, sugary skin, until a small red welt is left. She tilts her hips upward, begging for me to touch her. A devilish grin spreads across my face.

I loop my fingers into her panties and pull them down, tossing them aside. Before I go down on her, I pray that Riley and Rhys have moved into Riley's room, because I am about to make this beautiful woman scream my name, enough that she'll never be able to forget it. I place my mouth over her pleasure mound and kiss it repeatedly. Elissa rolls her hips, trying to ride my face, but when she does this, I pull away.

"No, you will wait and take what I give you," I grumble. Her body quivers and a squeak of a yes barely makes it out of her mouth. My mouth reclaims her clit, sucking it hard and slow, like slurping a milkshake. I take my time, lapping at her clit and sucking slowly, building her threshold for pleasure. Torturing her senses. A finger teases her outer lips, tracing their opening, and she wriggles to seat herself onto my finger. My finger plunges into her cavity hard and fast; not expecting it, she gasps sharply. I look up at her face and her head is tilted upward, her eyes are relaxed, her lids heavy, with furrowed brows and her mouth agape. Her breasts are soft hills, rising and falling rapidly as her climax builds.

"Brandt," she says on a breathy moan. *Not loud enough.* My jaw and mouth are glazed with her wetness and my fingers are pruning from being inside her. I thrust my finger in hard and withdraw slowly. Over and over. Building her tension. Her breathy moans and sighs of "Yes, yes" set my skin on fire, and I need her to find release. Finally, I crook my finger, finding the spot that makes fireworks burst and angels sing. I stroke it fast and hard. Faster and harder. Sucking her clit, I withdraw my finger for a moment and throw one of her legs over my shoulder as I muzzle my mouth to her. Her fingers lace into my hair and pull me harder into her and all I can smell is her arousal: musky, earthy, heavenly.

My tongue swirls around her clitoris before sucking it again. I feel her body tense. She's ready to come. I suck on her hard, ramping up the speed and force of my fingers inside her, three of them now. All of them hooked and stroking the spot that is currently making her moan and curl her toes. She's rocking against my face, one arm haphazardly thrown across her forehead, the other one tangled in my hair, tugging so hard she might rip it out of my scalp. I land one final stroke inside her and gently bite on her clit, sending her over the edge, convulsing on my face and pulsing around my fingers.

"Brandt! Yes! Brandt," she screams.

I lazily clean her up with my tongue, letting her come down from her high. I stroke her thigh with gentle pressure, helping her muscles relax after tensing for so long. She sighs as she strokes my hair, her breathing slowly regulating. Once she's caught her breath, I crawl toward her and place my lips on hers, letting her taste herself on me. My cock is granite-hard and ready to go. I reach over to her nightstand and pull out a foil packet, rip it open with my teeth, and roll it down my length.

Elissa places her hands on my shoulders and rolls us so that she's on top of me, her wet pussy sitting on my stomach and my cock pulsing between her butt cheeks. She grinds against my stomach, sliding her juices around on me, so fucking erotic. She leans forward, curling her ass upward and sliding me inside her one inch at a time.

"You feel so fucking good," she says breathlessly. I almost come undone right there. When she's fully seated, she starts rocking her body up and down on my shaft, rolling her hips and squeezing my dick as she reaches the tip before plunging back down on me.

• • •

We lay in a tangled, sweaty mess thirty minutes later.

"We shouldn't have done that…again," Elissa groans. I chuckle.

"But it was good. There's something here. Natural chemistry."

Elissa makes a noise of reluctant agreement. She rolls over to face me and tucks a hand underneath the pillow, I contort my body to match hers.

"Let's both agree that this thing between us stays casual. We're both adults. Busy adults. It would be easier to just hook up with each other every once in a while. Makes things easier." My heart sinks in my chest, but a small ember of hope burns. Maybe this is the step toward having Elissa to myself. A small step in the right direction. Her pleading eyes search mine.

"Er…fine, but as long as we don't sleep with other people." Elissa freezes at my comment.

"I just don't like sharing," I add quickly. Thankfully, she relaxes a bit.

"Fine. I can agree to that. For now."

CHAPTER

THIRTY

ELISSA

My father was always good at treating his employees like family, but the flip side was that he treated his family as employees. Ever since I can remember my father has always said, "Treat your employees right and they'll be loyal." I guess that's why every year for Canada Day he throws this big work function for the workers and their families. It's like a staff appreciation party. There's a barbecue, beach fun, and fireworks at the end of the night.

I've hated this function ever since I was little. Harold and Collette would act like a loving family in front of the employees, putting on fake smiles and making polite conversation. They even boasted about me from time to time, which, to my surprise, meant they knew of the awards I received in high school. Harold probably had his assistant keep tabs on my accomplishments so he could use it to his advantage, but without taking up any of his brain space.

There was a little respite the last four years because I didn't attend. I had the perfect excuse: school. I would take extra classes in the summer just to avoid going home, with the added bonus of being able to skip out on the work celebration. Unfortunately, this year I am head of the digital media department, so now it's mandatory to attend.

The good news about the event is that Lana will be there this year with her family, and it's been too long since I've seen her. I typically would spend Christmas break with Lana, her husband, and her son back in Chatham during my university years. Riley and I would pack up my car to the brim with presents and luggage and drive the insanely boring five hours, stopping halfway to switch up the driver. Sometimes we even made a pit stop at the Toronto Premium Outlets in Mississauga to do some final Christmas shopping (for ourselves, mostly).

I'm in the kitchen, busy loading the dishwasher when Riley comes padding in, still half-asleep. Her ratty sleep shorts are falling apart, almost as thin as cheesecloth, which makes sense, since she's had them since high school. Her t-shirt is in a similar state, a crop top that is a tad too small. She scrubs her face and, with her eyes barely cracked open, reaches up into the smooth mahogany cupboards to find a mug. I snicker to myself. Her top reveals a lot of plump underboob and *almost* allows her nipples to peek out.

"You really should get new sleep clothes," I say to her. She glances down mid-stretch with a tired look on her face. The corner of her mouth quirks and she lifts the rest of her top and flashes me with a snort of laughter.

"I don't sleep in clothes," she says matter-of-factly. I bark out a laugh and she winks at me.

"So, are you coming today?" Riley's head swivels around and her face is contorted into a concerned "what the hell is wrong with you, of course, I'm going" look.

"Okay, good. I was worried you would have plans with Rhys and leave me all to my lonesome," I say, pouting. Riley's eyes roll toward the ceiling as she shakes her head.

"I *do* have plans with Rhys today, they just so happen to coincide with my plans to attend the stupid family beach day that your father throws every year. Girl, you know I'd never ditch you on such an important day of loathing and family drama. Even my parents are invited and coming."

I breathe a sigh of relief. If Connor and Brianne were going to be there, that made six family-friendly faces I could hang out with.

"But you know," Riley says, in an awfully sly voice, "Brandt will be there, too. You could always sidle up to him. You guys are casual, I know, but companionship is nice." She nudges me with her elbow as she walks past me to place her mug under the coffeemaker.

"Stop trying to play matchmaker, Riles. It's not gonna happen. He's good in bed and he's a convenient lay, that's all."

Riley gives me a look of disbelief and chuckles to herself.

"What?" I ask indignantly. She smirks.

"Nothing, nothing."

• • •

The Beaches, a little neighbourhood on the eastern edge of Toronto, was always busy in the summer, and Canada Day was no exception. My father always rented out the Balmy Beach Club so people would have somewhere to take refuge from the heat and sun, but also because it came with a section of beach that was exclusive to the club, with a volleyball net and other activities for families to enjoy. It was a wonderful event for the families that worked for my father, I will say that. Although he doesn't have a familial bone in his body, he knows how to appreciate his workers.

The driver I ordered for the day calls me to let me know he's downstairs waiting. I holler out to Riley to let her know. She emerges from her room in a hot pink string bikini, pulling a flowy beach dress over her head. She grabs her phone off the island and drops it into a woven straw tote bag, then perches her sunglass on her nose and hooks the bag in the crook of her elbow. She walks over to the front closet and pulls out two wide-brim sunhats and tosses one to me.

I catch the hat and place it beside my phone, sunglasses, and bag sitting on the counter.

"Whoops, forgot my sandals," I exclaim. I run back to my room and dig through my closet to find my favourite strappy teal sandals that match the bathing suit I've chosen. Over the suit I've thrown on a black floral bathing suit cover-up that hangs to mid-thigh. I look into the mirrored door of the closet and tousle my hair before heading back to the living room and kitchen. I place my hat on my head, sunglasses on my face, sling my bag over my shoulder, and we head downstairs.

• • •

By the time we get to the beach, everything is in full swing. There are workers and their families sitting on blankets and towels, building sandcastles, or burying each other in the sand. There are some people resting on the grassy area by the tables where the caterers are setting up to start barbecuing for lunch. It's scorching for 11 AM, and the hot sun beats down on my shoulders and back. I can almost feel the sunburn starting through my bathing suit cover.

Riley and I find a spot close enough to the water to place our stuff without it getting wet when the waves come in. We unroll our towels, pop up the umbrella we brought, and spray ourselves down with sunblock. I settle down on my towel and lay on my stomach, pulling out the book I brought — a steamy romance novel, of course. I may not believe in love or relationships, but that doesn't mean I can't like reading about them. The tension, the push and pull, the heat.

A shadow cascades over me and Riley shrieks, jumping up and spraying sand all over my back as she does so. *Ugh.* I sit up on my knees and see that Riley is wrapped around Rhys, making out in the open. The shadow that's covering me, as I peer up, turns out to be Brandt. He's towering over me, hands on his hips. He's wearing dark bathing suit trunks and an open white linen button-down shirt. I've never seen him look more casual and gorgeous at the same time. His abs and golden hair glisten in the sun.

"We're going to be subjected to that all day," I grumble as I tilt my head at the two lovebirds. Brandt offers a non-committal groan. *Well, at least we're in it together, I suppose.* Brandt plops down beside me on the sand and runs his hands through his hair as it ruffles in the wind. He hunches forward, tucking his knees under his arms. His side profile is so masculine, with his broad, expansive chest and shoulders. The muscles in his neck are thick and strong, and my lips ache to kiss him.

I think he catches me staring at him because his lips turn up slightly. But those lips. The plush and full lips that kiss me tenderly and roughly, all at once. The way his mouth latches onto mine, claiming my lips as his own. I shake off the daydream and cross my legs to sit facing the water with Brandt, watching the calmness of the waves as they crest on the beach. Seagulls caw in the distance. Suddenly, down the beach, I notice a little kid is running toward us, his parents in tow.

"'Lissa!" the boy screeches.

"Knox, slow down, please!" a familiar maternal voice calls out. My chest swells, and my heart feels instantly full. A few seconds later, small, sandy arms wrap around my neck, checking me from the side and pushing me into Brandt.

"Hey there, buddy," I coo, wrapping my arms around Knox's little body and squeezing. When he lets go, I tousle his hair. "How was the drive down? Was it super boring?"

"Nuh-huh. I'm a big boy and had my twablet," he says proudly. Knox looks exactly like his father. Deep tan skin, dark, straight brown hair, but his eyes? His eyes were his mother's. Dark chocolate brown, almond-shaped eyes.

"Hey baby girl," a smooth, soft voice says from above.

Lana.

CHAPTER THIRTY-ONE

ELISSA

I push myself to my feet and Lana pulls me into a long, tight embrace. Tears bubble up and threaten to overflow, but I bite them back. She smells like apples and cinnamon and home.

"I've missed you, baby," Lana whispers. I choke back a sob.

"I've missed you, too, Mom."

"'Lissa! 'Lissa! Will you build a castle with me?" Knox is tugging on my hand, making me jerk up and down. A burst of laughter escapes me.

"Yes, Knox. I will help you build a sandcastle." I turn to Tiago, Lana's husband, and greet him with a hug as well.

"Hey mister, are you coming, too?" Knox asks Brandt. Brandt raises his eyebrows and points to his chest, then he looks to me, and I give him a gentle smile.

"Sure, bud. I'll help, too." The five of us move closer to the shoreline and settle in to make our fortress. Tiago, Knox, and Brandt take pails to go grab some water while Lana and I start to collect twigs and shells to decorate the castle. A warm breeze gently ruffles our hair as we walk and look for the best knick-knacks, wobbling over some of the uneven sandy terrain. Out of the corner of my eye, I catch Lana staring at me.

"Yes?" I ask. Lana's mouth curves into a delicate smile.

"He's handsome," Lana said, in a sickly sweet voice. I give her a questioning look. "The guy who was sitting beside you."

"Who, Brandt? I mean, yeah, he's good-looking. Anyone can see that," I say, staring over at the two men and Knox at the water's edge. There were women from other departments crowded around Brandt, touching him flirtatiously and positioning themselves so their breasts were prominent and their asses popped. Lana's husband Tiago was loving the attention, flexing his dadbod, and making the women laugh. Brandt's cool exterior didn't change. There was no toothy grin, just a pleasant, polite smile.

"Mhmm," Lana hummed. "Just be careful, sweetie. Sleeping with someone consistently, regardless of whether it's casual or not, leaves room for feelings to be hurt." It's just like Lana to know exactly what's going on. It's like she has a sixth sense when it comes to me.

"I won't get my feelings hurt, don't worry." She gives me a sad smile and places a soft hand on my arm and rubs.

"I know, dear. I was talking about him." I scoff in response.

"Him? Please, Mom. He's as much of a player as me, I bet. You should see all the articles." Lana gives me an all-knowing smile and continues walking, not saying another word.

• • •

A little while later, after the construction of a very impressive sandcastle, Knox, Tiago, and Lana run off to get some food from the barbecue, leaving me alone with Brandt. After the conversation I had with Lana, a brief feeling of awkwardness washes over me. I shake it off, telling myself that Lana isn't always right. She hasn't been wrong yet, but it's bound to happen; this is the time she's wrong.

"Do you want to go get some food too?" Brandt asks. I start to shake my head when Riley and Rhys make their way over.

"Yo, dude. Your mom and pops just got here," Rhys says. "They're just parking the car and said they'd be looking for you." Brandt's face contorts in confusion.

"What? Wait, why were you in the parking lot?" Brandt asks suspiciously. Riley and Rhys both turn matching shades of red and beam at each other. Rhys turns to Brandt, giving him *the look*.

"Oh, gross, you two!" I exclaimed. "Where would you even do it?" They glance over at Brandt guiltily. It takes

Brandt a moment to realize where they had sex. When it finally clicks, his face drains of colour as his lips curl in disgust.

"My car? Really?" Brandt asks gruffly. Rhys tries to look the picture of innocence.

"Sorry, dude. The public washrooms at the beach are way too dirty to do it in. Riley had wipes, so we wiped down the leather in your backseat."

I choke back a howl of laughter, instead making a grunting, snorting noise. Riley's eyes light up with laughter from the look on Brandt's face, and Rhys is giving Brandt his best "I'm sorry, but not sorry" expression. Brandt's hands scrub his face in annoyance, and someone calls his name from a distance. When he turns to see who is beckoning him, the three of us break out into a chorus of laughter.

Brandt walks away and toward the two figures, meeting them halfway. The two people pull him in for a synchronous hug, and I assume they are his parents. After they break apart, they continue walking over to where Rhys, Riley, and I are standing. As they come closer, I see how much Brandt resembles his father. Tall and broad, with linebacker shoulders and neat, wavy golden hair. I can see that Brandt is the younger version of his father. But he gets his olive skin from his mother. She's beautiful. The wind lifts her light brown hair, making the flecks of natural silver pulled through the strands sparkle in the sun, and she has sharp amber eyes with soft crinkles at the corners — laugh lines, I think they're called. She looks wholesome and welcoming and warm. Her beachy white linen dress billows around her ankles as she glides over to us, barefoot. The very essence of a goddess.

"Mr. and Mrs. Collins," Rhys says, making his way toward them and hugging Brandt's mother and giving his father a handshake.

"Oh, please, Rhys," Brandt's mother says with a playful lilt. "How many times do we have to tell you! Please call us Theresa and Hunter. It's been eleven years, Rhys. You're practically family." My heart warms at her sentiment toward Rhys and Riley's eyes shine.

"I'd like you to meet my girlfriend," Rhys says proudly, as he reaches out his hand for Riley to take. She walks over sheepishly.

"Riley, these are Brandt's parents, Theresa and Hunter." Riley gives them a polite smile and shakes their hands.

"Nice to meet you both," Riley says in a hushed tone, tucking some of her loose black locks behind her ear. Theresa clears her throat and her gaze shifts from me to Brandt. Her eyes widen with what seems like glee, or perhaps hope. For what? I'm not quite sure. When Brandt doesn't say anything, Theresa reaches out a hand toward me.

"And you, my dear, are…?"

"Oh, me," I say, and take her hand. As I do, her other hand envelops the rest of my exposed skin. Her hands are soft and warm, and the faint scent of Chanel No. 5 tickles my nose.

"Elissa Black. I'm Brandt's business partner. Well, my father is, but I will be when my father retires. Brandt is a great man; a good worker." *What the hell am I babbling for? And worse, I can't seem to stop.* "Everyone at the office loves him, he's a very popular guy. Well, would you look at him? Of course, he's popular." *Oh, my fucking god. Shut the hell up,*

Elissa. I feel my face burning, and I can't even say it's from the sun or heatstroke. Theresa's smile seems somehow knowing, and she glances between Brandt and his father, Hunter.

"Yes, he said he found everyone at the company rather welcoming. It's nice to know he's settling in okay. Coming from a humble background of a construction company family, I know it was a challenge for him at first to get his business going at twenty. But he figured it out," Theresa beams with pride. "We couldn't be prouder of him. If only he'd settle down and pop out a few grandchildren, I could die happily."

Suddenly it feels like an entire colony of ants is crawling on my skin, making me itch and squirm. My breathing quickens. I fold my arms together and rub my biceps, trying to banish the feeling of the tiny fuckers crawling over me. My breathing becomes more erratic, and I have to excuse myself from the conversation. I'm having trouble staying focused, and my head is spinning.

"Er, yes. Well, I need to…washroom. Yeah. Nice meeting you." I mutter incoherently. As I turn to leave, I see Riley's eyes are wide and worried. She excuses herself and hurries after me, calling my name and telling me to wait up. She doesn't realize I am holding back every single urge to fucking bolt right now.

CHAPTER
THIRTY-TWO

ELISSA

I keep speedwalking until I reach the parking lot. I need to get out of here, I need to breathe. *Why did his mom look at me like that when she mentioned grandkids? Does she think we're together because Rhys and Riley are? What if Brandt told them something? No, he couldn't have, right? We're just casual, there's nothing to tell.* My mind is reeling, spinning, and all the other *-ings* that a mind can do. Riley calls out from behind me.

"'Lissa, wait up! Seriously!"

I stop, turn to face her, then turn back around and continue walking, but slower. When Riley finally catches up, she tugs on my arm and brings me to a halt.

"What is wrong with you? All this anxiety and panic over her mentioning marriage and kids?" Riley's voice is filled with concern and disbelief. I nod my head slowly.

"But it wasn't even directed at you! Hell, she probably doesn't even know that you and Brandt are hooking up! Girl, you need to get ahold of yourself."

I look at her with wide eyes.

"You really think so?"

"Come on, how would she know? Brandt's not exactly a talker, so I don't see him telling his parents anything." Her words comfort me, allowing my heart to settle down and my body to regulate my breathing again.

"Now, can we go back and enjoy the rest of the day? Rhys and I wanted to play doubles volleyball with you and Brandt." My response is a glance that shoots daggers at her, making her laugh.

As the day winds down, I have successfully avoided my father and mother the entire day. My heart does a gleeful little skip before it capsizes in my chest cavity. Walking toward me are none other than my father and mother. And it looks like…Brandt's parents are with them. *Oh shit. Here we go.* A tight smile pulls at my cheeks as I grit my teeth, grinding away at one of my molars. *Fuck.*

My father and mother look absolutely like the personification of proud parents right now and it's making my stomach churn and a bitter taste rise in my mouth. They're talking jovially with Theresa and Hunter, and I wonder how such cold and distant people can put up such different fronts. *Shouldn't they be this pleasant and warm toward their daughter?* Anger stabs at my gut, making me grit my teeth harder.

"Ah, Elissa," my father says. "There you are. I'd like you to meet Mr. and Mrs. Collins, Brandt's parents." I offer a polite hello and turn to my father, ignoring my mother altogether.

"Yes, Father. I met them when they arrived. They were ever so kind, and it was great meeting them. Brandt is an excellent man and now I know where he learned it all, in a loving, caring, and warm family," I say pointedly. My father's nose twitches as his façade cracks just a smidge. He turns his stare back to Mr. and Mrs. Collins and starts talking about my time in university.

"Yes, she had the highest grades in both disciplines of business and English literature. She graduated top of her class and was even the valedictorian for Queen's University. She's spearheading the new digital division alongside young Mr. Collins and doing a fantastic job."

Yadda, yadda, yadda. Even though everything he says is true, none of it means anything filtered through his fake appreciation. I wish I could believe that they were truly proud of me.

"Well, please excuse me. I should go and find Riley," I interrupt my father. He shoots me a glare, and when I walk away, I hear him excuse himself and follow me. A rough hand clamps firmly around my elbow and yanks me to a stop.

"What the fuck was that?" Harold asks in a harsh, hushed tone. He smiles over at my mother and Mr. and Mrs. Collins before turning his mean face on me. "Do not fucking embarrass me. These people are important, even though they're nothing and just own some construction company." I scoff and roll my eyes at my father, ripping my elbow out of his grip.

"Then what are they to you if they don't fit into your standard of 'people of importance?'" I look down and see my father's hand twitch. His mouth opens to retort but he catches himself. I bet if we were home right now, or in private, that comment would have landed me a blow. I smile in triumph at his inability to do anything here, politely wave at my mother and Brandt's parents, and then glare at my father before turning and walking away.

• • •

Nightfall descends, as the pinks and oranges of the sunset are smeared with a darker blue as the sun sinks below the horizon. Fireflies and mosquitoes buzz around. Everyone has started settling back onto their blankets and towels to watch the fireworks. I head over to where Riley and I set up, but her and Rhys are laying down on both towels, cuddling together. I heave a sigh and walk in the opposite direction to find a secluded place.

I plop down onto the sand, pull my knees in tight to my chest, and rest my hands and head on them. I tilt my head to the side and look out at all the families. They're laughing happily, hugging, and spending time together. My eyes search out Lana and her family; they are sitting on a big blanket, her and Tiago side-by-side, legs outstretched, with Knox nestled between them. A little further down the way are Brianne and Connor Jaimeson, Riley's parents, enjoying a happy conversation with my parents, all of them laughing, with drinks clutched in their hands. A wild rush of jealousy flows over me. *Jealous of my parents? That's new.*

I'm not paying attention to the other side of me until someone exhales as they drop to the sand beside me. I turn my head and there's Brandt, brushing the sand off his hands. He nudges me with his shoulder.

"Hey," he rumbles. I give him a tense smile.

"Everything okay?" he asks. I shrug, not really wanting to divulge. He just nods and stares up at the sky, waiting for the fireworks to start.

"My parents told me about the weird moment in their conversation with your parents. They said that your dad was all huffy after he pulled you aside and talked to you. So, you're sure everything is okay?"

I look at Brandt, water pooling in my eyes. His parents noticed? They saw through the fake image my father and mother project. *I wonder if everyone else does, too.* Warmth kindles in my belly, making my heart glow. Brandt sighs, then continues.

"You know, people can tell that you're not really close with your parents. Most people see through the show they put on. I know I did. Your father is well known in the business community, and they know he's all about image."

I keep my eyes focused forward, blinking back the tears that have been building for the last twenty-four years.

"Your father doesn't do anything if it doesn't directly benefit him or his company. That includes having a daughter, and only using her when it's convenient." My heart melts at his words. I've never felt more seen by anyone I've kept at arm's length. My eyes shine, brimming with tears, when I glance over at him.

Brandt keeps talking, but I don't hear him. I'm lost in my thoughts of this man. How nice, warm, and caring he really is. And how I need to make sure he keeps his distance, because Lana might be right after all. He comes from a great, caring family, has great friends who respect him, and runs a successful business that he started himself. *I will break this man if I'm not careful.*

I glance over at him and watch his face light up, reflecting the colours of the first fireworks that burst and explode in the air. And, for a brief moment, I let myself be vulnerable. For a moment, I let myself be content.

I lean over and rest my head on Brandt's sturdy shoulder and sigh. He wraps his arm low around my waist and we sit there, watching the fireworks together.

CHAPTER
THIRTY-THREE

BRANDT

Elissa wanted to keep things casual, and for the last couple of months I've been busy. Busy planning the event coming up in a few weeks, busy getting the department running smoothly, busy fucking Elissa almost every night. We've even screwed on top of her desk a few times. The woman is insatiable. I feel a small pang of guilt when I think about how I got here. First, Harold set all this up. Second, she wasn't interested until Lexi stopped by our table at dinner that one night.

Since we were "keeping it casual," I still ended up going on that date with Lexi, even though I would have preferred to be deep inside Elissa. Lexi is nice, sweet, and definitely gorgeous, but since high school, it's always been Elissa. When I walked Lexi back to her apartment, I gave her a goodnight kiss, and I felt nothing. Not even a slight rush that could get my boy to stand and say hello to her.

Elissa has been opening up to me, too. Once you're in with her, the armour dissolves and falls away. She starts letting her guard down, and letting you in. She's told me all about her childhood and her "surrogate" mother (her words, not mine), Lana. I learned that's why she was so put off by me at first when I met her at graduation — she thought the third ticket her father requested was supposed to be for Lana. She's also shared a bit about her relationship with her parents, and I understand now why she's typically so closed off. Her parents really did a number on her, which I kind of suspected after getting to know Harold.

Speaking of Harold, he's been trying to keep me under his thumb lately. He keeps asking how it's going with his daughter, and trying to give me advice, as if he knows anything about Elissa that would help me. I think I am doing just fine, considering. We may be casual in Elissa's mind, but I know she's only seeing me, because I sleep over almost every night. We eat all our meals together and double date with Riley and Rhys.

Truth be told, when you look closely, we're in more of an exclusive relationship than a casual one. Whenever we leave the office, we leave together, then have a steamy makeout session in the elevator, and, once we're far enough away from the building, it's her hand that seeks mine and interlocks our fingers. She's come a long way from screwing me and kicking me out right after. When we were first casual, yeah, it still happened. Then one night, we accidentally fell asleep, and now sleepovers are acceptable — she's said nothing about me keeping some toiletries at her place, and I don't have to worry about clothes because I keep spares in my office.

I'm being careful not to say or do anything to freak her out because I don't want her to run. I don't want things to change because I've really fucking fallen for her. Sure, I *loved* her from afar, but I never really knew her. Now I feel like I know a bit more every day about who she is. Elissa makes me laugh. She's actually really easy to get along with, and she's fantastic in bed, which, true, I have limited experience to compare her to, but somehow I just know. My phone beeps in my pocket.

Eli: *Babe, are you coming over tonight? Riley and Rhys are going to his place.*

Elissa's need for privacy is understandable, but messaging me when I'm in the next office is just quirky. She could come to my office and close the door, but why do that? I see these texts as proof that I really have Eli. Because if anything were to change, I don't know if I could believe it ever truly happened.

Me: *Sure. I'll just have to run home and pick up a few things if that's OK?*

Eli: *Yeah, of course. I'll order Chinese for dinner.*

A knock sounds on my door, and I pull my attention from my messages. The door swings open and Harold and Elissa are standing in the doorway. I wave them in, shoving my phone back into my pocket. Harold plops down in a chair across from me while Elissa stands, probably so she can leave at a moment's notice.

"The launch party is in a few weeks," Harold says gruffly. "I assume you both will have dates in attendance?" Harold's eyes shuffle from me over to Elissa, trying to gauge our reactions. I speak up first.

"I haven't invited anyone to the party yet. I wasn't planning to, either."

"Me neither. I don't do dates, Father." Elissa's face contorts into a scowl, and her voice is sharp with ice. Harold's eyes light up at this and he rubs his hands together like an old Western movie villain.

"Perfect. If that's the case, then Brandt, you may escort Elissa to the party and be her date. It would be excellent for the press, too!" Elissa flinches, then straightens. I try not to take it personally, but it's hard not to.

"Father, like I said, I don't do dates." Harold scoffs at Elissa.

"Yeah, no fucking shit. That's why this is perfect. It gives you and the company a better image. No more pictures or news about you with different men, like in college."

Elissa looks like she's been slapped.

"How would you know? There were never any headlines and pictures. And isn't that a little sexist? If it were Brandt or any other male, no one would bat an eyelash." Harold jumps to his feet, his face red and eyes narrowed.

"How do you think I know? We own most of the Canadian newspapers and magazines, and if we don't own them, we fucking print for them. Who the fuck do you think keeps our name out of the news?!" Elissa's face falls and her fists clench until her knuckles are white and trembling with the effort to hold back an explosion of emotions.

"You will attend the party with Brandt and act like you are enjoying yourself." Harold stalks over to her and chucks her chin to level their eyes. "Elissa. You will have a two-drink minimum. No tequila, no drugs of any kind. If Riley is in attendance, she will also need to abide by these rules. If you are to leave the party, Brandt will escort you — even to the washroom. When it is time to leave for the night, he will escort you home. Do I make myself clear?" Elissa jerks her chin out of Harold's grasp.

"No, Father. You can't impose all these rules on me. I may be your daughter, but I'm a grown woman. And as for *Brandt*, in case you haven't noticed, he is also an adult and has no obligation to you. So why would you think it's acceptable to dictate such rules to him?" Harold is fuming, and a dark crimson, almost purple, flush stains his face. His jaw clenches and releases a few times before he responds. After searching Elissa's eyes, he whips his head toward me.

"Is this sufficient for you?" Harold asks me. I quickly glance at Elissa, and I find beautiful, sapphire eyes that are glazed with tears of frustration. My heart squeezes in my chest, but I turn to Harold and nod my head.

"Excellent. I'll leave you two to hash out details."

Harold's face has drained a bit of colour by the time he leaves my office. I risk a glance at Elissa, and fuck, is she mad. Her eyes are no longer full of sadness and pleading. Instead, rage now burns behind them. Glowering, she spins around and stomps her way back to her office, slamming her door so hard the wall between our offices wobbles and our assistants, who are sitting at their desks, nearly jump out of their skin.

It takes a few days, but soon Elissa is talking to me again. The radio silence felt like someone had cut my heart out of my chest. The launch party is only two weeks away and we have lots of loose ends to tie up and outfits to coordinate.

"Eli," I say, cornering Elissa in her office. "Is everything okay? With us, especially?" Her body stiffens, but then relaxes a moment later when she releases a long, pained sigh.

"Yeah. I should have known my father would pull something like this on me. Trying to set me up with you. I'm sorry on his behalf," she says, and a pang of guilt ricochets around my body. My heart sinks into my stomach, knowing she believes this was only the first ruse her father pulled on her when it comes to us. I suddenly feel sick to my stomach, and I pray she doesn't find out about how her father approached me months ago. I mumble an acceptance of her apology, and it only makes me feel worse. I should be the one apologizing.

"Did you want to have lunch today?" I ask, trying to change the subject. The smile that I love appears on her face and she says yes.

"Sushi?" She agrees and I leave her office, feeling simultaneously happy and remorseful.

Lunch comes around and I meet Eli at the elevator. Our assistants are also waiting there to go on lunch when Selena notices me. A giddy glint appears in her eyes as she plasters on a seductive smile.

"Mr. Collins. Ms. Black," she says, acknowledging us both but keeping her sight set on me. Lori nods at us but doesn't make eye contact. Ever since Eli told her off when the office was first being set up, Lori has remained quiet and distant.

"Would we be able to join you for lunch, Mr. Collins?" Selena purrs.

I look over to Elissa to see what she thinks. Her jaw is clenched tightly and her eyes are narrowed. I laugh inwardly.

"I wouldn't mind, Selena," I say, and Eli whips her head in my direction. She shoots me a look as if to silently say, *what the hell do you think you're doing?* "But unfortunately, today will not work. Ms. Black and I are having a working lunch to discuss the final details of the launch party. Perhaps another time?"

Selena's cheeks flush and she graciously accepts my apology. When the elevator arrives, the three women's heels click into the lift and I follow behind before pressing the button for the ground floor. Eli and I part ways with our assistants and head toward the sushi bar down the street. On the way there, we chat about work and the upcoming launch party.

"So, I was thinking I would just wear a black evening gown. That way it matches whatever you wear," Elissa explains. I nod at her suggestion.

"All right. I was probably going to wear a black suit, anyway."

"Great, now that's decided. Let's talk about interactions at the party. I think linking arms, hand on my back, and kiss on the cheek, those are all relatively safe to do. But I think keeping our distance is best." I listen quietly as she rattles off her expectations of intimacy for the evening.

"And when it's time to go home, my father has already expressed that you are to *escort* me home, so maybe pack a bag and drop it off at my place when you pick me up?" My head swivels to face her, my eyes pleading.

"Are you sure that's okay? I can always just go home afterward if it's more comfortable for you..." My voice trails off. *Please say it's okay, please say it's okay, please say it's okay.*

"Eh. It's fine, and it makes the most sense. Besides, I think Rhys and Riley are planning on staying either at his place or at a hotel after the party." *Not exactly a solid confirmation, but a baby step in the right direction. I'll take it.* We finally reach the restaurant and, since we settled most of the details on the walk over, we eat quickly, return before everyone comes back from lunch, and enjoy a quick rendezvous in my office.

The next two weeks fly by, and before I can wrap my head around it, it's mid-August and we've spent the *hottest* summer together. Almost three months of "casual." I was standing in the hallway of Elissa's place, waiting for her so we could head to the party. My hands are clammy from the nerves of being seen with her in public as a *date*. Maybe this would be a tipping point for us. Maybe this could even lead to bigger things for us.

"Eli," I call out, raising my voice so she can hear me from the hallway. "You almost ready? We need to get going soon if we're planning to get there on time."

"Yep," Eli shouts from her room. She rounds the corner with her head tilted as she fastens an earring to her lobe, just as my heart stops beating and time slows. She is mesmerizing. Her soft, copper hair twists into a low, messy bun on the right side of her nape while loose curls escape and frame her face.

My eyes trail down her body. Her exposed neck and bare shoulders glisten with some kind of superfine body glitter, making a necklace redundant. Her black strapless dress is a shimmery chiffon material and cinches around her curves. On the left side is a slit that teases the eye, rising to mid-thigh. Peeking through the bottom of her dress is a black slingback heel, elongating her toned legs and rounding her ass further. I gasp for air.

"Wow, Eli," I whisper breathlessly. "You look gorgeous."

Her ocean-jewel eyes twinkle at my compliment as a blush creeps up her neck and tints the apples of her cheeks. She whispers a thank-you and I move toward her to give her a kiss on the forehead. My dick hardens into steel and I have to reach down to rearrange my boys, which makes Elissa flush even more as she howls at me, her laughter echoing through the hallway on our way to the lift.

CHAPTER
THIRTY-FOUR

RILEY

Rhys and I arrive early, as I need to oversee the rest of the setup for the event. The event is being held in the Black & Wells Publishing and Press building's expansive lobby. I nod to security and a few of the hired waitstaff as I move through the lobby, making sure everything is ready to go. The tables are bar height, with a few tables at normal height mixed in, suited for a better mingling atmosphere. Black linens drape the tables, complete with glittery rose gold chiffon table runners. Flameless candles of varying heights flicker beside vases of hydrangeas in the centre of each table.

The sounds of light jazz dance through the air while the bartenders clang cups and bottles around, organizing the pop-up bar. There's a small kitchen off the backside of the lobby that was built for this exact reason when Harold first started the company, and the doors swish as waitstaff and caterers bustle through them.

It took hours' worth of work, but I am so happy I spent time hanging up fairy lights from the ceiling. The lobby has transformed into a banquet hall and is barely recognizable. Once I've checked in with all the staff working tonight, I find Rhys by the bar, ordering us two glasses of white wine. He passes me my glass and I press a kiss to his lips before taking a sip.

"Thanks, babe," I say. He smiles at me and grabs my hand.

"Let's find somewhere private for a moment, to talk." He tugs my hand and asks the security guard if we can use his office for a few minutes and winks. The security guard replies that he's going to do a perimeter check and will be back in fifteen minutes. Rhys leads me into the office, closes the door, and locks it.

"Rhys…we can't do that in here. People will start arriving at any moment." A dark look flashes in Rhys' eyes as a seductive smile spreads across his face.

"Don't worry, babe," he says in a gravelly voice. "I just wanted to talk for a moment." My heart flutters when he approaches me. He places the back of one hand on my cheek and strokes it softly, then grabs my hand with the other.

"I just wanted some privacy to say…I think I'm falling for you, and I want to be exclusive. I want you to be my girlfriend."

My heart stops and I forget how to breathe. *He wants me to be his girlfriend?!* I squeeze his hand as my eyes swim with tears of happiness. I can't say anything other than a breathy "Yes!" as I nod my head. I throw my arms around his neck and kiss him hard. When he kisses me back, it is full of hunger and want. He devours my lips as his hands travel down the length of my body, stopping at my waist. He bunches my long silk gown up around my hips and grinds up against me. Heat pools between my legs and I push back, letting our bodies speak.

My hands drop to fiddle with his pants until his hard dick springs free. He grips my ass with firm hands and lifts me up, resting my ass on the edge of the security desk. He reaches around to his back pocket to grab a foil packet from his wallet. Rhys breaks the kiss only long enough to tear the packet and roll it down the length of his shaft. I smash my mouth into his, gyrating my crotch against his. He pushes my panties aside and thrusts his cock into my soaking entrance.

Thrusting hard, he trails kisses along my jaw and down my neck to the tops of my breasts. When he slams his dick into my sweet spot, Rhys' hand muffles my moans so the people outside are not privy to our lovemaking. I bite down on his hand as he plunges into me faster, holding back my scream.

"Come, baby." Rhys growls.

As I let go, my pussy clenches around his cock, and I'm tingling from a full-body orgasm. I have just enough sense left in me to slap my hand across his mouth as he makes his final pumps to silence his moans. Rhys is breathing heavily as he rests his forehead on my shoulder, and I run my fingers through his inky hair. He holds my hand as I hop off the desk and we take a few moments to adjust our clothes and fix our hair so no one suspects we just copulated in the security office. Our eyes meet and we both burst out laughing.

I'm on cloud nine when we exit the office, and I notice people are starting to arrive. I scan the crowd, trying to see if 'Lissa and Brandt are here yet, but I don't spot them. Rhys escorts me around the lobby to mingle and welcome the guests, when someone taps my shoulder. We both turn around to see my parents standing there, smiling widely.

"Mom! Dad! You made it!" Rhys lets go of my waist momentarily so I can hug my parents. My dad pulls me in for a big bear hug and my mom kisses my cheek with a gentle embrace. I step back into Rhys' orbit as he places his hand on the small of my back. My parents look at me, their eyes questioning.

"Rhys, you remember my parents from the graduation dinner? Brianne and Connor. Mom, Dad, this is my boyfriend, Rhys." I look into Rhys' eyes and see the same love and happiness radiating in them that I feel. Rhys turns his attention to my parents and extends a hand to greet them.

"Hello, it's very nice to see you again. You've done a wonderful job raising your daughter. She is truly spectacular." He beams at my parents. My mom turns into a puddle of goo, her face flushing, and my father shakes Rhys' hand with extreme intensity but nods in approval. My parents start getting acquainted with Rhys when a waiter taps me on the shoulder and whispers in my ear. I dip my head slightly in acknowledgement and turn to my parents and Rhys.

"Please excuse me, I need to address something in the kitchen." I hug my parents quickly and place a soft kiss on

Rhys' cheek. "I'll be right back." I make my way across the lobby and disappear behind the kitchen door, my body and heart aching from being away from Rhys.

It takes forty-five minutes to deal with the caterers, and when I re-emerge the party is in full swing. Hundreds of attendees are fraternizing and laughing, some are even dancing already. I scan the crowd again to find Elissa, but Rhys shimmies into my field of view first, slow dancing with the air. My face breaks into a grin and I giggle as he dances goofily around me. He stops in front of me, bowing, with one hand tucked behind his waist and the other extended to me, like a prince asking a princess to dance. My face reddens as I slide my hand into his and curtsy. He clasps my hand and yanks me to him, wrapping one arm around my waist. He slowly twirls us around the dance floor, our bodies completely in sync. He folds me in closer and I rest my head against his shoulder. Safe and warm is what I feel when I am in Rhys' arms, and with every passing moment I'm with him, I fall deeper in love.

Across the lobby, I finally spot Elissa, but I notice right away that her body is stiff and her hands are curled into fists at her sides. Harold stomps away from her, pulling Collette in tow. Brandt moves closer to comfort Elissa, and she jerks away from his touch. She crosses her arms across her chest and turns on her heels, weaving her way toward me through the throng of people. She isn't paying attention and accidentally bumps into me, dropping her clutch. I bend over to help her pick up the contents scattered across the floor. She meets my gaze and her eyes are sad, broken — an expression I've never seen on her face before. She tosses everything into her clutch, and when we both straighten, she whispers her thanks and bolts out of the building.

Rhys and I exchange worried glances. *What the fuck just happened?*

CHAPTER
THIRTY-FIVE

ELISSA

The buzzer echoes loudly throughout the apartment, and I sprint into the hallway with my hair half-finished to buzz Brandt in and unlock the door before rushing back to my en suite washroom. I close the door behind me and get back to twisting and curling my hair into a low side bun. I tease soft, rust-coloured curls loose from the gathered hair framing my face. With my towel wrapped around my chest, I spritz a fine, glittery body mist along my collarbone and shoulders.

I make my way into my bedroom and dab some Chanel No. 5 on the nape of my neck and wrists before stepping into my sparkly, black strapless dress. I bend over and stick my legs out from the provocative slit that gives a glimpse of my lightly sun-kissed, toned thighs as I slip on my black slingbacks. Brandt hollers something about being late, but he doesn't understand that being late to these kinds of events is fashionable. Besides, we're the reason they're all gathering tonight. Might as well garner as much buzz as we can.

I step into the living room as I fasten my earrings on, and when Brandt sees me from the length of the hallway, his breath catches.

"Wow, Eli...you look gorgeous," he breathes. I feel my face flush and my eyes sting with a feeling I'm not sure I understand. I look away, embarrassed, then whisper a thank you. Brandt pulls me to him and places a soft kiss on my forehead. As he leans in, I can feel the strain of his pants against me, and he straightens up and adjusts himself quickly. I bust out laughing, as he's ruined the perfect moment with his dick. *Typical man for ya*. I cackle the entire way to the elevator and only stop when the doors have closed and his mouth is on mine, silencing the laughter with lust.

Out front, a sleek black limo is waiting for us. The chauffeur stands at the back of the vehicle, waiting with the door open. Brandt gestures for me to climb in first and then follows me. When the driver is back inside the cab, Brandt lets him know he can leave and asks for the divider to be rolled up. Brandt turns to look at me, then grabs my hand and clasps it between both of his.

"I know I already said this, but you really look gorgeous tonight." He lifts my hand and places a chaste kiss on my palm. I press my thighs together, trying to hold the wetness at bay, and I feel the heat rising to my ears. Brandt must have noticed because he leans in and leaves soft kisses along my neck. When he reaches the sensitive spot behind my ear, he takes a deep breath and whispers, "Fuck, you smell good. I bet your pussy does, too." He slides down to the floor of the limo, lifts my gown, and sticks his head inside.

He grabs the undersides of my thighs and tugs me forward, French kissing the soft skin on the inside of my legs. As his mouth reaches higher, his hot breath leaves steamy kisses on the outside of my underwear. He presses his nose into my underwear-covered slit and inhales deeply. A moan escapes my mouth, and I am panting like a dog in heat.

"Nope, I was wrong," he growls and then licks the outside of my panties. My stomach knots.

"It smells even better."

He pushes my panties to the side and, without warning, his tongue plunges into my wetness as his thumb finds my sensitive bundle of nerves. His tongue explores the inside of my hole and I clench my opening around his tongue, making him grunt. He rubs my clit faster, and I lace my fingers into his hair, tugging gently. Brandt moves his tongue to my clit and sucks hard as he dips two curved fingers into me, urging me to come. I'm almost there as his name tumbles from my lips.

"Brandt…yes."

My hips roll of their own accord, riding his face. The roughness of his five o'clock shadow against my sensitive skin only adds to the sensations overwhelming my pussy. The tingle starts to rise from my toes, and I curl them to stave off my orgasm for a little longer. But Brandt's mouth has other plans. His tongue swirls and bobbles on my clit, and he slips a third finger in my hole while slinging one of my legs over his shoulder. My head falls back, and I moan his name as I fall over the edge. Brandt laps up the essence that seeps out of me as my chest heaves as I come down. He fixes my panties, licking his lips and fingers as he reclaims his spot beside me. I notice his cock is firmly at attention, and I move to run my hands over his erection to return the favour, but he holds my wrist and shakes his head.

"We don't have time, sweetheart. We're here."

He tucks his cock into the waist of his pants, and when the driver opens the door, Brandt slides out and offers me his hand. As I exit the limo, the flashing of cameras obscures my view, but I plaster on a smile and allow Brandt to wrap his arm around my waist. We stop halfway toward the entrance of the building and take a few photos for the press before continuing inside.

Once we're inside, we don't have a chance to breathe. Waves of people come up to us for introductions and to congratulate us on the business venture. We make our way through the crowd to the bar. I order a beer for Brandt and a glass of red wine for myself. We stand at the bar chatting with a few guests, and I notice they look at us with odd, goofy expressions. I try to shake it off, but then the words of "congratulations" turn more vague. Instead, as new guests come up to us, they are saying the phrase "Congratulations, you two" — too strangely worded to be about business. I question Brandt with my eyes to see if he knows anything, but he looks just as confused as I am.

We continue to make polite conversation and I try my best to ignore the weird looks and funky phrasing, but I start to get a sinking feeling. I excuse myself to the washroom, disappear into the crowd, and make my way to privacy. But, instead of going to the washroom, I sneak into the stairwell, climb up to the second floor and take the elevator to the twenty-first floor.

The elevator climbs higher as my thoughts ping-pong around my head. *What kind of fresh hell is going on?* The atmosphere here just seems different than a regular launch party. Coming to a stop, I realize I pressed the wrong button and have ended up on the twenty-second floor — my father's floor. I shrug it off and exit the elevator, as I know I'm alone. I spotted my father downstairs earlier, and I know ditching my "watchdog" would piss him off. Slipping out of my heels to give my feet a break, I tiptoe down the corridor to find a quiet place to rest in one of the conference rooms.

As I near one of the conference rooms, I hear hushed voices coming from my father's office. I scurry toward a wall and press my back to it to avoid being seen. I slink my body closer to the door of my father's office.

"Harold, what the hell are you doing? Why are you telling people this without Elissa's knowledge? Did she even agree to this?"

My mother's voice reverberates down the corridor, causing me to hold my breath. When my father doesn't respond, it's safe to assume he shrugged off her questions.

"How is it going to look if she makes a scene? She'll ruin the launch party, and who knows what kind of press it'll create." My father scoffs in response.

"Don't act like you care, Collette. You only care about my money and your pool boy," he sneers. My mother inhales sharply, like she's been slapped.

"How dare you," she says quietly. Her words are soft, but her voice trembles with anger. "I've always cared, but you've never let me. You always pushed off my suggestions and interest, so don't stand there and tell me I don't care."

"As for Elissa," my father continues, ignoring her, "she won't do shit about it. Embarrassing herself is the last thing she will want to do, and she still has this incessant need to prove herself to me. Fucking weak little girl."

My heart stops and his words tear my heart apart, just like I'm eight years old again. Instantly I'm back to the little girl in the hallway, in the dark, hearing my father's hateful words. Again, at a party. Again, outside his office. And again, someone clasps my shoulder and shushes in my ear.

My hands fly to cover my mouth as I turn around to see who's caught me eavesdropping, and my heart swells as a tear rolls down my cheek. *Lana.* She grabs my hand and leads me to the stairwell, then I bring us down one floor to where my office is. I'm too stunned to say anything, so I lead her to my office.

Lana sits me down on the soft leather couch inside my office and closes the door. She's light as she plops down beside me, cups my face, and wipes my tears away with her thumbs. The tears only build up more, begging to burst forth, both from happiness at seeing her, and sadness at my father's words. A shaky laugh escapes me, and she pulls me into a tight embrace. Her hand locks behind the back of my head.

"It's okay, baby. Mom's right here," she coos, tightening her hold on me. I'm not sure how long we sit there for, but she lets my tears pour out and just holds me, telling me everything will be all right. My shoulders shake as my sobs tremble out of me. Once I've calmed, she holds me at arm's length and wipes away my tears. With her thumb, she carefully fixes my smudged winged liner, and we giggle together.

"I'm so glad to see you," I croak. I pull her in for another hug. "It's been too long."

"I know, sweetie. We won't let this much time pass again." I pull away and look at her, confused.

"Wait, how did you know where I was?" Lana gives me a soft smile.

"I was on my way over to say hello, but then saw you sneaking away. And when I spotted the elevator heading upstairs from the second floor, I thought I should follow you. Your parents had just taken the elevator a few minutes prior." She looks away and sighs. "I guess some things never change."

"Do you know what they were talking about, Mom?" Lana shakes her head with a sad, thin smile.

"Sorry, love. I have no idea what they were referring to. I just arrived here, myself. Tiago's downstairs in the garage, finding a parking spot. Fucking Tiago and his cheap ways! He refuses to use the valet." I laugh and immediately picture Tiago throwing a conniption because "No one is gonna touch my precious baby and I am not paying $100 to tip them to be gentle!" As if his Volkswagen Touareg is a Tesla or a Maserati.

"Oh, I've missed Tiago," I sigh. "I've missed you more, though." I grab Lana's hands and squeeze. Lana smiles sweetly as she smooths my hair and chucks her hand under my chin.

"I know Knox misses you, too. Let's get together for dinner soon. Maybe you can even come stay for the weekend. It really has been too long, my love." She brushes her lips against my forehead, stands, and pulls me up with her. "We should get back downstairs to the party before your parents notice you're missing. Something tells me your father is having you monitored."

"Ha! You have no idea. My monitor is actually my date tonight, and he's our business partner, Brandt." Lana raises her eyebrows at me.

"You mean the hottie arm candy tonight? Well, it can't be all that terrible," she says as she nudges my ribs playfully. My eyes drift off into a dreamy haze.

"No, it's not terrible at all. Actually, we've been sort of... hooking up the last few months. Nothing serious, but..." I notice Lana has stopped walking with me, and when I turn around, I see her staring at me with a woeful expression in her dark chocolate eyes.

"My love, you say it's not serious, but I see the way he looks at you. Sweetie, he's in love."

I freeze. Time stops moving. I can't breathe. I feel my body drain of all its colour and I am gasping for air. *He loves me? No, he doesn't love me. He's IN love with me. Since when? How did this happen? How did I not notice?* My eyes connect with Lana's, and suddenly she's in front of me, hands bracing my shoulders, but I can't quite hear what she's saying. Something about breathing, but I can't because everything feels and sounds like I'm underwater. I feel like I'm drowning.

CHAPTER
THIRTY-SIX

ELISSA

In love. He's in love. Brandt's in love with me. *What?* These thoughts whoosh through my head, again and again, as I struggle to catch my breath. Muffled words keep trying to break through the tidal wave of anxiety and panic that keeps pulling me into its undertow.

He loves me. Me.

What the hell am I going to do?

I should have seen the signs. One minute I'm kicking him out after sex, then suddenly he's snuggling me, and we're *pillow talking?!* And the next minute he's sleeping over and leaving his toothbrush and deodorant at my place. When the fuck did casual become less casual? Or exclusive?

Shit! I even told him to pack a bag for tonight. What the hell. Is he my...boyfriend? My stomach drops.

This is not good. I don't do attachments. Suddenly, a sharp sting slashes across my cheek, and I am thrown out of my inner turmoil. I cup my cheek and press it to help the sting subside while the fog clears from my eyes and mind. I see Lana standing there, her dark eyes wide with concern.

"Oh, thank God. You're back." Lana breathes a sigh of relief. "You went full-blown panic attack. I haven't seen you have one in years. I thought I was going to have to call the medics and get you something to calm down." I feel her grip on my arm; she's shaking like a leaf. She cradles me into a tight squeeze.

"Just breathe, sweets. I'm here, and I love you." Her words are like warm honey, soothing my panicked mind. Her hands clasp my face as she stares deep into my eyes. It feels like her gaze is piercing into my soul.

"Are you okay now?" I nod my head and she releases me. She leads me to the elevators and presses the button to call the lift. The elevator doors slide open and we both freeze when we see my father and mother standing inside. My father's face contorts into a scowl, and I feel bile rising up from my stomach and into my throat. Lana grabs my hand, squeezes tightly for reassurance, and pulls me along behind her into the elevator.

She turns to my father and says, "I ran into Elissa downstairs. You two have done a wonderful job with the new division. I asked her to give me a tour of her new workspace. I hope you don't mind." She has a sweet and innocent smile on her face, and my eyes seek her gaze, trying to convey my thanks. My father grumbles something unintelligible, but we both assume he's brushing off the incident. If anyone's worthy of being my monitor, it's definitely Lana, and for all intents and purposes, my dad trusts her. The elevator reaches the ground floor, but just before it opens, my father hits the emergency stop button.

"Elissa, when we exit, I want your best behaviour. No more running off, and it was terribly rude of you to leave Brandt alone at the party."

I flinch as he says Brandt's name. But Brandt is hardly alone. I'm sure once he noticed I left, he went to find Rhys and Riley, or our bimbo assistants found him and are hanging off his arms. Instead of risking a confrontation with my father, I decide to comply and nod my head.

"Good girl. Now, go find Brandt." He releases the stop button, and the doors slide open. "It was good seeing you again, Lana. We'll catch up later tonight." Harold and Collette push past us, and we exit after them.

"Well, darling, if you're okay, I should find Tiago. He's probably at the bar. I'll check in with you shortly, okay?" Lana pulls me in for a quick embrace and turns to find her husband.

I stand, frozen in place, scanning the party for any sign of Riley. I can't find her, and my search is interrupted by an arm slithering around my waist. Hot breath lingers on my ear.

"Where did you run off to, babe?" Brandt whispers. I stand rigidly in place at first, and an icy shiver runs down my spine. My skin feels like it has a thousand ants crawling all over it.

"Would you like to dance?" Brandt asks. Not sure what I should do, I bow my head ever so slightly to acknowledge his request and let him lead me to the dance floor.

Brandt and I have only done club dancing together, so when he stretches out his hand and swirls me to the dance floor, my other thoughts dissolve as he pulls me in close. He positions my left hand on his shoulder, places his hand gently on my waist, and guides me into a waltz. Brandt's movements are precise and flow perfectly with the music. His eyes capture mine and hold them hostage, not allowing me to look away. And, for a moment, for the briefest of time, the room and people evaporate. It's just me and Brandt.

He twirls us around and we're dancing in a wind of colour and music. I forget all about my panic from earlier, and a warm glow illuminates my chest. It spreads throughout my body as I look into the eyes of the man in front of me. My body vibrates from his touch. And though fear is clawing its way out of my stomach and trying to escape up my throat, when I look into his eyes, I am calm.

When Brandt slows down, the trance is broken, and I realize that the song is over. All at once I feel two hundred pairs of eyes on me as my entire body catches fire. I look around and notice that everyone is, in fact, staring at us. I quickly escape the dance floor and find the bar. I immediately order two shots of tequila and drain them, one after the next. My nerves calm down and the crowd resumes their conversations and dancing. Brandt materializes beside me and flags down the bartender for a beer.

"Are you okay?"

I side-eye him and force a tight smile. "Yep," I say, popping the "p." Brandt doesn't look convinced as he takes a long pull of his beer, his eyes never leaving my face. After a few moments of studying me, he relents.

"If you say so."

I turn to the bartender, ask for a whisky, and take a massive gulp when I have it in my hand. We make our way over to one of the standing tables and settle there for a bit. When the waiters come around, I grab a few appetizers to soak up some of the alcohol I just gulped down.

An hour goes by, and a dozen or so more people have come around wishing us luck and congratulating us. I've finally settled my nerves and am starting to relax and enjoy Brandt's company in between guests. I'm starting to believe that I can salvage this night and still end on a positive note — and with Brandt in my bed.

As Brandt chats about something Rhys said about him and Riley, my eyes settle on my father and mother across the lobby. They're standing and chatting with Brianne and Connor Jaimeson, Riley's parents. It's a jovial scene, and everyone is smiling and laughing. Mother and Brianne are hugging, and the men are shaking hands excitedly. A wave of dread crashes over me, but I try to shake it off. I turn my attention to Brandt and apologize, asking him to repeat himself.

"Oh, I just mentioned that when you were gone with Lana, Rhys was telling me..." Despite my best efforts, my attention is once again on the group across the lobby. *What the hell could have my father, mother, and Riley's parents so excited?*

"He even said the words 'love' and 'boyfriend.'" Those two words drag me from my thoughts like a bull dragging his rider across the ring. I focus my attention on Brandt and shake my head.

"I'm sorry, what?" I ask incredulously. Brandt furrows his brows and places a gentle hand on top of mine.

"I said, Rhys and Riley are dating now, officially. Are you sure you're okay?" Before I can answer though, Brianne and Connor burst out of the throng of people in front of us with clown-like smiles.

"Oh, honey!" Brianne gushes as she rounds the table and pulls me in for a big hug. "We just heard the news! When your father told us, we couldn't believe it!" Brianne seems to ignore my confused look and continues gushing.

"And to want to keep it a secret because of the launch! You are so dedicated to the company. Both of you are." Brianne's eyes dart between Brandt and me. Connor pipes up and pulls Brandt in for a manly hug, with two slaps on the back.

"Good for you, man. This is excellent news. And let me just say I have hopes for Riley and Rhys. He seems like a nice fellow…" Brianne and Connor's voices fade as I look past their shoulders and find my father and mother. I snap back to the conversation.

"I'm sorry. But what is it that my parents have told you?" Nothing could have prepared my heart for what they said next.

"Your engagement, of course!" Brianne says cheerfully. A small, manic laugh escapes me.

"I'm sorry, what?" With utter disbelief, I whip my head toward Brandt and all the colour from his face has drained. It's safe to say they have blindsided him as well. Brandt's body is rigid and he looks as though he's constipated. Brianne and Connor are still somehow oblivious to our shock and keep merrily chatting. Once I have my head on straight, I abruptly excuse myself from the conversation and hoof it over to where my parents are.

BRANDT

My heart plummets to my stomach when Mr. and Mrs. Jaimeson mention that Eli and I are engaged. Goosebumps crop up all over my body, and I break out into a cold sweat. I can sense Elissa's heated stare burrowing into the side of my face. I feel like I'm being squished in the trash compactor from *Star Wars*.

How could Harold do this to us? And blindside me, especially. I know what I agreed to, and this wasn't it. A gut-wrenching wave of guilt envelops me. Fuck. I agreed to this. *Yes, but I didn't agree to how this was accomplished!* Fucking Harold.

Elissa hightails it out of the conversation and makes a beeline toward her parents. I apologize for Elissa's rudeness to Brianne and Connor and excuse myself as well so I can follow Elissa.

"Oh, no worries, dear." Brianne says. "Best wishes. And tell 'Lissa-darling that we say congratulations, again." Mrs. Jaimeson pulls me in and kisses my cheek, and Mr. Jaimeson vigorously shakes my hand. I give them a weak smile and then zigzag through the horde until I reach Elissa and her parents. Elissa is already confronting her parents in hushed tones, so as not to alert the press or guests. As I settle beside Elissa, I try to place my hand on her back as an act of support, but she jerks away from me. There's pressure in my chest and I feel my heart cracking under the strain.

ELISSA

"Who the fuck do you think you are to announce an engagement for me?" I glower at my parents and speak through gritted teeth. My father rolls his eyes and my mother, for once, looks ashamed.

"I'm your fucking father and the owner of this company. Don't be a petulant child, Elissa. I have let you get away with all your ridiculous shenanigans over the last four years. Enough is enough. Finally, it's time for you to do something beneficial for this company. Everyone I have mentioned this *news* to tonight thinks it's wonderful!"

"I can't believe you did this to me. Wait, actually — I can. But I can't believe you did this to Brandt! I'm standing there, hearing 'my' news from the Jaimesons, floored, and here's Brandt thrown into the middle of it. And he sure as hell didn't know anything about it." My father's face twists into an unsettling smirk, making my blood curdle.

"Stop being dramatic, darling. Frankly, you could do worse than Brandt. He's a fine young man."

"It doesn't matter if he's a fine young man — he is. But it matters that you planned all this and didn't even tell us. How fucking inconsiderate of you. I don't want to get married. I don't want an arranged marriage. And I am sick of the bullshit you put me through."

Brandt tries to calm me down by rubbing my back, but I jerk away again, feeling my skin crawl and panic starting to rise inside me again. I try to quell the feeling by digging my nails into my palms, feeling the skin grow slippery with sweat and blood. Harold looks victorious and tucks Collette under his arm, closer to him.

"This conversation is over, Elissa. You don't have a choice. When I go up to give my speech, I am announcing it to the entire party. And we both know you won't embarrass me if I publicly announce it. Also, I know you've been fucking Brandt. So don't act all high and mighty. Might as well make it official." Harold takes my mother and walks away, chuckling to himself. Brandt's hand finds its way to my shoulder, but I shrug him off and whip around toward him.

"Thanks a lot for standing there like a mime and not saying anything. This affects you too, ya know?" Brandt's face drains of the colour he only just got back.

"I'm sorry. It seemed like you had it handled. And Harold isn't wrong. I wouldn't mind being engaged or married to you. Even if it's for the company." My mouth drops open, tears well in my eyes, and my heart is raging inside my chest, begging to be let out. I am floored.

"I can't believe you…" I whisper. I turn and start to push my way through the room, weaving as I go, as fast as I can. Running like Cinderella from the ball, until I bump into someone and drop my clutch, the contents skittering everywhere. I bite back my tears, refusing to cry here. When I see a familiar hand scooping up my things, I lift my head and see my best friend's concerned eyes staring back at me. I telepathically thank her and hope my emphatic stare conveys what I want — for her to keep the press, and Brandt, at bay, to let me have a head start. I straighten up and continue to the front entrance when a voice crackles over the sound system.

"Excuse me, everyone, if I could please have your attention. I would like to welcome and thank everyone for your attendance tonight. It's meant the world to me, to our staff, and to my daughter, who is heading up the new division." A polite applause ripples throughout the lobby. Unwilling to hear anymore, I race to the doors, kick my shoes off beside the security guard at the door, and take off, running down the street in my bare feet, my soles burning from the pavement, scorching under the summer evening's heat. My dress is gathered in my hands like Cinderella, tears blur my vision, and I'm not looking back.

I don't return home immediately. I run around downtown Toronto for a few blocks, burning off the rage that clings to me, clogging my veins like plaque. My feet burn and sting as they stomp into the ground. My heavy gait does not help, and only presses the pebbles and stones into my feet further. Sweat drips down my back, and the hem of my dress catches and pulls as it rustles over the asphalt. I don't look behind me; I'm too worried someone might be following me to take me back to my father. Worried it might be Brandt, trying to rescue me. Trying to trap me.

I'm huffing and puffing when suddenly I stumble to my knees, scraping my palms. Trying to catch my breath, trying to stay calm, I get my breathing under control, and realize I am in front of my building. I stand up on shaky legs, pain searing the soles of my feet, walk through the doors, and ascend to my apartment.

CHAPTER
THIRTY-SEVEN

ELISSA

I crash into my apartment, stumbling all the way to my bedroom, peeling off my dress as I go. I throw my clutch into the living room, where it bounces off the couch and lands on the floor. I barrel into my bedroom and slam the door shut, making my way to the en suite. I twist the tap open, full-blast, and hot water sprays out of the showerhead as steam fills the room. I step into the shower with my underwear and bra still on, but I don't care. I let the scalding water burn away the bugs creeping and crawling over my skin. I let the burn of the water override the burning I feel inside.

Standing under the stream, I let my emotions collapse. I let the waves of hurt and loneliness I've felt all these years finally wash over me. I feel them, then let them wash away with the water running down the drain, trying to cleanse my soul. If tears are streaming down my face, I can't tell, as the water merges as it streams down my body, taking my pain with it.

Eventually I twist the tap off and I emerge from the washroom, naked and dripping. I stand in my room, staring off into space. *Nothing I can say will change my father's mind.* It's too late now, he's probably announced it to the press and everyone in attendance. I'm stuck. Brandt's stuck. *Together.* The thought of being stuck together, with him, rolls a shiver over my body. When I realize I'm still dripping wet, I consider that I don't know if the idea of being stuck together is terrible or not. Small droplets roll down my legs and pool on the floor at my feet, when suddenly a loud banging comes from the front door. I snap out of my haze and grab a towel from the bathroom, wrapping it tightly around my body.

"Eli, it's me! Open up!" Brandt shouts. I stall in the middle of the hallway, wondering how he got inside the building without me buzzing him in.

"Babe, let me in and let's talk. Don't shut me out." A small chunk of my heart chips away at his pleas.

"I can't, Brandt. I can't do this. I just need some time." My words come out shaky. "Did you know? Did you know Harold was going to do this?" He stays silent a beat too long before he answers with a heavy sigh. I hear a soft thud, and I know Brandt's forehead is resting against my door.

"No, Eli. Of course I didn't know he was going to do that." A small stream of relief flows through me. "Please open the door so we can talk. I need to hold you."

Tears burn my eyes. Part of me wants desperately to open the door, but the stronger part of me stops me from unlocking the door and letting him in.

"I'm sorry." I whisper through the seal of the door. "Please try to understand."

I watch Brandt through the peephole. He's standing there, and I see a tear trickle down his cheek before he roughly scrubs it away. Again, I fight the urge to open the door and let him in. But I know, once I do, I'm letting him into something I'm not ready for, and it terrifies me. I stare at him through the glass of the peephole for almost an hour until he finally gives up, shoves his hands in his pockets, and walks away, his head drooping.

My body slumps against the door and I slide down to the floor, dropping my head to my knees. I take a big breath and sob into the stillness and quiet of my apartment.

BRANDT

I walked away. *But what else was I supposed to do? She'll never let me in.* She's only let me in this far because she didn't realize she was doing it. I don't know what the hell happened tonight. The evening started off great, and then Elissa disappeared for a while. Then, after that, she was on edge and…just different the rest of the night.

It took everything I had to walk away and give her time. I feel defeated, shredded, and broken. I hail a cab and take it back to the party to find Rhys and Riley. By the time I return, it's almost midnight, and I can see through the lobby windows that only the cleaning staff remain in the venue. I redirect the cab to Rhys' address to take Riley the key fob I borrowed and catch them up on what's happened. My phone vibrates and I realize I haven't checked it in hours; I pull it out of my pocket, praying it's Eli.

Rhys: *Dude. What the hell is going on?*

Rhys: *You're actually engaged? WTF? I thought there was gonna be a process.*

Rhys: *You're killing me, man. I need to know what's going on. Riley's fucking freaking because Elissa won't answer her phone.*

Rhys: *Please msg me when you can.*

Fuck. Rhys seems to be losing his shit, too. I message him back, apologizing for not answering earlier and letting him know I'm on my way.

RILEY

Brandt's a fucking mess when he shows up at Rhys' place. He's on the verge of tears, pacing back and forth, and minutes from being bald with all the hair he's tugging out. Rhys grabs him a beer from the fridge, guides him to the couch, and forces him to sit. After a half-hour of Brandt sitting in silence and staring into space, Rhys finally breaks the quiet.

"What the fuck happened, man? When the hell did you get engaged?" Brandt says nothing, just turns his head to stare blankly at Rhys.

"Is 'Lissa okay, Brandt? Did you see her?" I ask softly. He seems to accept my question.

"Yes...and I don't know. She wouldn't say much." His voice cracked, and I could tell his heart was cracking, too.

I move to sit beside him on the couch and wrap my arms around him, pulling him into an embrace. Once he's enveloped in my arms, he breaks; the floodgates open, and he just weeps. This tall, strong, Greek god-like man crumbles before me like a broken statue. Shattering, piece by piece. Pulverized into dust. My heart wept with, and for, him. I want to leave and go home to console Elissa, but I know that here, comforting Brandt, is where I need to be right now.

Elissa does best on her own when things get overwhelming. She needs space and time to breathe; a chance to come up for air. So, when Brandt settles down a bit, I sneak my phone out of my pocket and open the messages app to find 'Lissa's name.

Me: *Hey, lady. I know you need space. I'm here when you're ready. xoxo love you.*

The next morning we're all feeling sluggish, and we take turns getting ready in Rhys' one bathroom. Rhys pulls out some clothes for Brandt to change into. An hour later, we are on our way to my place to check on Elissa. We stop by Tim Hortons on our way to grab breakfast and caffeine. When we arrive, I press my key fob to the lobby's sensor, the door clicks, and we head for the elevator.

When we reach the apartment, I fiddle with my keys, eager to get inside and hug and console Elissa. My key swivels in the lock, and I burst through the door, calling Elissa's name. When I hear no response, I run to her bedroom as the guys collapse onto the couch in the living room. I stop dead in my tracks when I swing her bedroom door open.

Every drawer of her dresser haphazardly hangs open. Her closet door is open, and the drawers inside are the same, some random articles of clothing hanging out of them. My heart stutters. I race to her washroom, but all her toiletries are gone. I turn back to enter her bedroom when I notice a bag and a box on her bed. I race over and dig through the box, only to find a note inside and men's toiletries. A sob escapes me and my breath catches as I try to read the note through blurry vision. Hearing my sob, Brandt and Rhys barge into the room. Brandt snatches the letter away from me as I wail. Rhys sits down beside me and rocks me in his arms, trying to soothe me.

Brandt and Riley,

I know you two will be together when you read this. I am sorry for disappearing like this, but I just need some time alone. I can't live under my father's thumb anymore. I know you deserve more than a letter as an explanation or a goodbye, but I know if I were to do this face-to-face, Riles, you would talk me out of it. Or at least convince me to go to Fiji with you or something. Please don't try to find me right now. I need time to decompress and figure some shit out.

Riles: I love you and I'm sorry for everything. Stay in the apartment. I don't know when I'll be back, so feel free to take my room. I'll be in touch in a few days when my head is a little clearer. I love you. xoxo

Brandt: I'm sorry...I don't know how to... I'm just sorry.

All my best,

E. xoxo

CHAPTER THIRTY-EIGHT

ELISSA

I tear through my room like a hurricane, throwing things into my suitcases in a tizzy. Garments flutter through the air as they land on my bed and the floor, some pieces still hanging off the drawers I left open. I find a box that was untouched from my move with Riley and dump out the contents, random trinkets clattering to the floor. I collect Brandt's things from my washroom in the box and place it on my bed, along with the bag he packed for tonight. I tear a blank page out of a notebook and scrawl a note to Brandt and Riley, praying like hell one day they will forgive me.

Writing the note is breaking my heart, but I know that to sort out the chaos inside me, I need to leave. The walls of the apartment feel like they're caving in, shrinking, stuffing me into my own little suffocating box. I need to be as far away from my life, and my father, as possible. It takes me three trips to haul all my shit to my car, save the big items like furniture. I slam the trunk on my black Corvette and hop into the driver's seat. I press the ignition button, making a mental note to change my licence plate in the morning.

It's 2 AM as I speed down the Don Valley Parkway and take the exit to the 401 West ramp. I travel for about an hour and make a pit stop in Ayr, finding the first ATM I can, withdrawing the most cash I can at one time. I fill my car with gas; it will be the last thing I put on my credit card before I change everything over, so my father has a harder time finding me. My GPS tells me I'm still an hour outside of London. I put my car in gear and head toward the highway, ignoring the cell phone blowing up with calls and texts that's tucked in my centre console. I race down the 401, the blur of lights hitting my windshield as I pass oncoming traffic on the other side of the highway.

When I finally reach London, I head for the Homewood Suites by Hilton. I pull into the horseshoe driveway that's directly in front of the doors and turn off my car, then grab one of the bellhop carriages and wheel it to my car. Once I've unloaded the car's contents, I wheel the cart back inside and leave it by the front desk while I move my car to the parking lot, then head back in to check in — with cash.

I take the elevator up the fourteenth floor and find my suite, wheeling the luggage cart carrying all my belongings to the door. The lock beeps as I slide the keycard through the reader, and I twist the handle and walk in. I place the cart in front of the little couch and collapse on the bed, exhausted from the day. I look at the alarm clock beside the bed and finally take in the time. It's 4:30 AM and the sun will rise shortly. I roll off the bed and close the blackout shades, strip down to my undies, and collapse again on the bed before slowly drifting off to sleep.

Home. Sweet. Home.

ACKNOWLEDGEMENTS

First, I want to thank everyone who has purchased and read my debut novel. It took a lot of blood, sweat, and tears, but it was also a lot of fun getting it to this point! Your faith and interest in my novel are overwhelmingly heartwarming.

I would also like to thank the people who helped work on this project with me to get it to final perfection. To my editor, Lesley-Anne Longo, thank you for all the hard work you put into this to make me sound profesh. I don't know where I'd be without you on this book, that's for sure. You've been so accommodating and wonderful this entire process. And, to my cover designer, Laura Boyle, who endlessly worked with me, making my cover dreams a reality — your artwork is so beautiful.

Finally, to my family and friends, without whom this book would never have been possible. To my friends that supported me all the way, bringing a level of excitement to this I wouldn't have known without you. To my mother and sister for being my champions and reading every draft and chapter as I wrote. Especially a gigantic thank you to my husband for dealing with the chaos of publishing and raising our family while I was stuck behind a keyboard writing.

ABOUT THE AUTHOR

Kate Smoak lives with her husband, daughter, and fur babies in a small town in Ontario, Canada. When she's not writing, she can be found curling up with a good book, playing video games, or camping at the trailer with her family.

Instagram: @katesmoakwrites
Twitter: @katesmoakwrites
Website: www.katesmoak.ca

If you enjoyed this book, it would mean the
world to me if you would leave a review. Reviews
are like tips for authors.

For more goodies and exclusive content, please sign up
for my newsletter!

A
black
WINTER

Sample Chapters

Kate Smoak

CHAPTER ONE

Mid-August
The day after the launch party

BRANDT

Riley enters Elissa's room, and when she freezes in place, my stomach plummets. Something isn't right. She darts into the en suite bathroom, but quickly reappears. At the same time as Riley, Rhys and I notice my overnight bag and a box on Elissa's bed. I watch as Riley rushes over and throws open the box. My whole body goes numb as she pulls out a single piece of paper with trembling hands. Her face screws up and instantly drains of colour. Rhys and I look at each other and jump up, barging into the bedroom. I snatch the paper out of Riley's hands just as she falls apart with a wail. Rhys rushes to scoop Riley into his arms and comfort her.

I feel like a glacier. My frozen body aches as I read Elissa's hastily scrawled words. I can't move or think properly. Hell, I'm not even sure I can smell anything. It's like my brain has broken along with my heart. *She's gone?* I search the letter again for any information. My heart breaks a little more when I notice that the note is mostly for Riley, with just one small line meant for me.

Brandt and Riley,
I know you two will be together when you read this. I'm sorry for disappearing like this, but I just need some time alone. I can't live under my father's thumb anymore. I know you deserve more than a letter as an explanation or a goodbye, but I know if I were to do this face-to-face, Riles, you would talk me out of it. Or at least convince me to go to Fiji with you or something. Please don't look for me right now. I need time to decompress and figure some shit out.

    Riles: I love you and I'm sorry for everything. Stay in the apartment. I don't know when I'll be back, so feel free to take my room. I'll be in touch in a few days when my head is a little clearer. I love you. xoxo

    Brandt: I'm sorry...I don't know how to... I'm just sorry.

All my best,
E. xoxo

That's all I get? A "sorry," and nothing else? All the emotions I could possibly feel in this moment swirl around inside my core. My fingers curl into tight, white-knuckled fists. Only the sounds of the note crinkling in my hand and Riley's sobs fill the apartment.

"She'll be back soon," Rhys says quietly. I'm not sure if he's trying to soothe Riley or convince me. "Elissa probably just needs a breather. There's been a lot put on her the last few weeks."

That last part seems to have been enough to soothe Riley. She snorts, wiping her tears and snot on the blankets of Elissa's bed. She's left nothing behind other than her sheets and a few scattered items of clothing. Riley shuffles into the bathroom, closes the door, and the room falls silent. It feels like the floor has shifted underneath my feet and I'm free-falling into darkness.

November, three months later

The last three months have been a blur. After Elissa left, Harold lost his shit and dumped the entire department on me. So, instead of taking care of my other responsibilities within Collins Global Collective, I've had Rhys taking over most of the operations until I can get out of this fucking department. Rhys has been accommodating, but I pay him well for that, and he is the CFO, after all. He should do his share when it's called for.

It's been three months of long, grueling nights at the office. Burying myself with work to keep myself from thinking about her; then burying myself in someone else to keep from hurting over her. Sometimes I don't even go home—my office couch has gotten a lot of action these past few weeks. And when I say action, not only do I mean sleeping, but *sleeping*. Selena, my assistant, has been volun-teering to stay late and help me with the tasks that Elissa was supposed to be in charge of. I've unofficially promoted her at this point, but I keep holding out, like a fool, praying Elissa walks back through the door. But even if she did, I don't know what I'd do. She shattered me by running away.

"Brandt," Selena purrs. I shift my glance to her. I'm sitting behind my desk, typing on my computer, and she's lounging on my office couch. She hitches her black pencil skirt up to mid-thigh and traces little circular patterns on her legs with her middle finger while she sucks in her bottom lip, biting on it firmly. Her eyes are on me, dark with temptation.

"Come over and take a break for a bit." She pats the small space on the couch beside her.

Her eyes light up when I push away from my mahogany desk and stalk toward her, cuffing my sleeves around my muscular forearms. Her tongue glides along her lower lip and bites down on the soft pillowy skin. When I reach the couch, she shuffles off and sits me down. She straddles me, her skirt bunching up around her waist, and pulls me in for a kiss, the collar of my shirt gripped in her tiny fists.

Selena's soft lips crush against mine and she instant-ly probes her tongue into my mouth. Her hand slides around the back of my neck and up into my hair, tug-ging on it hard as she rolls her crotch against mine so I can feel her wanting heat through my pants. I break our kiss so I can French kiss her neck and she moans like a porn star in my ear. My dick gradually gets harder, and when I close my eyes, I imagine only the flash of silky copper hair and sharp blue eyes. Selena jumps off me and saunters over to my desk, pulling out a silver packet from the bottom drawer.

Selena settles herself back on my lap, her lips meeting mine in a slow, sensual kiss. She pulls at my bottom lip, softly sinking her teeth into it. Her hand slides down my broad chest, popping open the buttons of my shirt, and she rubs up and down my washboard abs for a few moments before descending further. Selena thumbs open the button on my trousers with one hand while the other grips my neck for support. She drags down the zipper of my pants and shoves her hand into the opening of my boxers, freeing my cock. Her long, manicured fingernails rake gently along my shaft, making me twitch before she wraps her tiny hand around me, priming me for the condom.

With the foil packet between her teeth and forefinger and thumb, she slides off my lap to her knees, tears open the condom and rolls the rubber onto my hard cock, pushing it down with her mouth. Before coming back up, she sucks both balls into her mouth and swirls her tongue around them. She leaves a trail of kisses along the side of my dick and up my chest, tickling the golden blonde hairs there, tonguing wet kisses over my abs.

Selena straddles me once more, pushing her thong to the side and positioning herself over my tip. She loops an arm around my neck, pulling me close. I wrap my large hands around her slim waist and thrust her down on my cock; she throws her head back and lets out a moan. I buck my hips upward, hitting her hard and deep. Her head rolls forward and she rests her forehead on mine as I slide her up and down on my dick. Her pelvis rolls simultaneously to hit her g-spot. Selena tilts her head and plasters her lips to mine, kissing me roughly and feverishly as she rides me harder.

One of my hands tugs her blouse out from her skirt and slides up her torso to cup one of her breasts, slipping my hand under the lacy bralette she's wearing. Selena has a smaller chest; cute little apple breasts, and my large hands cover them completely. As I touch the soft skin beneath my hands, I miss the feeling of my hands being full, the perfect amount of breast resting in my palm. I squeeze Selena's breast hard before rolling her nipple between my fingers and pinching it. She moans into my mouth; I pinch her nipple again and I can feel her tighten around my cock briefly.

"Oh, Brandt!"

I've learned Selena's biggest turn-on is getting rough with her nipples. I pinch her nipple repeatedly and she slams her tight pussy down on my cock, harder and harder. Her mouth moves against my ear as her hot, panting breaths tickle my earlobe, then she moves it to the sensitive spot behind my ear. She tongues it lightly, and I feel my balls tingle as a shiver runs up my spine. I thrust into her harder, moving both hands down to her perfect, juicy ass and giving it a good squeeze. My hand slides lower to gather some of her wetness on my finger. I trail it back to her small, puckered hole. Easing my finger into her hole, we're both breathing hard. As my finger gets deeper, her ass tightens around my finger. She is moaning so loudly that I bring my hand up from her nipple to cover her mouth to muffle the sound. I withdraw my finger before sliding it back in her asshole and slamming my dick into her hard.

It's enough to push her over the edge. As her tight holes spasm around my finger and dick, I unload inside her, filling the condom while flashes of blue eyes, bronze hair, and creamy pale skin play on my mind.

Selena collapses on top of me, both our chests rising and falling hard. I ease her off me, tug off the condom, and tie it up. I roll it into some tissues and dispose of it in the wastebasket. Selena is still sprawled on the couch, one leg hanging down, the other resting across the cushions. Her skirt is still bunched up around her waist and her legs are wide open, putting her pussy on display. Readjusting my clothes, I excuse myself from the office to give her some privacy, but also to head to the break room to get some coffee.

"Want a coffee?" I ask her. She grins and nods. "Find something to order while I grab coffee. I'll put it on the company's tab." Selena stands, adjusts her clothing, and follows me out of my office, heading to her desk to sift through the takeout pamphlets.

CHAPTER TWO

BRANDT

At the end of the day, I order a car for Selena and walk her out of the building. I open the door for her and she lowers herself off the curb and onto the street with one foot as she leans in to kiss me. I turn my cheek slightly so she doesn't connect with my lips. Instead, she lands a kiss on the corner of my mouth. She sighs, disappointed.

"Good night, Brandt. See you tomorrow." I offer her a silent nod and close the door behind her.

I take off toward Rhys' apartment, and a few blocks later, I approach Riley's building, I am filled with rage when I think about how that was Elissa and Riley's place. A haze of red floats into my vision and my breathing becomes ragged. In the crisp November air, I no longer feel a chill as I continue walking down the street.

Fire burns inside me, and any time anyone mentions or makes me think of her, it stokes the fire. Every mention of her name is like another log being thrown on, making the fire last longer. If I'd truly known how she was, I never would have entertained the deal. Perfectly manicured hands tore my heart from my chest and then served it to me on a plate, raw, with a *bon appétite* note attached.

Oh, who am I kidding.

I would take the deal, over and over again, because the time with her was amazing. The only thing I would change is the way I left my heart unguarded. I dove in headfirst, with reckless abandon, and allowed my heart to run my emotions.

When I finally reach Rhys' place, I buzz up. I wait for a minute, and nothing. I buzz again. Again, nothing. I reach into my pocket and pull out my phone, thinking that calling him might be a better way to get his attention. Just as I'm about to press the green call button, a loud screeching noise echoes throughout the lobby of the building. There's giggling in the background and Rhys' voice is fragmented between heaving breaths. I grumble inwardly.

"Yeah?" My eyes drift toward the ceiling as I shake my head at his casual tone.

"It's me. But clearly you're busy tonight." Someone, I assume Riley, cackles in the background, then makes their way to the speaker.

"Brrrraaandtttttt," a plastered Riley shouts through the speaker. "Where are you? Are you here?" I mumble back, telling Rhys to get ahold of Riley and buzz me up for a moment. A minute later, the door clicks and a long buzz drowns out the silence of the lobby. I make my way toward the elevator and my phone beeps in my pocket. I extricate it from my jacket to see who messaged me.

Selena: *Baby, you seemed off when we left. Let me know if you wanna talk.*

Me: *Thanks. And please don't call me that.*

Selena sends an embarrassed-looking emoji, and a gif of Puss in Boots giving kitty eyes.

Selena: *Sorry. But let me know if you want to come over soon. I'll be up a little longer. I'm not wearing much...*

As I close in on Rhys' door, I look at the message Selena sent and chuckle to myself, knowing Riley would say "this girl is thirsty." The door flings open suddenly and a squeal jars my mind as a tiny body jumps on me.

"Oof." For a tiny girl, she sure can knock the wind out of you. "Hey Riley," I say flatly.

She happily greets me with "Oh, Brandty," but her mood changes when my phone's text message alert sounds twice in quick succession.

"Who the hell is texting you so much?" She rips the phone out of my hand and scrolls through the messages. Riley's brows furrow and her cheeks redden. The grinding of her teeth ruins the stillness in the air.

"*Selena?*" Riley sneers. "As in, your assistant?" I make a noncommittal noise in response and avoid her stare. "Are you fucking joking, Brandt? Elissa—" Riley and I both freeze, our eyes darting to find each other's as the blood drains from our faces at the mention of *her* name.

She shakes off the frost before me and changes the direction of the conversation, clearing her throat as she hands me my phone.

"I mean…damn, this girl is thirstaaay." Riley turns to Rhys, pats his shoulder, and stumbles into the bedroom. Rhys gives me an apologetic look and gestures for me to come in. I take off my shoes while shrugging off my jacket, tossing it over a kitchen chair as I make my way to the living room before collapsing on the couch. My sprawled body takes up the length of the couch, and I close my eyes and drift off for a moment. Suddenly, cold glass rests against my cheek and I shiver from the abrupt sensation. Rhys is pressing a beer bottle to my face.

"I was just resting my eyes," I say.

"Mmhm. So, why are you here so late?" Rhys asks me. I falter for a second. I haven't been sure what to say to him as of late because of Riley, who is in the next room, probably listening to our conversation. The bottle of beer hovers in front of my lips before I take a long pull, still debating on what I should tell him.

"Just didn't want to go straight home. Had a long day and hooked up with my assistant again, but now she's getting clingy. I told her it was just casual," I say to Rhys with a long sigh. "She wants more, and I just can't give it to her. Elissa fucked me up, and I'm not ready for anything…more." Rhys nods his head in understanding. This thing with Selena started a few weeks ago, out of necessity—I needed to try and erase Elissa's skin, body, and taste from my mind. Her being is burned into my brain like a searing brand, leaving her mark on me forever. But, as great as Selena has been, she's just a temporary distraction, and one that's not working very well, either. It's not her fault—it's Elissa's, for fucking me up.

"Maybe you need to get out and hook up with someone else, and break it off with her," Rhys suggests. I contemplate his words. *But is another random hookup going to help this aching, suffocating feeling I have in my chest?*

"Sure, easier said than done when all I do is work until 11 PM. When or how am I supposed to see anyone when I'm always at the office?" My mind meanders to Lori, who had been Elissa's assistant. She's a solid eight with a great, voluptuous rack and an ass for days. She rarely wears skirts, but the dress pants she wears with her pumps make her ass look fantastic. I shake off the thought, slightly disgusted with myself. Is this how businessmen usually act when they're sleeping with their assistants? I decide to message Selena to break it off, and I look over at Rhys and ask him what I should say. He shrugs.

"Just say something like you had fun, but you should break it off before it gets complicated."

With every tap my fingers make on the screen, I feel as though an immense pressure is being lifted off me, but at the same time, a slow, sinking feeling creeps into my stomach as my heart pangs. I'm finding it increasingly hard to believe I'll ever get over *her*. Even when I'm not actively thinking about her, I'm still thinking about her; I see her everywhere I go. I can't get her out of my system. She's stuck onto me like a tiny, prickly burr on the cuff of my pant leg.

"How's Riley doing with everything?" I ask, Rhys shrugs and rakes his hands through his hair.

"I don't know man, she…she just won't talk about it. It's like she's pretending everything is okay, or like Elissa is just on some vacation," Rhys mutters. My lips thin and I nod my head, not quite sure what to say. My mind still wrestles with Elissa's abandonment of us daily and it's been three fucking months. *Get over it, dude. But it's easier said than done when my heart aches for her every damn day.*

"How are you holding up with everything? Sorry I've been so absent at CGC." Rhys' head falls forward and he sighs.

"It's all right man. A lot of fucking work. Doing your job and mine, it's exhausting. But I know it's only temporary, so get out of there fast," he growls. A sympathetic chuckle rumbles out of me, and I feel for him, I do. He's been a great sport for letting me lean on him and stepping up to the plate to take on all the extras that I can't do right now.

I keep the message with Selena open, and the three dots pop up and disappear a few times, indicating she's typing a reply. The anxiety of awaiting her response bubbles in my gut. But, after half an hour, there's no response. I finish my beer as Riley walks out into the living room in nothing but a small tank top and cheeky pink underwear. Rhys' eyes bug out and a small drop of sweat forms on his brow. He's clearly embarrassed that his girlfriend is walking around practically naked in front of me. It hardly matters to me. Riley is a gorgeous woman, no one can deny that, but there's really only one woman who's ever caught my attention. My hands twitch, and I'm itching to feel her in my arms again; to feel her silky creamy skin under my fingertips again…

However, as my eyes linger on Riley's form, I notice something different about her. As long as I've known her, she's always been petite, but now she's so small I can see the faint ridges of her ribs through her skintight tank top. Her midriff, and even her cheeks, look especially hollow. I make a mental note to talk to Rhys about this when we're alone. Riley grabs a beer cap from the counter, twists it in her hand, and tosses it onto the coffee table. She takes a long pull of Rhys' beer and tries to wrestle the remote out of his hand. When she's unsuccessful, she moans and licks his ear.

"And...that's my cue. See you guys later." I stand up and walk out of the apartment, not looking back. Before I close the apartment door behind me, I hear Riley say, "Yes!" I assume she won control of the remote by distraction. Riley: 1, Rhys: 0.

Back at my apartment building, as I walk out of the elevator and down the hallway, I loosen the tie around my neck. I yank my apartment door open I start removing clothing as I make my way to the bedroom. I'm too revved up to sleep, so I decide to change into my workout clothes and make my way downstairs, to the building's gym. Once there, I hop on the treadmill and zone out as I start to jog.

"Haven't seen you here in a while," a smooth and delicate voice murmurs into my ear, and the hairs on the back of my neck stand up. I turn down the treadmill to a brisk walk. I don't need to look to know that it's Lexi, the petite, busty blonde who asks me out constantly. I nod in her direction.

"Yeah, work's been killing me." Work, Elissa. Same thing. They both suck.

"You don't say," Lexi drawls. "And here I was thinking you moved to another place, so you didn't have to evade me asking you out." A playful smirk stretches across her face. My face heats and my heartbeat quickens at her insinuation. She steps onto the treadmill beside mine and the air thickens; tension radiates between us. Our eyes lock and the heat creeps down my face to my neck, swirling the contents of my stomach. I break our connection, turn off the treadmill, and stalk to the bench press to set up the weights.

I'm doing quick presses of two hundred pounds for about ten minutes when I hear the beeping of Lexi's treadmill, signalling the cool-down period. Keeping my focus on the presses and my form, I don't realize she's come over to me until she materializes above me, staring at me upside down. Droplets of sweat glisten on her forehead as some roll down the length of her neck.

"Need a spot?" She extends her tiny hands so they hover under the bar, following my movement. I puff my chest and cheeks simultaneously as I keep pumping my arms, letting small puffs of breath out in between.

"Not an imperfect form there, Collins." My mind falters at the casual nickname, throwing me off. Typically, she'd flirt a bit more, or coo my name, trying to seduce me at every chance. I've obviously pissed her off, even though I've done nothing. I quirk my brow at her, and she lets out a small chuckle.

"What? That is your last name, right?" she taunts, her mouth upturning on the right corner. I nod and return the bar to its resting position. I sit up and she walks around the bench, now facing me, toe-to-toe. She cocks her leg and plants her hands on her hips.

"You gonna move? My turn," she says, rolling her tongue against her bottom lip before pulling it in. I bend over, grab my towel, and wipe some sweat off my brow before I stand up. We're millimetres apart. She's still got her bottom lip between her teeth, only now she's nibbling on it nervously, like she's debating something.

Two small, but firm, hands push against my chest, slamming me back down onto the bench while Lexi's legs wrap outside of mine, straddling me. Startled, I stay frozen as her fingers lace into my damp hair and she pulls me into her, pressing her soft, enormous chest into my collarbone. Her lips descend to mine, slowly, like she's giving me a moment to stop this, but right now I'm not thinking straight. For the first time, I realize I'm fighting to keep from getting hard for someone who isn't her. For the first time since Elissa left, I find my mind blank. I lean in, not stopping her, and her lips are full, but a little rough from all the nibbling she must do; a small habit I can tell she has by the feeling of her lips against mine.

Her tongue sweeps against my mouth, parting my lips. I let her tongue explore my mouth as my tongue finds hers. Her hands slide down my torso, and she tightens her grip around the bottom of my shirt and tugs. My hands grip her wrists to stop her as I break the kiss, both of us panting.

"Not like this," I say, heaving for air.

Made in the USA
Columbia, SC
16 October 2023

24142206R00171